Crucible Heart

To Robert
Thank you so much
for your awesome talent
and help. Many Blessings
Dianna

Crucible Heart

Diana Symons

GOLD PEN
Press

ISBN: 1-934995-04-5
ISBN-13: 978-1-934995-04-4

Photo Credit to Celleni
www.sxc.hu/photo/859734

Cover design by Robert Duvall

To my son, Christopher.
May God always draw you closer to His heart.

Acknowledgements

Grateful thanks to Lynn Squire, Julia Loren, Katie Vorreiter, and Robert Duvall for making my book readable and beautiful. I love working with talented people.

Thank you to my friends and family who lovingly support my writing, especially my sister Danette, who is so excited to see this finally finished.

Thank you to all of you.

Prologue

My heart did a little dance as I shoved my suitcase under the bed and turned to take in the room. I'd finally moved into my dorm at SFU. After all the shopping, all the planning, all the parental lecturing, Victoria Jennifer Johnson was actually in college in San Francisco. I tapped my fingers on my hips and turned to the unmade bed across from me. My roommate hadn't checked in yet, so I didn't know how that was going work out, but I was so freaking excited it didn't matter. I just couldn't believe I was really on my own and in San Francisco. After growing up in Connerville, I'd moved to a real city—a place pulsing with life and energy, not farm reports and grange meetings.

I smoothed out my bedspread, then nudged the green and white striped garbage can that matched the desk set my Mom helped me buy. Everything was in place. My new life was official and I was ready to live.

I grabbed the pink leather purse I bought on my last shopping trip with my friends, fished out my car keys, and all but hopped down the hall. I had to get out to see the city, the traffic, the people, the buildings. I'd visited San Francisco with my parents a few times, but now it was time to see it my way.

I decided to just drive around and be a tourist in my new town. It didn't matter which direction I went—everything was going to be awesome. With my MP3 player plugged in, I tapped the steering wheel to the music as I pulled out of the parking garage. Soon I found myself in a quiet neighborhood with tall houses mashed together and moms and strollers all over the place. I bounced with the music and wished my best friend, Cassie, was with me. We talked forever about being in college together, but it just didn't work out for her.

Not surprisingly, my phone chirped. It was Cassie.

```
Hey V. What r u doing?
```

I held the phone to the steering wheel and texted back as I drove, glancing up at the road. It was a quiet side street by a small park.

```
In my car
Where u going?
Anywhere. I'm in SF!
Is it cool?
Way cool
Tell me everything
I will
```

I tapped send and wondered if I would need to keep her posted on every bite I took, when something hit the front of the car. I looked up from my phone and slammed on the brakes. A woman ran out from the park and dropped an armload of presents on the pavement. I turned the music off and tried to make sense of what I saw in the rearview mirror. People ran out to the street, shouting. The woman who dropped the presents was screaming. She was screaming. A birthday balloon floated away on the breeze.

A horror began to rise up in my stomach. The nightmare that played out on the street behind me didn't seem real. Nothing made sense. Another second and the horror rose up to my throat.

An old man opened my car door and shouted at me to get out. He leaned in and grabbed my car keys. "You hit that boy!" he yelled in my face. A vein bulged in his neck as he glared at me. "You hit my grandson."

I couldn't understand what he said. It was as if he spoke another language, an ugly, horrible language that stripped everything good and beautiful from life. I got out of the car and mechanically groped my way to the back. I tried so hard not to look, but I had to. A small boy lay in the street, unnatural and twisted. He looked about five years old with a head full of blond curls. Blood pooled on the pavement underneath him, staining the perfect curls the color of my favorite nail polish.

I whirled around and threw-up. Nothing made sense. None of that could be real. I tried hard to wake up because nothing that was happening could be real. And then the screaming grew louder. It wasn't until later that I realized that the sound came from my own throat.

One

I did two years in prison for gross vehicular manslaughter. Totally my fault. I had been ticketed for texting and driving four times before the accident, so they threw the book at me. Why did they let me out? I knew who I was when I was inside—guilty, convicted, prison scum. Outside, I was supposed to find a life back in society, but I was still guilty, convicted, prison scum. There was no life.

I tapped ash from my cigarette as I watched normal people drift past my bench in Golden Gate Park. Crazy Igor and Crazy Ahab were going at it over part of a burrito tossed in the garbage. I named the homeless guys because I lived in their world now. Not that I'm homeless. I was supposed to find a life, now that I was back in society. But, seriously, how was that going to happen? Like those guys digging through trash cans, I live in a world ignored by normal people. I didn't blame anyone for that. If I actually had a life, I'd ignore me too.

A teenage boy stopped in front of me, white T-shirt, pants hanging off his butt. "Got a cigarette?" He had his hand out like he expected a cigarette to magically appear in it.

"Sure." I pulled one out and helped him light up.

"Thanks, man." He walked off in that exaggerated sway they used to be bad as smoke trailed behind him.

I sighed as I watched him walk away. Who sees me? Clueless teenage mooches. Awesome. I ground out the last of my smoke in the dirt and tossed it in a metal garbage can. I sat back against the bench barely noticing the row of Edwardian houses across the street. It was my day off from the only crummy job I could get as an ex-con and I'd spent it doing nothing. Somehow I'd managed to waste hours staring into space. The mooch made me look up and realize how late in the day it was getting.

I was about to head back home when God decided to play a malicious joke on me. Just as I stood up, a woman and little boy walked past. A little boy with blond, curly hair. My throat closed up and pain slammed through my head and throbbed at my temples. I couldn't take my eyes off the kid as he laughed and looked up at the woman, holding out a melting ice cream cone for her to share. I gasped, trying desperately to breathe, but couldn't take my eyes off him. I kept flashing back to blood on the street and a small mangled body. I blinked several times, but tears poured down my face.

Suddenly, my view of the boy was blocked by a man peering down at me. He was handsome. He had silver hair but I could tell he was only a few years older than me. But it was his blue eyes that that unsettled me.

"Are you okay?" He looked at me like a doctor, checking to see if my pupils were dilated.

I couldn't answer. Couldn't even try. My head throbbed and my stomach queased. I was just grateful the kid was out of my line of sight so I wouldn't throw up in front of the handsome stranger.

"Sit down," said the guy.

He sat me down on the bench and perched next to me. "What's going on?"

I wiped my face with both hands and struggled to take a deep breath.

"That's it. Just relax." His voice was soothing, like an ice cube melting against skin on a sticky, hot day.

I exhaled and glanced at him. "I'm okay."

He smirked and leaned back a little, then watched me rub my temple. "Your head hurt?"

"Yeah," I answered with a wispy, little voice. I didn't have the energy to deal with him.

"Can I pray for your headache?" He asked with a straight face even.

I stood and swayed a little as I got my bearings. "You can leave me alone."

He remained seated but leaned forward on his knees and pointed a finger at me. "God can take care of it, whatever it is that's causing you so much pain."

Seriously? "I think God's having enough fun with me right now." I glared at him and walked away through a cloud of pain and nausea.

I stood at the stoplight and willed the light to turn green. I felt like I had evil super powers drawn from pain and bad temper. I couldn't get the image of the guy on the bench out of my head. He was just the kind of guy that Cassie and I used to flirt with. The clean-cut kind we knew we'd marry and have kids with. But that was before.

The light turned and I crossed over to Broderick. I ignored the SUV trying to park in a space a Mini couldn't get into. Usually I liked to stop and watch the show, but I wasn't in the mood. I stopped in the middle of the block and pulled out my keys to the glass street door of my building. Inside the lobby, I shoved a tricycle out of the way with my foot. The Garcias upstairs have two little boys, living normal lives.

I unlocked the apartment door and heard the TV. Trish, my roommate, was in the front room with a bottle of wine.

Our apartment building was one of the few on the block not updated since the 1906 earthquake. It was old. We still had the old gas fireplace, crown molding, and yellowing wallpaper. Trish's worn furniture fit right in.

She lifted her glass to me like a toast. "Jenna!"

I go by Jenna now. Victoria Jennifer Johnson died in prison, along with everything that I used to think was good and right.

"Want some?" She reached down and lifted the bottle.

I hesitated. "Yeah, sure. Just a minute." I went down the long, narrow hallway to the kitchen and grabbed a bottle of ibuprofen from a cupboard and shook some into my hand. I brought back a wineglass and held it out while Trish filled it. I settled on the couch, put my feet up next to hers on the coffee table, and swallowed my pills with something red.

"What is this?" I held the glass up and looked at the color.

"Merlot. Do you like it?"

I sipped again and winced. "Kind of harsh for me, but what do I know?"

"It's not for everybody." She winced as she watched me drain my glass. "What's going on?"

I held the empty glass on my lap and rested my head against the couch with my eyes closed, hoping the alcohol would work faster than the pills. "I was in the park. A little kid came by. Blond. Curls."

"Oh, geez." She reached over and patted my arm. "I'm sorry. Here." She grabbed the wine bottle and poured some more.

"Thanks." I was glad that I didn't have to go into it. She knew. She was a good friend, a good person, someone willing to let an ex-con make a fresh start.

"It's not like you intentionally murdered someone," she had said when I told her about the accident. "I mean, when you think about it, it could have been me behind the wheel." She said meeting me changed her mind about ever texting in the car again. I think she was hoping to make me feel better.

I was halfway through the second glass when the alcohol kicked in. My head still throbbed, but I was starting to relax. I waited for a commercial and rolled my head to look at her. "So how was your day?"

9

She swirled her glass and shrugged. "Haircut, couple of color jobs. No good gossip." She finished her glass then refilled it.

For a hairdresser, Trish looked nice. I'm just saying. Hairdressers tended to practice on each other. Sometimes it worked, sometimes it didn't. Trish was Japanese and wore her shiny, black hair cut blunt at the shoulders. It was a good look. She swirled her wine and eyed me as if I were customer. "You could do with a trim soon."

I pulled at my curls. She'd showed me before how to mousse them to keep birds from nesting, but I didn't do much else. I looked just like my Mom—same brown curls, same brown eyes. I was just a slimmer, taller version. "If you say so." I finished my glass and set it down. I wasn't in the mood to find out who was going to be voted off the island. "Thanks for the wine." I stood and rubbed my eye with the palm of my hand.

"You should probably lie down for a while." She looked up with a caring but helpless look. "Oh! Your mother called."

"Great. What did she have to say?" Mom was okay. Of course, she was seriously disappointed in me. Who wanted to admit they had a daughter who'd been in prison? Still, she kept in touch and wanted to know how I was doing.

"She just wanted to check up." She looked into her glass and swirled the rosy liquid. "You know, you can get a cell phone that you add minutes to. It's cheaper than having full service like mine." She tipped her glass back and drank, then looked at me with her eyebrows up, an exclamation point to get me to respond.

I nodded. We'd been through this before. Apparently I was the last person on the planet without a cell phone. Certainly the last one in San Francisco. For some reason it was a big shock to everyone when they found out I didn't have one. It was like admitting you voted for Bush. In San Francisco, that was a big deal. There were plenty of people who didn't own cars here, but no cell phone? It was almost illegal.

"You want to call her?" She put her glass down gently then set her hand on the cell phone lying next to her.

"Maybe later." I wasn't up to dealing with Mom wanting me to visit. I hadn't been home since I got out. I'd only told a few people that I'd been to prison—Trish; Laurel, my friend at work; and my boss Brenda, because I had to for employment. I could deal with them.

But talking with family? No. Family remembered how you used to be. They remembered your potential and your dreams. I heard disappointment in Mom's voice every time I talked to her. When she'd come to visit me inside, I could see it in her eyes. She used to be proud of me. Now that place where pride used to be was just empty. She wouldn't even talk about what Dad thought. I had no idea and I was afraid to ask.

I went to my room and lay down on the mattress on the floor. Besides it, my room was pretty empty—a couple of boxes to hold my clothes, a few books, and that was it.

I rolled on my back and rested my arm across my eyes. Whenever I saw a little kid, I relived the accident in excruciating detail. I saw everything. I heard everything. It was my fault that a mother would never watch her son grow up. I even felt the sudden loss of my own life as dramatically as if it just happened. That little boy died and I lost myself. All my plans, all my hopes, all my respectability—gone in one stupid moment. I sat up and pulled my wallet out of my back pocket. I took out a folded piece of paper and opened it. It had been in my wallet so long the folds were worn and the edges were bent. I set it on the bed and pressed it flat. I didn't read it, just looked at it and wiped away a wet trail from my cheek.

I closed my eyes and settled back against the wall. I couldn't take it anymore. I just couldn't. My whole life was working a stupid job at Copyland and trying to forget. It wasn't a life, it was a long, slow death. I was young and I was going to be alone and trapped by the horror of my past forever. The image of silver hair and blue eyes flashed through my mind. What kind of guy would want to be with me after he knew the truth? I didn't care how nice he was, I'd always be the monster who killed a kid. I grabbed my pillow and sobbed into it.

The Bible said something about suicide being bad, but God wasn't on my side anyway. I wiped my face and sniffed. I needed to think very carefully. What exactly would be the best way to kill myself?

Two

"Stupid, stupid monster!"

I kicked the machine hard enough to hurt, then leaned against it to pull myself together. Losing my temper wouldn't make it work right, but releasing vengeance sure felt good. I ripped open the side panel, pulled out the paper jam, then slammed the panel closed. When I punched the green button again, the monster roared back to life. Stacks of paper dropped onto a neatly collated pile as innocently as baby lambs. As if.

I glared at the thing, then turned and glanced nervously at Brenda, a small black woman perched on a stool behind the counter. She lifted an eyebrow at me then turned back to her computer. I know, I wasn't supposed to get mad like that, especially with customers in the store. At least I didn't swear. Out loud. I grabbed the dolly like it was the monster's evil offspring and wheeled it to the storage room. That's my blow-off-steam move so I don't actually detonate in public. I dropped paper boxes on the dolly as penance, then leaned against it with my head down. I still had a headache from the day before, but it wasn't as bad. I tried to keep up with the ibuprofen, but it never really chased the headache away.

I pushed the dolly out of the storeroom and parked it by the monster, then made sure the beast was behaving itself. I almost wished it were a monster. I could feed it and make it do tricks for me, then sic it on the next customer who yelled at me for not having enough time to do their stupid print job because they brought it in at the last minute. Monster sit! Roar! Attack! Good monster.

The beast did seem to be behaving itself for the time being. I liked to think it was afraid of me, but I knew it smirked at me from behind that metal plating. We both knew who was boss.

"I'm going out for a smoke," I said to Brenda as I passed her desk.

She threatened me with cancer again then smiled sweetly to a customer walking in.

Outside, I pulled a pack of smokes from a pocket of my cargo pants, lit up, then leaned against the wall to watch the show. San Francisco was the best city in the world. In ten minutes you could watch every kind of freak walk past, then go back to work. It was awesome. I especially liked the ones with giant hair spikes. I heard they used glue to keep the spikes up straight. Seriously.

"Hey, Jenna!" Bats came slouching towards me.

In the old days, my friends and I would go to the mall to shop for shoes, then head to Starbucks. Now I was friends with a guy from a tattoo parlor down the block. He was a little seedy looking, completely covered in ink, but harmless.

"Hey, Bats."

He dropped back against the wall and pulled out his cigarettes.

"How's life?" He cupped his hand around the lighter until the end of his cigarette glowed red.

"Cool." That's what you said when you had absolutely nothing to say but didn't want to be rude.

"Cool." He took a drag then blew out a long stream of smoke. "Gotta love the fresh air, you know?" He looked around at the air and smiled.

I just shook my head. "Bats, you're smoking a cigarette. How can you even tell if you're breathing fresh air? Do you see any irony here?"

"What!" He looked hurt. "We're outside. We're breathing the air. It's fresh." He took a deep breath then coughed.

"You smoke too much," I said. "Stop smoking, then you can enjoy the fresh air."

"I know." He sounded apologetic, then frowned at me. "Hey, you smoke as much as I do."

"I know." I waved my hand up. "But I don't have any delusions about the fresh air."

He looked like he was going to tell me more about the freshness of the outdoors and why I should stop smoking too, when someone called him from his shop.

"Oh, man!" He jabbed out his smoke and stretched his back. "I'll see you later, Jenna." He walked away and waved over his shoulder.

"Later, Bats."

I watched him walk away and glanced down at my ankle where Bats had done a tat of a diamond for me. Once upon a time, I was going to major in geology, but a tat of a rock or dirt wouldn't be all that impressive. A diamond was geology at its best.

I finished my cigarette and ground it out to carry the butt inside. Been through that lecture too many times. Brenda saw all.

The monster burped a few times during the afternoon, so I had a mess to fix when a print job came out with every-other page blank. I had no idea how. Somehow I managed to make it through the day without dismembering the monster or a customer. I was pretty proud.

My friend Laurel and I loitered outside after we got off. We'd usually wait so Brenda wouldn't be left alone to lock up. It wasn't a bad neighborhood, but was still the city. You looked after your people. Brenda might've been tough on the outside, but she was still a head shorter than either of us.

"How you doing?" Laurel eyed me like she knew something was going on.

I rubbed my temple. "Just a nagging headache."

"Did you take anything?"

"Ibuprofen."

She glanced back into the doorway. "You want something stronger? I can get you anything you want."

"No, that's okay," I lied. "I'm on parole. I'll be all right,"

Brenda came out jingling keys and locked the door. She looked up at Laurel then me. "See you two tomorrow." She walked off to try to find her car somewhere in the eight blocks where she'd snagged parking. I'd tried to get her to take the bus, but she had kids to pick up.

"You want me to drive you home?" asked Laurel as she pulled out her keys.

I zipped up my army jacket and stuck my hands in my pockets. "No thanks. I'll walk. The exercise might help. See you later 'gater."

She grinned and shook her head as she turned the other way.

The nice part about where I lived was that it was close and I didn't need a car. I didn't even have a car. Not anymore. I walked down Divisadero to Fell and over to Broderick. I saw some of the same people a lot 'cause I walked the same way every day. We didn't chat, so I didn't know names, but we'd nod, throw the chin up, say hi. The brothers with the BBQ joint did a mean tri-tip and audacious sweet potato pie. I couldn't afford to spend a lot on carryout, but sometimes it was perfect. There were all kinds of little hole-in-the-wall places to eat—Chinese, Mexican, pizza, coffee shops, even some kind of French bistro. If you had the money, it would be fun to check them all out.

Sometimes I'd stop at the corner market run by the Chinese lady. I think she was Chinese. She had stuff in there that I wondered about—black, shriveled-up stuff in plastic bags. I didn't even want to know. I usually picked up soup and crackers, and she always tried to get me to buy some kind of meat or weird vegetables. Probably should have, but I wasn't a cook. Not at all. Opening soup and frying baloney was as good as it got with me.

When I got to my apartment building, I had to stop and groan. It smelled like pee again. That place by the steps to the basement was not a public toilet! I felt for the wretch who lived on the street, but stop peeing in front of my building, it was nasty. I pulled a hose out from the basement and washed the steps down before going in.

Trish wasn't home yet, so I opened some soup and ate it with crackers. Nothing was as good as Mom's homemade chicken soup, but oh well. My expectations were not very lofty anymore. I dropped a small handful of crushed crackers in my bowl to soak up the last of the broth and mashed them up. Mom would have worried about how much weight I'd lost since she saw me last, but I couldn't afford real food on my little salary. But at least I had a job. I was grateful for that. Otherwise, the homeless guys and I would be getting to know each other a lot more.

I cleaned up my mess in the kitchen, pulled on my jacket, and headed out. San Francisco usually had pretty decent weather and as long as it was still light, I wanted to be outside. It beat staring at my bedroom walls or TV.

I knew that any time I stepped out my front door there was a risk of seeing some kid who would blow up my day, but I wasn't ready to lock myself inside forever. Not yet.

A little nip in the air made me zip up my jacket as I waited for the light at the corner. The traffic was still busy as commuters tried to get home from work. Lots of people lived in the city but drove down to the South Bay where most of the high tech jobs were. I didn't have their big paychecks, but I liked that I was walking-distance to work.

Just as the light was about to change, I saw a teenager staring at his cell phone, thumbs flying, as he drove slowly by. Suddenly, something snapped inside me. I yelled at him as loud as I could. "*Hey!*"

The kid looked up, startled.

"What do you think you're doing?" I shouted like one of those crazy people you saw talking to themselves in the Tenderloin.

He flipped me the finger and roared off as other cars hurried to get through the light.

I'd scared the daylights out of an old lady standing next to me, but was so mad I didn't care. No, I wasn't mad. I was way past mad. I crossed the street in a fury as hot tears ran down my face. I stormed through the park, dropped onto a bench, and covered my face with my hands.

I hated that I exploded like that, but there was just no stopping it. It came out unleashed and full of venom. If that kid had been standing in front of me, I would have slapped him senseless. I rocked forward and moaned into my hands. I hated that I was so angry. I hated myself for being such a waste of space and air.

"So, having another bad day?"

Someone sat down on the bench.

I wiped my face and looked up. It was Blue Eyes. I looked away and wondered if I could pretend I hadn't seen him.

"Seriously, everything okay?"

I took out a cigarette and lit up with shaky hands. I blew out smoke and glared at him. "Yeah, everything's just peachy."

"I told you yesterday that God can help. He can fix anything." He stretched his arms out along the top of the bench and crossed his legs. He had that relaxed attitude like he knew he was right and he was waiting for me to catch up.

I don't think so. I glanced at him out of the corner of my eye then looked away. Sometimes you have to just ignore the loonies.

He looked out across the park and started talking, like I was listening. "Sometimes we get to the end of our rope and there's nowhere to go. You can't go back up, and there's no more rope to go down. If you let go, you lose it all. That's the best place to find Jesus. He can pull you right along next to him and you'll be safe as kittens."

I grunted and puffed a cloud of smoke his direction.

He chuckled and waved the haze away from his face. "I'm just saying, there's help if you want it. When people get desperate and they don't think there are any options, they do stupid things." He gave me a knowing look that sent a chill down my back.

"You don't know anything about me." I folded my arms across my chest with my cigarette lifted up away from my face and looked off at nothing.

"I don't, but God does. Believe it or not, he really wants to help you." He sounded less obnoxious and more caring, like the sound in his voice I heard the day before.

I couldn't help glancing at him. His look was serious. I could tell he saw me. I wasn't one of the unwashed masses. He saw *me*. That look released panic in my stomach. He wouldn't want to know me if he knew. I could feel the rejection already.

He watched my reaction and leaned forward gently. "I don't know what it is, but something is going on with you and I'd like to help." He reached into his pocket and pulled out a small leather case and took out a business card. "Here, call me if you want to talk." He held out the card even after I didn't take it. "You never know—you might think about it later and change your mind. Just take it."

I don't know why, but I did. I shoved it in my jacket pocket without looking at it, then leaned down to rub out my cigarette in the dirt. I stood up, flicked the butt into a garbage can, and walked away. I didn't look at him or say anything. I didn't know what his agenda was, but I wasn't buying.

I walked down the park, the opposite way from home, just to think. Who did he think he was with all the answers? What was he going to help with? He had some magic wand that erased your screw-ups? What kind of weed was he on? I shook my head and laughed to myself, but fingered the business card in my pocket.

Three

I leaned against the kitchen counter the next morning and sipped my coffee while Trish peeked in the toaster. She always looked like a little kid in the mornings, with her fuzzy pink robe and slippers.

I looked at my jacket hanging off the back of a kitchen chair and remembered the business card in the pocket. "I keep running into this guy at the park," I said as I cupped my hand around the hot mug.

She looked up curiously. "What kind of guy?"

"Weird. He keeps telling me that God wants to fix all my problems. I'm not sure even *God* is aware of how big a job that is."

She caught the toast that popped up and buttered it. "Why is he telling you that? What does he know about you?"

"Nothing!" I glanced away because it came out with a little more passion than I intended.

She hesitated with her toast half way to a bite. "So why is he talking to you if he doesn't know you?"

"Because he keeps running into me right after I freak out about something. First was when I saw that little kid the other day and then again yesterday when I saw an imbecile texting and driving. Apparently I'm not very subtle in my reaction to stupidity." I drained my cup and rinsed it out in the sink.

Trish chewed her toast thoughtfully. She had that far-off look in her eye like she was really working it over. She looked up with big eyes. "Maybe he really does know something and God is using him like a messenger. Like an *angel!* What did he look like?"

"An angel? I don't think so." I stretched my arm into my jacket and pulled it on.

"Come on." She insisted. "What did he look like?"

I tugged the sleeves to straighten them out and sighed. "Silver hair, blue eyes, khakis, white button-up shirt."

She stared off again. "Hmm. Well, you never know. Why would it be so impossible for God to send an angel? You know you need help. God probably knows that too." She looked up at me and cocked her head.

"Yeah, well, unless God uses angels named—" I pulled the business card out of my pocket—"Jess Brown, Property Investment Manager, I don't think so." I stopped to think. Did I know that name?

She looked disappointed. "Still, that doesn't mean that God isn't using him to help you. You should consider the possibility."

I smiled. I liked Trish. We should all have someone in our lives who believed in impossible things. As long as I didn't have to.

"Right, well, see you later." I zipped up my jacket and left for work.

***

Laurel and I sat in the break room later that day and laughed.

"An angel?" She cackled.

I glanced out the door to see if we were going to incur sidewalk sweeping for being too noisy.

"Yeah, I'm not kidding," I said. "She was so disappointed when I pulled out the guy's business card."

"Yeah? Let me see it," she said with her hand out.

I started to reach for it then stopped. "It's in my jacket pocket."

"Humph." She sat back and swung her foot off her crossed leg. "I'd be careful if I were you. Creeps in the park trying to get into your business? I wouldn't trust him."

"I know." But then I thought about it. "I don't think he's a creep. He seemed okay, but the whole God thing . . . "

"You ever been into that?" She picked at the Styrofoam cup she'd used for her coffee and threw the pieces into a garbage can by the door.

"Yeah, when I was in high school. I got saved and the whole bit."

"Yeah? So what happened? You found Jesus, then you lost him?"

"Something like that. I lost a lot in prison."

She looked uncomfortable and glanced away. Something about my time in prison always made her act weird.

"Still," I said. "It's not like I believed that much before I went in."

She reached down and picked up Styrofoam bits that fell on the floor. "Too bad."

"What do you mean?" I frowned.

She mashed the rest of her cup and tossed it. "Wouldn't it be cool if a real angel came sweeping into your life and fixed all your messes?"

"Uh-huh. And I could wear a glass slipper and live happily ever after."

She sat and stared at the garbage can for a moment. "You know what we should do?" She looked around at me and studied my face. "We should go out tonight. Have some fun. Maybe we could find ourselves an angel or two." She grinned and bounced her eyebrows. "What do you say?"

I tapped the table and thought about it. "Okay. Where were you thinking?"

"There's a warehouse club I've been to a couple times. You'll like it."

I looked down at my Tweety Bird T-shirt and cargo pants. "This is as dressy as I get, you know."

She looked me over with a half sneer. "Come on, Jenna. Want to borrow something?"

"No," I said, like she asked if I'd rather go naked. "I don't girly up very well, you know that. This is who I am, baby. Love it or leave it."

She rolled her eyes and nodded. "Fine. But you're going to look like my gay partner."

"So what? This is San Francisco!" I patted her on the head and smirked as I got up and left the room.

***

Laurel met me at a bus stop south of Market. She was wearing tall heels, a very short, tight dress, and showing plenty of boobs. She looked me over, head to toe, rolled her eyes, then turned on her heel to lead me to the warehouse. It wasn't hard to find. The outside walls practically vibrated from the volume coming from inside. A crowd lingered around the door, giving the eye to everyone who walked past. I got the OMG look from a boobified mini-skirt crowd, obviously shocked that I showed up in cargo pants and tennis shoes. So what? My feet weren't going to kill me at the end of the night like theirs were.

We paid the door fee, got our hands stamped, and then followed a small group of giggling Asian girls into the darkened hall. It was packed with moving, bouncing, flailing bodies and the music was deafening. Laurel looked at me and nodded to the dance floor. I followed her out and we danced with each other. Then we danced with the people next to us. After a while, I lost her. I didn't know if she ditched me or just drifted into the crowd.

I was hot. Sweaty hot. I squeezed through bodies and made my way to the nearest wall and dropped against it to cool off. I watched couples undulating so close to each other it looked a little obscene. Back home, Cassie, Sherrie, and I used to practice dancing like that. Mom would never let me go to clubs then.

Connerville didn't even have any, so we had our own dance parties—with boys. We let on like they were good, Christian dance parties, until the adults left us alone. It was amazing how fast those boys could feel up a girl when they thought no one was looking.

"Hey!"

A guy next to me was trying to get my attention. He was cute, Indian. In the Bay Area, that means from India not America. He had that cleaned-up look of a geek, and his smile was brilliant.

"Want to dance?" he yelled, leaning toward me.

I nodded and followed him back to the dance floor. We did our best. No one would be asking us to dance with stars, but it was fun. Eventually we stopped and he nodded toward the door.

I found my jacket where I stashed it and went out after him. The air was cold after the heat and sweat inside. It felt great. I followed the cute geek out to where we could hear each other.

"What's your name?" he asked, pulling on a light jacket.

I ran my hand through the wet hair at the back of my neck. "Jenna. What's yours?"

"Manish."

"What?"

"Manish," he said more emphatically.

"Oh. Nice to meet you." I grinned and held out my hand.

He smiled and shook it. "Nice to meet you, too." He looked around at the crowd that looked exactly like it did when I went in. "Have you been here before?"

I shook my head. "No. I came with a friend. I lost her somewhere inside though." I looked over the crowd mingling outside and wondered if I'd see Laurel again that night.

"You want to get a drink?" he asked.

Suddenly a warning alarm went off in my head. "What time is it?" I checked to see if he wore a wristwatch.

He did. "Eleven forty-five. Why?"

"I have to go," I said and pulled my jacket on.

"Why? Do you turn into a pumpkin at midnight?"

I couldn't believe I didn't see that coming. "No. The busses stop running." I zipped up my jacket and gave him my guess-I'll-be-leaving smile.

"I can drive you home," he said. "I have a car in the garage down the block." He turned and pointed.

"No, I'm good." I said. "Nice to meet you Manish. Bye."

"Wait." He grabbed my arm lightly as he pulled his wallet out. I thought he was going to give me bus fare, but he handed me a business card.

"Manish Patel. Software Engineer," I read. He *was* a geek.

"Call me?" He held his hand up to his ear with thumb and finger extended like a phone.

I smiled mysteriously and walked away. Just then Laurel came running up out of the crowd.

"Hey! You leaving?" She grabbed my arm as she tottered on her heels.

"Yeah. I need to catch the bus."

"But it's so early." She pulled at her skirt and looked up with glassy eyes.

"I know. Maybe you should call it quits too. You look like you've had enough."

She giggled and waved me off. "Don't make me laugh. Besides, I met Mr. Right. He's so cute, Jenna." She looked back toward the club and shifted her boobs in her dress.

"Are you sure?" I asked. "How are you getting home? You don't look like you should drive."

"Who said I was going to drive?" She tossed her head and walked away. "See you tomorrow," she called over her shoulder.

I shoved my hands in the pockets of my jacket and trotted off. It was a long walk home if I was late.

Four

A commercial blaring from the clock radio by my bed jarred me awake the next morning. I gave it a vicious whap to shut it up. I blinked a few times against the gray light that tried really hard to break through the blinds. Then I remembered the night before. Manish—what a cutie. I smiled just thinking of that handsome face. For some reason, I thought about my parents being unfazed by me dating an Indian because I had already ruined any expectations they had for me. Dating—what was I thinking? I just met the guy.

That made me roll out of bed and stumble down the hall. We had an old claw-foot bathtub that always made me smile. It had a wire bar that held up a shower curtain like in the cartoons. I always expected to hear singing and see a long-handled bath brush poke out the top of it. The shower was hot and comfortable. I wanted to stay in it all day, but I wasn't the only one who needed to get ready for work.

After I was dressed, I followed the scent of coffee down the hall. Trish always set up the coffeepot the night before so it would brew before we got into the kitchen in the morning. I poured myself a cup then grabbed another mug as Trish shuffled in.

"Oh, thank you," she said, reaching for the cup I held out for her. She pulled creamer out of the fridge and splashed it in. "How was your night last night?"

I clinked a spoon as I stirred in sugar. "Not too bad. I met a guy." I dropped the spoon on the counter then leaned back.

"You met a guy? Like an angel?" She winked.

"This guy is Indian, and cute." I took a sip and set the cup down. "That's about all I know about him. And he's a geek."

"Cute, Indian geek. Sounds promising. Are you going to see him again?" She shuffled back to the fridge to put the creamer away.

"He asked me to call him." I waited for it.

"Bet you wish you had that cell phone now," she said, right on cue.

I shook my head. "I'll call from work. There are actually other phones in the world you know."

"Uh-huh." She carried her coffee down the hall and left me to work out my need for a cell phone.

I put my jacket on, went out the back door with my coffee, and sat on the top of the steps that ran down into the small, sad yard. There wasn't much to look at, just a courageous little tree, some scraggly bushes, and dirt where cats came to poo. I pulled out my cigarette and lit up in the cold air. In one week, I collected two interesting business cards, probably polar opposites. Not that—what was his name? I pulled the cards out of my pocket—Jess. Not that Christian Jess was good and Manish was evil, but they probably had different agendas. I guessed Jess was after brownie points, and Manish was after, well, he was a guy.

What Manish was after didn't bother me. I wasn't the saintly daughter my parents thought I was before the accident. Dustin Barns and I spent enough time in the back of his car after youth meetings to pretty much tarnish my imaginary halo. Maybe that's why I thought making the call to Manish was more of a probability than calling Jess. I couldn't see Jess and I ever being on the same page.

***

I was sorting through a shipment of paper in the storeroom when Brenda came in. She stopped in the doorway and folded her arms and watched me with her lips pressed tightly.

"What's up?" I asked. Whatever it was, it didn't look good.

"Laurel," she said.

"Yeah? Where is she? She's late." I figured she had a pretty late night, or early morning. "Everything okay?" I shoved a stack of boxes against the wall with my foot and turned to her.

"She's in the hospital," she said flatly.

"Wait, what? What happened? I was just with her last night."

"She got beat up. Where did you go?"

I stared at the floor while my stomach knotted up. "We went to a warehouse club, south of Market. She wanted to stay when I left because she said she met a guy."

"Did you see who it was?" she asked.

"No, I went home. Criminy. I should have stayed with her. She looked out of it when I left. I should have known better." I kicked a nearby box hard and hurt my foot.

"Don't beat yourself up. I just thought you would want to know."

"Where is she?" I asked.

"San Francisco General." She reached out and touched my arm then walked out.

It felt like the air had been ripped out of me. I bent over and leaned against my thighs. How did that happen? How did she let that happen? Was it because she was high she didn't see the signs? She put too much trust in someone who looked good. How were you supposed to know who you *could* trust? Oh, Laurel, Laurel. I should have stayed. I shouldn't have left you there like that.

***

Three buses later, I got to the sprawling complex that was San Francisco General. The huge brick buildings looked part prison, part English university. The balloons and flowers I saw other people carrying in made me feel bad. I didn't bring anything. I forgot about that.

Nurses ignored me as I passed their stations and navigated turns. The hallway had that disinfected smell that always seemed to do a poor job of masking the stench of sickness. When I found the right room, I stood at the door and watched Laurel sleep. She looked like hell. Half her face was purple, and her arm was in a cast. Who knew what else was beat up in her body? Her blond hair was a mangled mess against her pillow. She just didn't look like the Laurel I knew.

I snuck into the room and sat down quietly in the chair next to her bed, trying not to wake her up. A nurse took care of that without even flinching. She marched in, put a blood pressure cuff on Laurel's good arm, puffed it up, and then wrote in her chart.

Laurel opened her eyes and watched her.

"You have a visitor," said the nurse, nodding at me.

Laurel turned her head slowly, like it hurt to move.

"Hey, Laurel," I said quietly.

She didn't change her dull expression, though I'm not sure she could have with her face as swollen as it was.

"Jenna," she whispered. "You shouldn't have left."

Knife, right through the heart. She was right. If I had stayed?

"I'm sorry, Laurel. I'm so sorry."

The nurse glanced at me with that you-must-be-pond-scum look, then picked up her things and left the room.

"He was so cute, Jenna. I trusted him." She stared at me with eyes she could barely see with.

"I'm so sorry." I reached out and touched the fingers extending out of her cast. "Could you tell the police who it was?"

She looked away and pulled her arm back with a grimace.

"Do you know who the guy was, Laurel?"

30

A tear leaked out of one eye, and she squeezed both eyes shut.

I looked around for a tissue and grabbed one from a box. I dabbed at her face and smoothed her hair.

"It's okay, Laurel. You're going to get better, and it's going to be okay."

"He raped me, Jenna." Her look accused me, like I was the one who did it. Or it could have just been the puffiness around her eyes.

"Oh, God." I sat down and leaned my head against her bed.

"You should have stayed with me."

She barely spoke out loud, but the impact of her words landed with explosions of pain. The headache came rushing at me like a beast let out to ransack my head. I didn't have anything to say. What could I say? I sat back and held my face in my hand. My head was pounding and I knew she was watching me, waiting for me to admit my guilt. How could I say I wasn't guilty when she lay there in a hospital bed looking like a human punching bag? I looked up at her and sighed heavily. She was crying.

I reached over and squeezed her good hand. "You'll get through this and go on. You will." I sounded insincere to myself.

She didn't say anything. She just turned her head to the window.

Five

A small boy stood up from the middle of the street. His hair was matted with blood and grime. One arm dangled sickeningly and a leg twisted the wrong way. He raised his bent arm and pointed. A woman came running up with a face like a fright mask. Her shrieks filled the whole world. She turned and lunged with hands like claws. Laurel sat up in bed with her bruised face and pointed with her good arm. She mouthed something, but the sound of the other woman's screaming drowned it out.

I cried out and woke myself up. It was still dark. Another nightmare. I stared at the shadowy ceiling while my heart raced. Great—now Laurel joined the cast to accuse me and haunt my sleep. Sleeping had become as dangerous as stepping outside. I honestly didn't know which was worse, the nightmares or the memories. I rolled over and pulled my blankets up under my chin and stared. I couldn't go back to sleep. I knew who was waiting for me. I laid still and watched the dawn slowly fill the room with gray light.

The sound of the front door closing startled me awake. I must have drifted off. I lifted my head and listened to the quiet. Trish must have left for work. I dropped back to my pillow and thought about the day before. I went to see Laurel, but she was miserable, and I didn't know how to make it better. Brenda bit my head off for screwing up a print job, and Trish got mad at me for not cleaning the bathroom.

I stared at the water stain on the ceiling and wondered if the earth could just open up and swallow me away. I lived in San Francisco; it wasn't an unreasonable request. I had a day off with no will to live and nothing to live for. I thought for a brief moment about just staying in bed all day, but was already bored.

I got up and had my coffee and smokes on the back steps. A sparrow hopped around on the ground hoping for something. Idiot bird. I wasn't eating anything. I flicked ash at it, and it flew to a weed growing tall by the railing and cocked its head at me.

"I got nothing. What are you going to do about it?"

It chirped and hopped over to another weed then flew over the fence. Okay, not a total idiot. At least it knew where not to hang out.

I spent the morning cleaning the bathroom and the kitchen and dumping garbage. Then I washed up, threw a fried baloney sandwich and bag of chips into a grocery bag with a bottle of water from the fridge, and grabbed my jacket.

I walked down the block and caught the number five bus on McAllister and headed down Fulton. Gotta love public transportation in the city. The buses were usually on time and you could get anywhere you wanted if you were willing to walk a little. Just stay away from the trolley cars. The tourists didn't actually care if you had someplace to be, they just wanted to ride up the hills and get their pictures taken. Those conductors were so patient.

I shifted over in the seat to let an old lady with her shopping bag sit next to me. She glanced at me then looked away like they do on the bus. It's okay to watch people, just don't make eye contact. Makes them feel uncomfortable.

I looked out the window and saw my stop coming up, so I got up, slid past the old lady, and held onto the pole as we rolled to a stop. I got off at Ocean Beach by Playland. Well, used to be Playland. Everyone still called it that. I waited for the light then crossed the Great Highway and went down to the beach. It was gray and a little cold, but not terrible. Even in the rain, the beach was always a great place to go. There were joggers on both the beach and the paved trail that ran next to the old highway. Old people shuffled along, moms pushed little kids in strollers, and of course dogs in the sand chased anything that could be thrown, though I wasn't sure dogs were really allowed there.

I found a spot in the sand, leaned back against a big piece of driftwood, and stretched out my legs. I missed my old friends, from before. Most of them found other things to do rather than come visit me in prison. Could you blame them? I heard from some, but it was always stilted and awkward. No one ever knew what to say. I never heard from Cassie again. I never asked about her. We used to be such good friends—best friends. The kind you'd talk to about stuff you wouldn't tell your mom. The girl was a mad texter.

I opened the bottle of water and swallowed a mouthful, while a seagull landed in front of me and stared at my baloney sandwich and chips. I didn't know how they always knew when there was food around. Probably because everyone always had food at the beach. It was tempting to feed them, but they said it was bad for them. Though I wasn't sure it was worse than giving them cancer with cigarette smoke. Still, I wasn't sharing. I shooed the bugger off, but he only drifted away a foot and stood there watching, waiting.

Too bad for him. I finished my lunch, shoved the plastic bag in my jacket pocket, and stretched. The sky made brief appearances as the day warmed up a bit. It was nice. A big-footed Labrador puppy came bounding up to me and started licking my face before a guy ran over to pull him off.

"Sorry about that," he said, lugging the puppy away.

"No problem." I wiped slobber off my face with my sleeve.

"Bucky! Come on!" The guy was slapping his thigh to get the dog to follow, but Bucky clearly wanted to chase the seagulls instead.

Good luck, dude. Get a leash.

The waves crashed and sent a toddler screaming to his mother before turning around and following the water back. That water was cold. I so didn't understand the people who wanted to get in it. The ocean here was really for listening to. You know how you watched the water and listened to the waves and willed yourself to be someplace else? There was probably some Vedic principal that helped you train to really do that. People probably studied for years for the day they went to the beach and mediated or whatever, then disappeared, never to be seen again. Did it ever happen? Heck no. Wasn't that the way it went with religion? People studied and bowed and prayed and gave money or fruit, but nothing ever happened. What was the use?

I thought of Laurel, all beat up and swollen in her hospital bed. Part of me knew I wasn't to blame, but part of me wanted to die for leaving her. Would God punish me for that? Was God for real anyway? I thought about Trish and her angel thing. I didn't think she was religious, so it was surprising for her to talk like that, like God cared at all.

I sighed against the wind and watched the ocean roll in small waves. Somewhere there was a place of peace without nightmares and haunting visions. Or maybe we just ended it here, like this was the end of the line. No heaven, no reincarnation. That was okay, too. I could live with that, so to speak. Was there hell? I hoped so. You'd like to think that those SOBs doing unspeakable things out there got it stuck to them in the end, but what about everyone else? I think there would be some mercy in being hit by a bus. No more mystery. You were done. Bye-bye. I just wasn't wild about pain.

I pulled out a cigarette and lit up with my hand cupped over the end. Too many questions. If I could go through life with blinders on and some alert system so I knew not to look a certain direction, I think I could make it. Even then, I needed a brain washing, like a real brain washing, to clean out the ugly memories. And then I needed something that would stop me from hurting anyone ever again. Then I'd be just fine. Blinders, brainwashing, and no hurting people. I'd be just fine. If only.

Sometimes it got so hard. I tried to carry on like it was all good. But it wasn't. It so was not. I pulled out my wallet and took out the worn, folded paper and held it out against the wind. I took a drag and the paper flew back against my other hand. I didn't really need to read it. I knew what it said. I just needed to look at the words again and see if this time it would help.

I forgive you . . . you didn't plan it . . . a terrible thing that happened . . . five-year-old son . . . find peace.

Find peace. Murderers shouldn't find peace. Why should they? Murderers should rot in hell. I almost envied some of the women I knew inside prison. They'd right out stabbed, shot, or tried to kill people—usually boyfriends who'd been beating the hell out of them—but they were proud of it. They didn't feel guilty one bit. I killed a kid by accident with my car and I couldn't live with myself. Find peace. Why should I? How would that bring the kid back to his family? I didn't deserve to live while someone's son was dead.

I wiped a tear and folded the letter. Yet another time it didn't work.

I tried to pull myself together before the headaches started again. It didn't take seeing a little kid with blond hair or a good friend in the hospital to send me to hell. Sometimes I could go there all by myself. I closed my eyes and let the cold wind blow against my face. Stop thinking. Stop thinking about anything. Just sit and feel the wind. Peace, peace, peace, forgive. I could see the words from the letter scroll past my eyelids like the credits in a movie. They grew larger and larger and flew at me like Cecil B. DeMille was directing the epic production of my own personal tragedy. Stop it! Just stop it.

I stood and brushed sand off my pants with a stubby cigarette in my mouth. The wind blew cold through my open jacket. I zipped it closed, but was still cold. Maybe it had more to do with fighting my demons, but the chill seemed to go deep. Suddenly I had an urge to soak in the old claw-foot bathtub. The thought of it made me feel better. I walked back across the highway and caught the bus to go home.

Six

I got off the bus at the top of the Panhandle and walked down through the park. It wasn't as windy there, so it was warmer, nice even. I drank the last of my water and tossed the bottle in a garbage can. The homeless guys would pull it out later during their evening collection. I started to reach for a cigarette but remembered I was almost out. Best to hold off until later so I could stretch them out before I bought more. So expensive anyway. I needed to stop.

"Hey, hi."

I turned around and saw Blue Eyes walking up with a folder in his hand. He smiled like we were BFFs.

I gave him the stink eye. "Why are you always in the park?"

He folded his arms and lifted an eyebrow. "Why are you?"

"I asked first."

He smirked and pointed the folder up the street to a row of old Edwardian houses smashed together to maximize as much space as possible on the block. Gotta love those tall, narrow houses with the old fashioned detail that builders can't afford anymore. "I'm looking at some properties for sale. I always check out the neighborhood and see what it's like before I buy. You know: location, location, location. The right house in the wrong place is the wrong house."

"You're moving there?" I asked.

38

"I'm a property investor. Sometimes I resell them, sometimes I rent them out." He turned and gave me the look. "So, I told *you*."

"Yeah, well, you keep running into me so you must know how bad the neighborhood is." I didn't feel like telling him what I was or wasn't doing there.

"Not from my perspective," he said. He looked around and nodded to a bench. "Sit down and tell me what you like and what you don't like about the area."

I so didn't understand why he wanted to talk to me, but I could tell he was harmless. Anyway, I learned some things in prison. I could defend myself. I followed him over to the bench and sat with my hands in my jacket pockets. He sat half facing me and waited.

"I don't know," I said lamely. "It's okay."

"What about the homeless people?"

I gave my head a shake. "They're all right. They don't hurt anyone. But they do pee in front of my building sometimes."

He nodded. "I've heard that from others. And you like the park." It was a statement really, like he had that figured out.

I shrugged. "Yeah, I like the park."

"What was going on the first time I saw you? You seemed pretty distressed." He looked at me with those blue eyes that made me feel just a little calmer. Kind of made me stop thinking about anything for a second.

I didn't know what to say. I couldn't come out and tell him about seeing the blond kid. I didn't care how nice he was, he was a stranger.

He just waited, patiently.

"Just something that brought back a bad memory," I managed to get out.

He nodded but kept his eyes on me. "I told you before that God can fix things that we can't. I mean it."

"Uh-huh. You know, my roommate thinks you're an angel."

His laugh was genuine. The kind of laugh you'd love to hear again. He shook his head and looked down. "No, I'm not an angel. Tell her I said so."

I knew it! Of course he wasn't an angel. Still, I felt a tiny sadness inside. If he were an angel, maybe he really could help me fix things. Like magic or something. Was there such a thing as angel magic?

"She'll be disappointed," I said. I kicked a pebble with my tennis shoe and watched it bounce away.

"Why did she say that?" he asked.

I shrugged. "I don't know." I looked him over. "The hair. You keep talking about God."

"Mmm, the hair. Yeah, that started turning when I was in high school." He ran his hand through the silver and sighed.

I had to ask. "How old are you really?"

"Twenty-seven, believe it or not." He glanced at me to see if I did believe him.

"Weird."

"I know." He settled back against the bench then turned those eyes on me. "So why are you always in the park?"

I bounced the heel of my tennis shoe on the ground and avoided his eye. "It's my life, what can I say?"

He tucked the folder under his leg to keep it from blowing open in the breeze. "Say you'll let me help. I may not be an angel, but I know God can do anything."

I looked out across the park and shook my head. "I don't really know anything about that."

"That's okay," he said. "If we knew everything we needed to know, we'd be perfect." He shifted his weight and turned more toward me. "Here's the thing. God pointed you out to me for a reason, because He wants to do something extraordinary for you. All you have to do is let him. It's that easy."

"What do you mean God pointed me out to you?"

Just then Crazy Ivan stopped in front of me in a cloud of I-Haven't-Bathed-In-A-Decade aroma. It was enough to make your eyes water. "Gotta smoke?" he asked sheepishly.

"Yeah, sure." I pulled out my pack of cigarettes, looked at my last one, and handed the whole thing to him.

"Thanks," he said, still standing there, expectantly.

I reached in and pulled out my lighter and helped him light up.

He waved his cigarette at me and looked at Jess. "She's a good person."

"I know she is," said Jess. He reached in his pocket and pulled out a bill and handed it to him.

Crazy Ivan took it but stared at it like he didn't recognize what it was then looked at me. "He's a good man. You should marry him." His gargly laugh exposed a bunch of missing teeth and made him look like an old pirate.

"All right, all right, move along," I said and waved him off.

The old man gargled again and jabbed the air at me before shuffling away.

I waited for the breeze to clear the air then thought about the conversation before being interrupted. "So, what did you mean God pointed me out to you?"

Jess folded his hands like he was going to explain something to a child. "Sometimes when you talk to God, he shows you things he wants to point out," he said, glancing at me. "It may be a picture of something that has meaning or something he wants you to start thinking about."

I listened, but I'm not sure why. It sounded stupid.

"So, the other day I was praying, and God showed me a picture of you sitting on a bench in the park here." He looked to see if I was tracking with him.

"What do you mean you saw a picture of me?"

"In my head." He touched the side of his head for emphasis.

"How? Have you ever seen me before?"

41

"Not that I know of, but God has, so it wasn't hard for him to show me who you were."

"Seriously?" I really didn't know how to believe him.

He nodded. "Seriously. It's true. I saw you before I actually saw you. That's why I know God really wants to help you."

I looked away, sincerely missing that last cigarette. Maybe Laurel was right. Stay away from crazies trying to get into your business.

"Look, I know it's hard to take in," he said leaning toward me. "But check this out. I'll bet you that you'll have the best night's sleep of your life tonight. God will do that just to show you he's real and serious about changing your life."

"Uh-huh," I said, the way you did when Crazy Ahab told you about the little people who lived in the bushes.

Jess sat up and picked up his folder. "Call me and let me know." He checked his watch and stood up. "I have to go. Call me, okay?"

I didn't agree. I sat and watched him walk away. Would it be wonderful to have my life cleaned up? Yes. Did I believe it could ever happen? Not in a million years.

Seven

Trish went out with friends so I stayed in my room all evening and read a mystery novel I picked up for free at a garage sale. Around one o'clock, I heard the sound of keys, the front door open and close, and then heels clicking down the hall.

I glanced up at soft tapping at my door. Trish poked her head in slowly, like she was trying to sneak in behind the teacher's back. "Everything okay? Your light was on, so I knew you were up."

I put my book down and nodded. "Yeah. I'm fine. How was your evening?"

She leaned against the doorframe and dangled her girly purse. She had the glazed eyes of a night drinking. "It was all right. Cat got drunk early, so we took her home." She leaned forward with a serious look. "How is your friend, Laurel? Did you see her today?"

I shook my head. "No. I couldn't do it. She blames me for leaving her there at the club."

Trish frowned and leaned back against the doorframe. "You know it's not your fault. If she wasn't kidnapped, she went off with that guy on her own."

"Yeah, I know," I said. "But if I'd stayed with her, maybe she wouldn't have."

"You don't know that and it's not right that she blames you." She pushed a curl out of her eyes and cocked her head. "Did you call the cute guy?"

"Which cute guy?" I asked.

"There's more than one? The guy you met the other night at the club."

"Oh. No. I got a little freaked out about what happened to Laurel. I was afraid to call him." I adjusted the pillow behind my back and scrunched into it.

"I don't think you should be afraid to call him," she said. "Not every guy out there is going to do that to a girl. I think you should give him a chance. You don't have show up at his apartment. Go somewhere public. Get to know him. You never know!"

"Hmm. Maybe."

She yawned violently and looked at her watch. "Yea for Cat getting drunk early so I can go to bed. I wish I could go out and have fun and still get a good night's sleep. I'm getting old! See you tomorrow."

She closed the door and clicked down the hall to her room.

I picked up my book again and tried to figure out if the killer really was the sweet old lady with the great sausage recipe. After a while, I got sleepy. I woke up with daylight seeping into the room and the book on my chest. I looked at the clock on the floor. It was seven o'clock. Traffic was already picking up on Broderick.

I sat up, a little confused. I didn't remember going to sleep. I just remembered reading, then waking up. So strange. I blinked a few times and tried to remember dreaming. Nothing. No nightmares, just sleep. Tears started from my eyes and I squeezed them closed. A night of peace without the haunting images. Even as the guilt slammed back to my consciousness, I was happy for a small favor. Was that God?

I closed the book then got up and stretched. I felt oddly rested. I heard Trish shuffle past in her fuzzy slippers. I wanted to tell her, but I felt a little funny about it. It was something real that happened, or was it? For sure I didn't want to tell Jess. For some reason, I just didn't want to admit that he was right.

***

I took a break at work and went out to smoke with Bats. I passed him my lighter and watched him flick it.

"Bats, you believe in God?" I asked.

He took a drag as the cigarette lit then blew it out and handed the lighter back. "Yeah, I do."

"Really?" I had to look hard at him. A guy like him, tats everywhere, you didn't think of him being religious.

"I mean, I don't go to church, but like, I believe there's a God out there." He waved his cigarette around vaguely then started looking intently at the street and the sky. "Like universal love." He smiled and looked pleased, like he just came up with the idea.

"Universal love." I repeated it so he could hear how stupid it sounded. I pointed up and down the street. "Does this look like universal love to you?"

He shrugged. "It's probably as good as it gets, you know what I mean? I mean, if it weren't for universal love, we'd all probably kill each other and stuff. So universal love is, is like, cool." He looked at me and nodded evenly, mystery solved.

I laughed at him. "Bats, how did you get your name anyway?"

He took a drag and looked down. "I don't even remember," he said in a low voice as he flicked ash on the sidewalk. He pulled up his sleeve on one arm. "I started getting these bat tats a while back, but I don't remember what started it."

"Lost a few years, did you?" It was easy to see.

He nodded. "Yeah. I started getting messed up pretty young." He hugged himself and looked at me. "What about you? You believe in God?"

"I don't know," I shrugged. I told him about Jess seeing a vision of me in the park.

"Whoa! Dude! He must be like a, a guru or something." His eyes got big and he looked at me like I was the guru.

45

"Naw, he's not a guru. He's a just a guy, but he says he prays a lot and God tells him things."

"Like what kind of things?" He frowned. I could tell he was trying to work out how God would tell people things and still fit into universal love. I could see the wheels trying to turn, but they were rusty.

"Like telling him to talk to me, for one. I don't know." I threw my hand up and looked at him.

"Whoa. Hey, did he say anything about me?" He looked so hopeful.

I giggled. "No, he didn't. Maybe next time."

"Yeah, okay," he said, looking disappointed. He wandered back to his store and left me wondering how he managed to do the intricate artwork he did every day. He was good. A little scary, but good.

I went back inside and got a print order blasting away on the monster then looked around the store. It was quiet. I pulled two business cards out of my wallet and looked at them. I flicked them together while I thought about making the call. What would I be setting into motion? I went into the break room and picked up the phone and punched in the number.

"Hello?"

"Hi, this is Jenna."

Eight

I'm not usually a Starbucks person—coffee at home is way cheaper—but I've been known to indulge in a tall caramel macchiato every so often. I heard my name called from the counter and grabbed a cardboard sleeve to slip over the hot cup. I took a careful sip and went to sit outside before somebody grabbed the only table left.

Saturday mornings in San Francisco were about finding a seat at a coffee shop—didn't have to be Starbucks—getting a pastry and coffee, and sitting back. It was even cool to be by yourself. However, a laptop definitely added cred to your coolness if you could look like you were deep into something terribly creative. Wearing the right scarf seemed to be important, too.

I was without laptop or scarf, but wasn't particularly worried about it. I drank my expensive coffee and wondered how my day was going to go. I was nervous. What was I really getting into? Yeah, I was waiting for Manish.

I called him the day before, wondering if calling him while he was probably working was a bad idea. I wondered if he'd remember who I was or how we met. How embarrassing to have to tell him.

"Hi, Jenna," he said when I gave him my name. "I'm glad you called. I didn't think you would."

"So, you remember me?"

"Of course. We danced and you had to leave before you turned into a pumpkin."

"Yes, that's always a problem," I said. "It's so hard to get home that way, being a pumpkin." Stupid! Stupid! Stupid! What was I saying?

"So, we should get together," he said.

"I'd like that." I was thankful he didn't mind stupidity. There was hope.

"I'm going on a hike with a Bay Area hiking group tomorrow. Want to come?"

"Hiking? Yeah, I can do that. It's like walking a lot, right? I do that all the time."

As I sat outside Starbucks, I wondered what it would really be like. Exactly how much "hiking" were we talking about?

"Jenna?"

It was a question. I could tell he wasn't entirely sure what I looked like in the daytime.

"Hi, Manish."

He looked as good as ever. He was wearing a tan jacket with his hands tucked in his jean pockets. He relaxed and smiled. "Ready?"

"Did you want to get something?" I asked and pointed back inside.

"No, I don't drink coffee. I'm fine." His smile was so sweet it made my heart ache.

Cute geek that didn't drink coffee or smoke. This could be trouble.

"One second." I ran back inside and grabbed a lid for my cup and fitted it on. "Okay. I'm good."

"Good." He led the way down the block and across the street to his car. It was a little red sports car. No caffeine or tobacco, but he did like style and performance in his car.

He beeped the lock and opened the door for me. "You brought a lunch?"

"Yep." I patted the small backpack I tucked down by my feet as I got in.

"And water?"

"Yep."

"Alrighty then." He buckled up and we roared off.

I'm nervous in cars anyway, because of my accident, but sitting so low in traffic, I couldn't help clutching the arm rest. I hoped it didn't make him feel like a bad driver. I glanced at him, but he didn't seem to notice. Or maybe he just ignored it. We were on the freeway in a matter of minutes, and I realized I had no idea where we were going.

"We're really going hiking right? You're not taking me out to the hills somewhere where I'm going to be found dead and rotting in six months?" I smiled at him weakly.

He gave me an appalled look. "Yeah, we're really going hiking. What did you think? I'm some kind of ax murderer?"

I shook my head. "No, hiking is good." I watched the cars and listened to the sound of the engine. "It's just that the friend I was with at the club that night got so beat up by the guy she met, she ended up at the hospital."

"What!" He jerked his head toward me with wide eyes. "Seriously?"

"Seriously. She's pretty messed up."

"Is she the girl who came out when I was leaving?"

"Yeah, that was her."

"Oh, man. Did they catch the guy?"

"No. I don't think so."

"Wow. Okay, I guess I see why you'd feel a little insecure. It should be a nice day. That's the plan, honest." He tried to smile but still looked a little horrified.

It was hard to carry on small talk after that.

Eventually, we pulled off the freeway and drove for another forty-five minutes, climbing into the mountains on smaller and smaller roads. We finally slowed down and turned into the entrance to a state park where several people already stood around, coffee cups in hand. Another Indian guy was eating a mcbreakfast sandwich. My kind of hiking fuel.

We got out, gravel crunching under foot, and stretched. It was kind of cold in the shade, and everyone wore light layers. I wondered if I was going to be warm enough. Even though we stood in a parking lot, the wind sighing in the tops of the trees and the echo of ravens cawing gave the place that far-off feel of being further than an hour drive from one of the most famous cities in the world.

"Hey, Manish!"

Manish spoke to a few friends and introduced me. Most of them were Indian or Asian, all in their twenties.

"You guys all know each other from work?" I asked.

They looked at each other awkwardly.

"Some of us work together, but the rest of us met through the online hiking group," said an Asian guy, Ken.

They all nodded and pointed to Adam who started it. Adam blushed like a little girl. For real.

We waited another ten minutes until a few more people showed up, then started off at a trailhead near the ranger station. I glanced at a map on a big wooden board, but there were trail paths leading all over the place. How did people not get lost out there?

"Have you been here before?" I asked Manish.

"Yes. Several times."

"How do you know where to go?"

He pulled out a folded map that looked identical to the one on the board. "You follow the signs on the trail."

"Where'd you get that?" I looked around for a map dispenser.

"I printed it from the website," he said, folding the map and shoving it back into his pocket.

"Of course you did."

I decided not to stress about being lost forever in the woods and to follow people who, apparently, knew where they were going.

It was a beautiful trail through redwood trees and ferns. Absolutely gorgeous. I was surprised the path under the redwoods felt spongy, like carpet. I didn't expect that. Manish and I walked at the end of the line behind everyone. I wasn't having a hard time keeping up, but I walked slower because I liked looking at things.

"Check it out," said Manish. He pointed to something long, fat, and yellow in the dirt by the side of the trail. "Banana slug."

"Eww," I said, peering down at it. It was as long as my hand. "It's gross, but fascinating. It's like a prehistoric slug. Like a dinosaur slug. Look at it moving!"

"Yeah," he laughed. "They're all over here."

Sure enough, I started seeing them along the trail, on the side of trail markers, stuck to small branches. Some were long and thin, others were smaller, but they all looked creepy.

Pretty soon we were out of the cool shade of the redwoods and into an open field where the sun was hot. No more spongy path, it was hard-packed dirt. I hadn't thought about wearing a hat. Everyone else did, even Manish. It was too bad the whole hike wasn't through the trees. I liked that. The field was just a field. I wondered about the allure of walking through the heat when it wasn't even that pretty, but kept my thoughts to myself. I was the newbie, and these guys did this all the time. All the jackets and sweatshirts had been taken off and wrapped around waists or stuffed into backpacks. One guy who'd started out with his T-shirt looking like it had been balled up under his bed had steamed all the wrinkles out with sweat.

Then something caught my eye. "Wait. Are those cows?"

The guy in front of me laughed.

51

"Really? Is that weird?" I asked. "Cows on a trail through the redwoods?"

"Some rancher must lease property here," said Manish. "Just watch where you step."

Thankfully, the path headed down a shallow valley into more redwoods and ferns. It was so refreshing and cool after the open heat. We followed a stream for a while, then we slowed down. I could hear conversation at the head of the line, but couldn't make out what they were talking about. Apparently it was agreed that we would group up there, because everyone dropped their backpacks and found a place to sit.

"Ready for lunch?" asked Manish.

He stepped carefully to a large flat rock next to the stream and held his hand out to help steady me over. I was conscious that it was the first time we touched. For some reason, I felt a little embarrassed.

A pretty, dark-skinned girl with sleek black hair pulled into a claw clip dropped down nearby.

"What was your name again?" she asked with a lilting accent.

"Jenna," I said. I tried to get comfortable on the rock and sat cross-legged next to Manish.

"Oh yeah. I'm Nalla." She motioned to herself and opened her backpack. "How did you two meet?"

I looked at Manish to see if he was going to answer, but he was pulling out food from his pack, apparently ignoring the question.

"At a dance club, in San Francisco," I said finally.

"Oh? I bet that was fun." She took out a plastic container of rice and vegetables and started eating with a plastic fork.

"How can you eat that cold?" I asked.

"I don't mind," she smiled. She looked over at my sandwich. "What are you eating?"

I swallowed. "Um, fried baloney."

"What? Fried baloney?" She crinkled her nose.

I pointed to her lunch. "Let me guess, vegetarian?"

She grinned and bounced her head.

Manish smirked and bit into what looked like a giant roast beef sandwich from a sandwich shop.

"Is it good?" asked Nalla, looking at my baloney like I was eating something still wiggling.

I swallowed hard. "I like it!"

"Hey, don't feel bad," said Manish. "Fried baloney isn't any stranger than what the rest of us eat."

"So how do you two know each other?" I asked Nalla.

She pointed at Manish with her chin. "We work together." She held her hand up to whisper loudly behind it. "Manish is the bad boy of the office." She grinned at him and laughed when he rolled his eyes.

"Really? Tell me more."

Nalla stayed quiet and poked at her rice so Manish had to answer. "I told my parents I wasn't going to marry the girl they arranged for me to marry."

"Why?"

"I didn't know her!"

I could tell by the emotion of his answer that it had been a serious fight.

Nalla grinned mischievously. "Now he's an American boy."

"Yeah? Is that bad?" I looked from one to the other.

"No," said Manish. He took a bite of his sandwich and looked defiant.

"Don't ask his parents," said Nalla in a low voice.

"Ok." It felt a little like sitting next to an open flame with a box of firecrackers, so I decided not to press anymore.

"Where do you work?" asked Nalla, flicking at a leaf that drifted onto her food.

"Copyland on Divisidero," I said.

"Oh? What do you do?" she asked.

Manish seemed to drop a little of his rebelliousness and listened.

"I make copies of stuff. It's a copy store." I tried not be embarrassed, but it was the truth.

Nalla shrugged. "I bet you're good at it."

"Why do you say that?" I asked.

"You seem smart. You want smart people doing that. When you've got a big presentation to make, you want everything to be perfect. I'm glad they have someone like you working there."

I smiled at her. What a nice thing to say.

I looked around at the others sitting in small groups along the steam. A raven cawed, and it echoed in the trees. The only other sound was the murmur of voices against the water flowing past. It was so beautiful.

"You guys hike a lot?" I asked, hoping to settle some feathers a little.

Manish looked at Nalla. "Yeah. Probably once a month, sometimes more often. Depends on who can make it."

"And the weather," said Nalla. "I don't like to hike in the rain, but some do." She pointed behind her to three guys sitting together.

I looked at Nalla's worn boots. "So is it better to wear boots than tennis shoes?" I felt stupid, not even knowing what I should have worn.

She kicked her boots together. "Depends on the trail. If it's pretty smooth like this one, no, your tennis shoes are fine. If it's rocky and it's a little rough, it helps. You want to protect your ankles if you stumble."

"Oh," I nodded. "That makes sense."

"Look!" Nalla pointed behind me.

I turned quickly and saw a doe and a fawn step neatly through the ferns and trot up the hill.

"Wow," I said. "They didn't seem that concerned about us. That's so cool."

"We've seen a lot of wildlife on our hikes," said Nalla.

"Yeah? Like what?"

Nalla and Manish looked at each other to think.

"Coyote, deer," said Manish.

"Remember the bobcat?" asked Nalla.

Manish nodded. "Bobcat, snakes, turkeys."

"Oh, you gotta love seeing turkeys on a hike," I said.

"Lots of turkeys," said Nalla.

"Banana slugs," I suggested.

"Banana slugs," added Manish.

"Ever see a mountain lion?" I asked.

"No, but that would be cool," said Manish.

Hmm. I wondered.

I finished my sandwich and watched the water bubble past a clump of ferns. We were only a few yards away from redwood trees towering massively above us. "It's so pretty here."

Manish nodded. "It's one of my favorite places to hike. It's hard to believe that we're so close to a major tech center. If you didn't hear airplanes overhead, you could feel like a pioneer discovering these redwoods for the first time."

I smiled at him. Cute and poetic.

"You should come again," said Nalla.

I shrugged and smiled at Manish. "Maybe."

We finished our lunch, and everyone got up reluctantly and started down the trail. Sadly, the rest of the hike was not in the cool shade of redwoods. It was hot and sweaty, and I really wished I'd worn a hat.

In the end, I enjoyed the hike. I mean walking; it was just walking. It wasn't like we climbed over mountains, though there were plenty of hills. Good thing I lived in San Francisco. I was used to hill climbing. The hike was good exercise and I met nice people. I got to see Manish with his friends. Nothing to not like.

The group wanted to go out to dinner when we got back to the parking lot, but I bowed out. They might've had giant paychecks from their geek jobs, but I did not. Manish didn't seem to mind as we drove back to the city.

"You want me to drop you off at the Starbucks or where you live?" he asked.

"Starbucks is fine. There's never parking anywhere on my block."

He got lucky and found a spot on the street near where we met up. I didn't jump out right away, so he waited. He seemed like the kind of guy who could sit patiently and not be bothered by it. He leaned his head against his fist with his elbow on the steering wheel and watched me. He had such a kind face.

I looked at him looking me and made a decision. I hesitated but decided to go for it. "Manish, you seem like such a nice guy. I want to tell you something."

His peaceful expression changed to worry but he didn't say anything.

"I mean, I had fun today. It's not anything about you. It's something I wanted you to know about me." I ran my finger along the wood grain dash and glanced at him. He looked scared.

"I went to prison for killing a little boy because I was texting and driving."

The shock was almost physical. He stared at me in horror then looked away and turned to his window.

I waited. I knew I just blew up any paper-doll idealism he might have built up about me. Best to be honest about it all.

He looked back and studied my eyes. "How long were you in prison?"

"Two years."

He turned back to his window. "You killed a boy." He said it quietly, as if he were pronouncing judgment to an invisible court.

When he continued to stare out the window without looking at me, I realized I had crossed the line. Taking a life, no matter how, was something unforgiveable. I understood. I got out and walked away.

Nine

Half a block from Manish's car I lost it. Tears poured out faster than I could wipe them away. That was the way it was going to be, wasn't it? I'd admit who I was to people and then live forever with the rejection. Could you blame them? Sitting that close to a murderer? No one wanted to sign up for that. I didn't blame Manish. Killing a child was about as horrendous as it got. I was amazed there wasn't some kind of cosmic aura that flashed *Child Killer* over my head. Unclean! Parents Protect Your Little Ones!

I dug into my front pants pocket. Nothing. Not in the other side or the back pockets. Finally I found a used tissue in my jacket pocket and blew my nose. What did I expect? Did I really think that it was going to be okay? Just like that, people would suddenly accept that killing a child wasn't that bad? What about in twenty years? Would the horror of it start to fade so I could be just me, without my past? I wondered if I could think up a good lie that would cover all the bases so I'd never have to admit the truth to anyone again.

I wiped my eyes with my sleeve and stopped to avoid bumping a waitress serving coffee in a sidewalk café. I was inching around her when someone stood up from one of the tables and blocked me. I tried to walk around him when I heard his voice.

"Jenna," he said quietly.

I looked up in surprise. "Jess."

He touched my cheek lightly with the back of his finger. "You've been crying. Sit down. Let me order you some tea or something."

I shook my head and tried to push past him, but he put his hand on my shoulder.

"Look at me, Jenna."

I tried not to but couldn't help it. He looked so kind. Would he still look at me like that if he knew?

"Sit down."

He maneuvered me into a chair at his table and sat down across from me. He picked up a stack of papers and dropped them into a briefcase by his feet.

The waitress stopped and cocked her head. "Can I get you anything?" she asked, mercifully not commenting on the emotional mess I clearly was.

"Coffee? Tea?" suggested Jess.

"Yeah, okay. Coffee." I dropped my little backpack by my feet and wiped at my face.

When the waitress left, Jess handed me a napkin. "I'm so sorry."

"What for?" I used the napkin to dab at my eyes and wipe my nose.

"For whatever hurt you so badly." He folded his arms on the table and leaned against them. "I hate seeing you like this."

The waitress came back with a coffee pot and poured into a cup she set in front of me. I tore open a few packets of sugar and stirred. It gave me something to do so I didn't have to respond to him.

"Just so you know," he said softly. "I'm not judging you for anything. I just want to help."

I sipped the hot coffee and had to set it down quickly because I couldn't stop the tears that broke out. I grabbed another napkin and pressed it against my eyes. I struggled to control myself and breathe normally. I dabbed my eyes and tried to blow my nose delicately without looking completely gross.

I was struck by how comforting it was to have someone say they weren't judging me, even if they didn't mean it. I mean, he probably did believe it, but he didn't know me yet. The judging would come, but for now, it felt good that he wanted to be nice.

"I'm sorry," I said. I looked around and people were either ignoring me or didn't notice.

"Don't be sorry." He pushed my cup toward me. "Drink your coffee. Relax."

I picked up the cup and took a drink. It was good coffee. Tasting it wrenched me back out of my free-fall.

"It's good." I set the cup down but still held it gingerly with both hands.

His smile was tinged with concern.

"Jenna, if you had a thousand dollars in your pocket and you passed a homeless person on street asking for a dollar, would you give it to him?"

"Yes," I said, wondering where he was going.

"You'd probably give him more than a dollar wouldn't you?"

"Maybe."

"Would you accept it if it was the other way around? If you needed it?"

"I don't know." I picked up the cup and again and took a sip.

"Pride keeps us from receiving what we need the most sometimes." He toyed with his spoon and watched me. "I have more than a dollar to give you. I have the answer to what you really want to know."

"What are you talking about?"

"I can show you how Jesus can save your life," he said, leaning forward. "That hurt in your heart won't ever go away otherwise. You'll just cover it up with other things and it will fester and make you miserable."

"Too late." He had no idea.

"I'm serious Jenna. Jesus can save your life and give you the peace you really want." He sat back and twirled the spoon while he waited for me to cave.

I set my cup down and sighed. "I know you mean well, Jess. I appreciate it, I really do, but I don't think it's going to do any good."

"I understand," he said. "I just want you to trust me so I can help you."

Trust him. That was going to be a really hard call. I pulled out my wallet and set down my last three dollars. He started to stop me, but dropped back looking defeated.

"Sometimes life just isn't that easy to clean up," I said and walked away.

I went home, trying not to replay the day in my mind. I could almost see black clouds forming over my head as I sank into despair. When I got home, I sat out on the back steps with my head in my hands. I was in the mood to hate life. Laurel got beat up like no one ever should. If I'd stayed with her, would she have been safe? I wish I knew. Manish thought I was a monster. He was right. How was it possible for the pain in my heart to keep getting bigger, deeper? It felt like an infection, gnawing away at flesh and tissue. This was how cancer started, wasn't it? Life was a cancer. It was deadly and poisonous. No matter how hard you tried to avoid it, the poison seeped in and everything you swallowed tasted rotten.

I looked across the yard and the scraggly bushes that grew along the fence. What should I do? What exactly should I do? I thought of Jess and his seriousness in wanting to help. Should I talk to him about it before I decided to cash it in? I couldn't see myself telling him. But really, I knew I wasn't ready to punch out either. I was scared. What if hell was real? I didn't have any illusions about going to heaven, if there was one. It would either be fire and brimstone or nothing. How did you gamble on that? I wiped a tear from my face. If I lived, it was hell, if I died, it was hell.

There wasn't any way to win.

Ten

I picked at the beef stir-fry with little enthusiasm. I just didn't have an appetite.

"You don't have to eat it if you don't want to," said Trish.

I set my fork down and sat back. "I'm sorry. I know you're being nice and making extra for me. I even like this. I'm just not hungry."

She chewed thoughtfully then swallowed. "I'm sorry. Thing is, I understand how shocked Manish was. It's not an easy thing to hear from someone you're interested in."

I nodded. "Yeah, Mom, Dad, meet Jenna. I know there's this whole cultural difference and all, but never mind, that won't matter after I tell you that she went to prison for killing a kid. Pass the *naan?*"

She started to smile then stopped. "So maybe it was a mistake telling him so early. I do think he should know at some point, but maybe it was too soon. If he got to know you better first, maybe it would have been different."

"Maybe. And then I saw Jess."

Her fork stopped in mid air as she stared at a bowl of rice. "Jess?"

"The angel guy who's not really an angel. I was walking home and he was sitting outside at a café and saw me. He kept telling me that Jesus has all the answers." I sighed heavily and pushed at my plate with my thumb. The smell of food when I wasn't hungry was making me feel sick.

Trish finished her bite and leaned her elbows on the table. "You know, Jenna, he might be right. Maybe God is behind this after all. I mean, seriously, how is it that in all of San Francisco, you keep running to this guy? Don't you think that's odd?"

I cleared my throat and waited for her to get serious.

"Well?" She did look serious. "Maybe he *is* right. Maybe there's something to this that neither you or I know about and he does. Just because you don't believe doesn't mean God isn't there to help. Maybe you should check it out." She stabbed a water chestnut and looked at me with eyebrows up.

"Right." It didn't quite come out with contempt, but maybe a little scorn. I was disappointed she would suggest that.

Then she really surprised me. She set her fork down hard and glared at me.

"Look! You mope around here like the world is coming to an end. Yes, you've been through tough times, but life goes on. People came out of the Holocaust and made better lives for themselves than you."

"Yes, but they weren't guilty of taking a child's life were they?" Stupid tears started in my eyes.

"So what?!" she shouted. "Jenna, get a life! I'm sorry, but someone out there is trying to help you and you are refusing to even think about accepting it. You'd rather sit around and pity yourself than see if this Jess guy really does know what he's talking about."

We stared at each other while she let her torrent sink in.

I finally looked away and wiped my eyes. "Okay," I said quietly. "Maybe I should." I looked back at her, hoping she'd soften up again, but she was still fuming. "But I don't know if I can tell him. Look what happened when I told Manish. I can't do it."

She exhaled and relaxed a bit, thankfully, then grabbed her glass of soda so the ice tinkled softly. She took a sip then set it down carefully. "So don't tell him." She looked at me then looked off, like she was still thinking it through.

"You mean, just see what he has to say without going into the gory details?"

"Yeah, why not?" She started to sound pleased with herself and picked up her fork again.

I leaned back in my chair to think about it. She was right that I really did need help. And yes, it was amazing that there was someone out there who kept trying to help me.

"The thing is, he's going to tell me all the stuff I heard in church when I was younger. It didn't help me then, how's it going to help me now?" I looked at her miserably, hoping she would change her mind.

"How old were you then, when you were going to church?"

"High school."

She pushed rice round her plate with the edge of her fork. "I heard a lot of stuff in high school, especially from my parents that I didn't take seriously until I was out on my own. I still think you should give him a chance. If it's total crap, then at least you tried." She set her fork down and leaned against the table and waited for my answer. She had spoken.

I rolled my neck and let out a deep breath. "Okay."

She pulled her cell phone out of her pocket and handed it to me without saying anything. I grunted thanks and took it to my room, feeling like I was going into time-out for being bad.

I sat on the edge of my mattress on the floor with my feet crossed and felt the weight of the phone in my hands. I really didn't want to make that call. I really, really didn't want to make that call. Was it fear? Pride? I don't know, but the only thing that made me fish Jess's business card from my wallet was the thought of having to face Trish if I didn't. I punched in the number and hit send before I could change my mind.

"Hello, this is Jess . . . Hello?"

"Yeah, this is Jenna."

" . . . From the park, Jenna?"

"Yeah."

"Hi." His voice got softer, sweeter. It was amazing how one small word changed his tone.

I looked up at the ceiling and wished it would fall in, right then, right where I was sitting.

"You want to talk about something?" he asked.

"You said I should call." If he would just say he was busy . . .

"I'm glad you did. Let's talk. In fact, you know that diner on the corner of Hayes and Divisadero?"

"Yeah."

"Want to meet there? Say, twenty minutes?"

I said "Okay" and punched the end button before I was forced to say anything else. Great, now I had to sit and listen to him tell me I was going to hell if I didn't find Jesus. I really didn't need anyone helping me understand my situation in life. I had a pretty good feeling for where I was headed. I leaned my face into my hands and moaned. What was I getting myself into?

Eleven

I paced outside the Home Cookin' Diner and smoked. Trish was right. If what he had to say was crap, I could say I tried and be done with it. But I was nervous. I even blew off some guy asking for change, and I almost never did that. I needed to get it together or I'd say something stupid, something I didn't want to get into. I turned in my pace and saw Jess coming up the sidewalk, smiling like he already saw me. I stabbed out my cigarette in the sand bucket next to the door and shoved my hands in my jacket pockets as I bounced on my heels. Here we go.

"Hey, good to see you," he said as he stopped in front of me.

I nodded and looked away so I didn't need to hold eye contact. I got a whiff of soap or something from him. It smelled good.

He watched me squirm for a second then reached for the door. "Let's go in."

The waitress seated us at a booth by the window and left us with menus and coffee.

Jess studied every page like he was ordering his last meal. He finally looked over the top. "Have you eaten?"

"Not really. I wasn't hungry."

He disappeared back into the menu and I heard mumbling.

The waitress came back and stood with her pad and pen ready. "Whatcha having?" she asked, looking at me.

I shook my head. "Nothing."

"We have pie," she said in a singsong voice.

"My treat," said Jess looking very interested at the dessert case.

The waitress winked at him. "We got cherry, choc . . . "

"Cherry," I said, handing her the menu.

"How 'bout you?" she asked, turning to Jess.

"Cherry, chocolate . . . ?" he looked up at her for more information.

She tucked the menu under her arm so she could count her fingers. "Cherry, chocolate cream, lemon meringue, blueberry, and . . . coconut cream."

Jess looked a little dreamy and handed her the menu. "Coconut cream, please."

"You got it," she said and walked away.

I glanced at Jess. He was fingering his spoon and watching me. He had that patient look like he could take all night waiting for me to say something.

"So, my roommate said I should call you." Best to get things started by blaming Trish.

"What about?"

I slumped against the back of the booth and looked up at him. Might as well get it over with. "About what you said about God."

"Do you really want to know?" The spoon never stopped turning in his fingers.

"What? I thought that's all you guys needed to get you on your soapbox."

"Look, I'm happy to talk about God all night, but only if you're really interested in listening, not because you're doing it for your roommate." The spoon stopped while he waited.

I stared at the salt shaker, thinking of all sorts of smart-alecky answers. Just before I said something stupid, the waitress set pie

67

down in front of me. I didn't even look up, I just picked up a fork and started eating. It's a real shame, because I like cherry pie, a lot. I just don't remember if this cherry pie was any good because I was so uncomfortable, trying to think of how not to have a conversation with Jess about God.

My pie was about half gone when the waitress came back and refilled our coffee cups. She glanced at me and then at Jess and walked away singing "I Left My Heart in San Francisco" under her breath.

Jess was patient. He ate his pie, moaning occasionally, clearly enjoying every bite, and waited. He sipped his coffee and scraped his plate of every bit of crumb and whipped cream until the plate looked clean.

I swallowed my last bite, shoved the plate forward, and pulled my coffee mug in front of me. "Okay, I'm interested." I glanced up at him and he smiled, not a big toothy smile, but one that looked very pleased.

He leaned forward and started talking in a low voice, like he was telling me battle plans the enemy wasn't supposed to hear. "God knows everything you've been through, and it breaks his heart that you've been through so much pain."

"What do you know about what I've been through?" I got a panicky feeling that he had some kind of vision about my past.

"I don't know anything. All I have to do is look at how unhappy you are. I've seen you in distress. I know you're going through something very, very hard. All you have to do is give it to God. Jesus said that he would carry our burdens for us so we wouldn't have to."

"Look, I've been there and done that," I said. "That didn't stop God from letting my whole world go to hell."

He pulled back a little and studied me. "It's not God's fault when bad things happen. Sometimes it's our own actions that get us into trouble."

"What about the ones who are young and innocent and bad things happen to them?" My mind went back immediately to a small body lying in the road.

"Jenna," he said softly. "It's not God's fault that people don't listen to him. You know that saying—'no man is an island'? It's true. Good or bad, our lives affect other people." He leaned down to look into my face. "I don't need to know what happened. I don't want to know. I just want you to understand that Jesus died on the cross so that you can let go of your pain and live, finally live, in peace."

I didn't know what it was, but something about his words went straight to my heart. Live in peace? Was that really possible? I looked up at him and stared into those blue eyes. He did have peace inside, I could see it. He knew what he was talking about.

"You said you've been there and tried that," he said. "Let's give it another shot. Let's make sure that this time you really connect with the King of Kings and Lord of Lords. It's time to live without pain in your heart."

I looked down at the table and wondered what that would feel like. A life without guilt? Sleep without nightmares? Passing small boys on the street without anxiety attacks? I wanted it. He was offering me a magic pill, and I wanted it. I felt emotion well up behind my eyes, but I forced myself not to cry. Unfortunately, I couldn't talk either. I looked up at him and nodded. It was all I could do.

"Okay, this is what we're going to do. I'll pray a prayer and you repeat after me. Okay?" He held my look and I nodded.

And so I prayed, choking it out as best I could.

When we finished, I sat back to check myself out. How did I feel? Was it different? Not really. "So, when does the peace kick in?"

"It comes as you begin to trust God. You just gave your life to him, now it's his turn to take care of you. But you have to let him. The more you trust him, the more peace you feel. Want lots of peace?" He left the question hanging.

"Trust God a lot." I finished for him. "Got it. So, how does that work anyway?"

"Talk to him. Tell him everything you're tired of carrying. Ask him to fix it. What you just did, receiving Jesus in your heart, that was the easy part. Letting God change your character will take years. Baby steps."

"Okay." I felt like I could really look at him now. I didn't feel—I don't know—guilty. That right there was major. I looked off across the room as I realized that something did feel different inside.

"More coffee?" The waitress stood holding the pot over my cup.

I glanced at Jess. Did he want to stay longer?

He raised both eyebrows and pushed his cup toward her so she refilled both.

We stayed another hour and he told me about prayer and reading the Bible and how that was going to let God change me the way I needed to be changed. He pulled out a Bible he brought with him and gave it to me.

"Read through John to start." He opened the book and showed me where John was.

"That's one of the gospels," I said. Memories stirred from another lifetime.

"That's right," he nodded.

It felt weird that I knew about the gospels but didn't know how much it was supposed to change me. I held the book to my chest as I slumped back against the booth. "Thanks."

He drained the last of his cup and pulled out money for the bill, then glanced at me. "You're welcome. But it's really God going after you. He just used me to do it."

"Yeah, but I didn't make it easy."

He smirked. "No, you didn't. You kind of scared me."

"Great." I slid out of the booth.

"I'm just saying, I'm happy to see you friendly," he said, following me out the door.

I stopped to give him a fake glare, but he was zipping up his jacket.

"Did you drive?" he asked.

"No, I live really close."

"Let me walk you home then," he said.

"You don't have to do that." I zipped my own jacket with my new Bible held tight under my arm.

"I know." He stood with his hands in his pockets.

"Fine. This way."

We crossed the street and walked down the block. I couldn't believe I was walking this guy to my apartment, but it seemed different now, like we were friends. I kind of wondered if there was anything more than that as I glanced at him out of the corner of my eye. Cute guy, even with the silver hair.

We stopped in front of my building, and I nodded toward it. He sized it up with his real estate eyes and seemed to find it acceptable.

"Okay, well, have a good night," he said. He pointed to the book under my arm. "Read, read, read."

"I will." I bounced my head.

"Can I call you and see how you're doing?"

"I don't have a phone. I used my roommate's phone to call you." I suddenly felt stupid not having a cell phone.

"So, how about we plan to meet again and you tell me what you're learning?" He stepped forward to let a couple walk past.

"Okay, but what if I don't have anything to report?"

He smiled. "You will. How about Wednesday? Same bat time? Same bat place?"

"Sure, fine."

"Okay then, Jenna." He gave me a quick hug, like you do with aunts and cousins and wretches who are trying to find their way. "Have a good night."

"Sounds good to me." I turned away the same time he did, but I glanced at him as I unlocked the door. He wanted to see me again.

Twelve

I sat up reading the gospel of John for quite a while, then went to sleep. My dreams were strange. The old nightmares came back, but I dreamed Jesus was whacking at them with a sword. I woke up feeling rested, but I couldn't get the picture of Jesus hacking at the nightmares out of my head. I thought about the stories I read in John. I wished I could have been there to see it all happening. Jesus sounded like someone I would listen to.

I went to work feeling kind of happy. It was hard to put in words, but it was like I felt hopeful, like maybe my life wasn't a total loss after all.

It must have shown on my face because Brenda asked me, "What's with you? You get lucky last night?"

I stopped feeding the monster for a second and shook my head. "No." I pushed the paper drawer closed with my foot and picked up the empty carton. I went over to where she was working on the computer and leaned the carton on top of the counter. "Brenda, you ever read the Bible?"

She looked up a little startled and gave me a funny look. "Is that what's going on? You found *Jesus?*"

"Well, kind of," I said. "I prayed with a guy and I started reading the Bible. It's pretty amazing, Brenda. If you've never read it, you should. I feel better today than I have . . . I don't know, ever."

She didn't say anything, just watched me walk away with the empty paper carton. I knew what she was thinking because I knew what went through my head when I heard people go off in Jesus talk. I was okay with that, I understood.

**

I got off the bus on Geary and walked a few blocks to a plain looking apartment building. I buzzed room number seven on the keypad next to the outside door and hugged my jacket close because the wind was cold.

"Who is it?" asked a staticky voice from the intercom.

"Jenna. Jenna Johnson, from work," I said, leaning in close to the small speaker.

No response. I wondered if she was going to let me in. Finally the door clicked and I pushed it open. I climbed the narrow, carpeted stairway that deadened my steps to the second floor, found number seven, and knocked.

Laurel opened the door and stood aside. Her casted arm was in a sling and her face was still bruised a little, but not swollen like the last time I saw her.

"Hi, Laurel," I said as I followed her in.

"Hi." She walked into the living room and sat gingerly on a couch next to a pile of magazines.

"I brought Chinese food," I said, holding up a bag.

"You didn't have to do that," she said dully. She rolled her big eyes up at me with no enthusiasm at seeing a friend.

I tried to gauge to see if she was mad at me, but I couldn't tell.

"You want it now, while it's still hot?" I asked, feeling the bag for warmth.

She dropped her head back against the couch and shrugged. "Sure, why not."

"Okay." I went into the kitchen and found plates and spoons and took everything out to the small coffee table and spread it out.

I pulled out chopsticks but I realized it was her right arm in the cast.

"Fork for you," I said, and brought one back from the kitchen.

She watched me quietly as I opened up all the little boxes and stuck in spoons.

"Want me to fill your plate for you?" I asked.

"Sure."

I gave her some of everything and handed her the plate and fork. She balanced it on her lap and started to clumsily stab at food with her left hand.

I filled my own plate and sat cross-legged on the floor in front of her.

"You look better," I said, trying to ignore the fading green bruises on her cheek.

She gave me an irritated look and swirled up chow mien awkwardly.

"Laurel, I'm so sorry for this happening to you."

She didn't say anything.

"Maybe I could get some movies," I suggested, and dipped an egg roll in hot mustard.

Nothing.

I decided to eat and let her be quiet. When we were done, I cleaned up everything and put the leftovers in her refrigerator. I went back to the living room and sat in a chair near her and leaned forward.

"Laurel, talk to me."

She seemed to suddenly get emotional. She took a deep breath and let it out shakily. "I can't, Jenna. I can't talk about it."

I nodded. "I understand. When I had my car accident—it's completely different from what you went through—but it was trauma. I couldn't talk about it for the longest time. It's okay."

She looked a little relieved and wiped her eyes with her free hand.

"I don't mean to get sappy, but I just wanted you to know that I'm here for you," I said. "I mean it."

She didn't look particularly encouraged.

"Look, none of my friends were there for me after my accident." I looked down at my hands as old memories rushed in. "No one. Yeah, my Mom, but all my friends bailed. I know what it feels like to be left alone with pain, and I don't want you to feel that."

"So, where've you been?" she asked sharply.

I sighed. "You were so mad at me. And I felt guilty for leaving you that night. But I've been thinking about you a lot and hoping that you were getting better."

She seemed to be studying the flower pattern on the couch cushion for irregularities.

"But I'm here now," I said. "I'm still your friend."

Her face unclouded a little. "Thanks."

It felt like something broke. She relaxed, and I felt like we were okay again.

I pointed to the TV. "So what's on?"

She gave me a guilty smile. "I've been watching Cagney and Lacy reruns."

"Cool." I settled back in the chair, and she picked up the remote.

Thirteen

"What up, Jenna?" Bats took his lighter out for me then pulled a cigarette from behind his ear.

I blew out a stream of smoke and pulled my collar up against the nippy air. "I've been reading in the Bible," I said and hugged my jacket close to my body.

"Oh, yeah?" He looked genuinely interested.

"It's pretty good. But there's a lot of stuff I don't get. Like, they used to kill their enemies for not believing in God. And if you did something wrong, you had to kill an animal to make it right."

"You mean, just go out in a field and shoot a cow?" He wrinkled his nose as he thought about it.

"No, you had to take it to a priest, and he did it," I said. "And that story about Moses? Do *not* get God pissed off."

"No way," said Bats. "I thought the Bible was all holy and stuff like that."

"I don't know," I said. "I've been reading it like Jess told me. Remember the guy who saw the vision of me?"

Bats looked up quickly. "The guru?"

"He's not a guru," I tapped ash and shook my head. "He's just a guy. Anyway, he's helping me. He helped me pray and ask Jesus to forgive me and come into my heart."

Bats puckered his lips and nodded. "That's cool." He looked me over like he was checking for anything new. "Universal love," he said, eyeing me, and took a puff.

"Yeah, there's a lot about love actually. And how you treat people. It's a big deal. It's just not good to act all pretentious, know what I mean?"

"Pretentious," he repeated, squinting a little.

"You know, acting like you're all that when you're not. You have to be nice to people."

"Yeah, that's cool," said Bats. "I never like to act pretentious. It's bad for business."

A guy covered in black leather roared past on a motorcycle and yelled something.

Bats looked up and waved. "Hey, Stevie!" He settled back against the wall. "That guy . . . still owes me money." He cocked his head toward me and looked serious. "I heard about that Laurel girl. You know how she is?"

"Doing better," I said.

He shook his head. "That's rotten to beat up a girl like that. I hope they find the SOB that did it."

"I know. Me too."

"Was she . . . raped, or anything?" he asked.

I didn't know what I should tell him, so I hesitated. He pressed his lips and nodded. I guess I didn't have to say anything. Maybe Bats had more going on than I thought.

"Let me know if there's anything I can do," he said.

"Okay." I didn't have a clue what he could do, but it was nice of him to offer.

"I better get back," I said and stubbed out the butt on the ground.

"Okay, see ya Jenna," said Bats.

***

Wednesday night I paced outside the diner for a good twenty minutes. A homeless woman sitting against the wall took all the

78

change I gave her and watched me with an amused look. I burned through two cigarettes and thought seriously about a third. I'm not really a chain smoker, but I was anxious. Not anxious in a scary way, but more like excited. I wanted to talk to Jess about what I had read. I had so many questions.

I turned around and saw him crossing the street with a small mob of people. You just can't miss him in a crowd with that hair and those eyes. He looked so happy to see me. It made me feel good that someone would be that happy to see me.

"Hey," I said.

"Hey ho!" He grinned and stopped with his arms crossed, looking cocky. "So, you came back for another round. I'm glad."

"Yeah, I'm back," I nodded.

"How was your day?" he asked.

I smiled automatically as I thought about it. "It was a good day. I mean, it wasn't perfect. I still got mad at the stupid copy machine I work on, and then I got mad that I got mad." I pulled out the Bible I was holding and looked at it. "Then I read some more and I felt a lot better."

"Good." He turned and opened the door to the diner. "Tell me about it inside."

We ordered coffee from the same waitress, and Jess sat back with his hands in his lap and waited.

I put the Bible on the table and patted it. "I read through John, and a bunch of other places."

"Really?"

"Yeah. Jesus is kind of like Hamlet, isn't he?"

"Hamlet?" His forehead wrinkled up.

"I mean, except Jesus didn't kill anyone, and he came back alive after he died." I thought it about it a little more. "I guess he's not like Hamlet at all, it's just that Hamlet is my favorite character in Shakespeare, and Jesus seems larger than life like that."

I thought Jess would say that Jesus *was* larger than life, since he came back from the dead, but he didn't, he just sat there. "I've never thought about him like that before—Jesus or Hamlet," he said finally.

I laughed. "I know, it's stupid." I looked up and smiled at the waitress as she set down the coffee in front of us. I stirred in sugar as she rattled off the pie offerings.

"Apple, cherry, pecan, lemon meringue?" She held up her coffee pot and rested her free hand on her hip while she looked back and forth between us.

Jess tilted his head and raised his eyebrows at me.

"Yeah, okay," I said. I got paid that day so I was prepared to pay for both of us.

"Good, so what'll you have?" she asked.

"Lemon meringue sounds good to me," I said.

Jess looked over at the pies in the display case. "Pecan, please."

She brought us both huge pieces of pie. They seemed much larger than the last time. It was kind of ridiculous.

"Seriously?" I looked up at her.

"You'll love it," was all she said before walking away.

Jess looked at his piece like a starved man.

"Have you had dinner?" I asked.

"Uh-huh." He never took his eyes off the pie. "This looks so good."

We stopped talking while we ate our pie and drank our coffee. I remembered my grandmother would make lemon meringue pies like that—tart custard, sweet, flaky crust. Just the way it was supposed to be.

I took a sip from my cup and set it down carefully on the little paper circle. I asked him my questions, stuff I just wasn't sure about. Jess had a good answer for everything. No matter what I asked him, he always seemed to know how to explain it so it made sense.

I looked at the Bible then smiled at him. "Thank you. This is just so . . . nice." I meant it. I felt happy inside. I looked at Jess's smiling face and realized I was looking at him like he was a guy, like someone interested in me instead of someone being nice because I was a basket case who needed God. I had to be careful. My luck with guys hadn't been that great, ever.

"I'm glad you're happy." He ate the last of his crust and pushed the plate aside. "You look like a new person compared to the first time I saw you."

"Oh, man!" I thought back to that day. How embarrassing it seemed now. I must have looked like a freak.

"You know, it still takes time," he said. "Sometimes God takes away things that hurt us just like that." He snapped his fingers. "Others take more time. They just get better and better as we let him fix us."

"Okay, that's good to know." I folded my napkin into squares and wondered how fast I was going to get rid of all the bad stuff. I had a lot to get rid of.

He drained his coffee and looked up expectantly. "Ready to go?"

"Yep."

He picked up the bill that the waitress pushed by his coffee cup.

"Hey! I was going to get that," I said. "I didn't see her set it down."

"I appreciate that," he said. "But I'll take care of it."

I pressed my lips together as I watched him pay. I hated feeling like a mooch.

He saw my look and held the door open for me. "Don't rob other people of the opportunity to bless you."

"What?" I zipped up my jacket and tried to work that out.

"Seriously," he said. "When we bless other people, God blesses us back. Don't take that away from someone who wants to do something good for you."

"But what if I want to be the one to do something good?"

He smiled. "You'll get your chance."

We walked back to my house like friends, and I wondered what this really was. Was he only interested in me because he wanted to see God fix my life, or did he like me like I was starting to like him? I was afraid of what this wasn't. I didn't want to set myself up for getting hurt again.

We stopped in front of my apartment and looked at each other.

"Want to meet again tomorrow night?" he asked. He asked it so casually that I couldn't tell what was behind it.

"Um, not tomorrow night. I can't." I lied. I lied to the man who brought me to Jesus. That was probably pretty bad. I'd have to talk to God about it later.

He just nodded. "That's okay. If you want to save up your questions and get together once a week that's okay too."

Once a week! Did I really want to wait that long to see him again? No, he was right. I needed to focus on the stuff I was supposed to learn from the Bible. Anything else would just confuse me even more.

"That sounds okay to me." I didn't lie about that.

I started to turn, but he took a step that made me stop. I thought he was going to do something else, but he just asked me a question.

"How do you feel about going to church on Sunday? It's a really good idea to connect with other Christians. It will help you get stronger in your faith, trust me."

"Okay. I guess I should." It had been so long since I'd been to church, I was curious about what it would be like now.

"Good. I can pick you up Sunday morning, about 9:30." He gave me a thumbs-up and walked off.

Trish was in the kitchen, pulling cookies out of the oven with her big oven mitts with owl faces on them.

"Perfect timing!" she said, looking up. "They're still hot, but give them a minute."

"Oh, no," I said. "I just had a huge piece of lemon meringue pie. I mean huge." I leaned against the counter and watched her.

She looked around at me surprised. "You did?"

"I met Jess at a diner. We've been talking about God. I had a lot of questions about what I've been reading in the Bible."

"Good!" She picked up a spatula and started moving cookies to a wire rack.

"I prayed to ask Jesus into my heart," I said. I forgot we'd been missing each other for a few days so I hadn't told her yet.

"Really?" She turned and faced me, the spatula dangling from her hand. "How'd that go?"

"Pretty good. He told me I'd find peace with God if I did. And I did, find peace."

"Did you tell him?"

I knew what she meant. "No. He said he knew I was going through some bad stuff, but he didn't want to know what it was. I'm glad. I don't know why I don't mind talking to you about it, but I don't feel comfortable telling him. Not after Manish."

She shrugged. "You just met him. You might later on."

"Yeah, maybe. He's going to pick me up and take me to church on Sunday."

"Yeah? Is he cute? Do you like him?" She toyed with the spatula and made a goofy face.

I think I blushed a little. "He is cute. That silver hair and his blue eyes . . . he's just so attractive. But!"

"But? You don't think it's the right thing to start liking him since he's trying to help you and all." She sighed with the air of knowing it all.

"Yep." I reached over and took a broken cookie off the tray. "I think he's just being nice. I don't know. I'm not very good at that stuff."

Trish turned back to her cookies. "Give it time. If it's meant to be it will work out."

Encouragement and wisdom, I loved that in a friend.

Fourteen

I kicked the monster in the stomach as hard as I dared. Really I was closing the paper tray with my foot. I just did it with excessive enthusiasm. I couldn't get the beast to work. I did all the checks I knew to do, and it wouldn't start. I leaned against the control panel and growled. It was half way into a print job that I would have to finish on Mini Me, which was smaller, slower, and even older than the monster.

I glanced over at Brenda. She was having a bad day too. Something about a phone call from her kid's school. She wasn't going to be in the mood to let me sit outside and smoke for the next two hours while I cooled off.

I growled again at the beast and started pulling out the sheets that had printed like they were supposed to. I was lucky it was just a straight-up print job with no duplexing or collating. I started up Mini Me and dared it stop. It did tremble a little, but I'm pretty sure it wasn't because of me. It was just old.

I turned to go to the break room and saw Manish standing by the counter. Brenda looked from him to me and went back to work.

"Hey," I said, as I wiped my hands on my pants and walked over to him. Manish? Really?

"Hi," he said sheepishly.

We stood there staring at each other for a second. Then I realized he didn't know what to say. I walked past him and nodded to the front door, and he followed me out.

"Mind if I smoke?" I asked.

"I'm not sure I knew you smoked," he said.

Great. Probably just cancelled out what ever goodwill brought him to find me. I shrugged and put the cigarettes packet back in my pocket. I really wanted one though. I folded my arms, leaned against the wall, and watched him.

He stood with his hands in his pockets looking down at the pavement. "Jenna, I came to apologize."

I shrugged again. "You don't have to. I told you something completely shocking. I understand."

"But that's just it," he said looking up. "You told me something very hard, and I let you go without acknowledging how hard it must have been. I shouldn't have done that."

I looked down the sidewalk and shook my head. "Manish, what I told you was terrible. Just because I told you about it doesn't make me a good person."

"But it was an accident, wasn't it?" The question hung there like he really needed to know.

I nodded and looked in his eyes. "Yeah. It was an accident. Are you kidding? A five year old boy?" I had to look away. I was starting to remember too much.

He stepped up to me and held my shoulders until I looked at him. "Accidents don't make you a bad person, Jenna. I'm sure you've learned a lot about texting and driving, am I right?"

I smirked. "I don't even own a car or a cell phone now."

He smiled. "See? You're not a bad person. If anything, I was the bad person for letting you feel hurt. Will you forgive me?" He rubbed my shoulders then squeezed them.

"Are you kidding? Of course." Whatever he was offering, I wanted in.

He exhaled then pulled me into a warm hug. I almost cried. Having him come find me to apologize and hold me was more than I would have ever thought possible. I leaned my forehead against his shoulder and closed my eyes. It was like a dream. Suddenly I didn't care what Mini Me did or didn't do to the print job. I was in heaven.

He pulled back and looked in my eyes. "Can I come back when you get off and take you to dinner?"

I nodded like an idiot.

He grinned. "Good. What time?"

"Five," I managed to say.

"Okay. I'll see you at five." He squeezed my shoulders again and walked away.

I went back inside in a daze. Did that really just happen? Did Manish just come out of the blue and change my day from horrible to heavenly like Prince Charming?

Brenda didn't look up, but pointed with her pen to Mini Me. I didn't even care that it was stopped when it wasn't supposed to be. I pulled out the crumpled paper inside and started the machine up again without a single evil thought. I even patted it on its grimy head and watched it chug for a while. I had a dinner date.

***

Five o'clock could not come fast enough. You know how that is? Every second on the clock actually takes half a minute. I'm not sure how that works, but when I really need time to slow down, every second takes minus ten seconds. It's weird like that.

I wondered about wearing my Sylvester the cat T-shirt, but it wasn't like I had other options to change into. Manish was going to have to love me T-shirts and all. We came as a package set. I was just pulling my jacket on when he walked in.

"Hey!" I said as I went up to him and tugged at his jacket collar.

"Ready?" He held the door open and followed me out.

86

"You came back." I put my hands in my pockets and looked up at him.

"Of course I came back," he said. "You didn't think I would?"

"I knew you would," I said. "I was just so surprised to see you earlier, it didn't seem real."

"Oh." He smiled and put his arm around me and walked me down the street. "It's okay though, right?"

I nodded. "Yeah. It's most definitely okay."

His car was parked around the block. He unlocked the passenger door, and I let myself down on the soft leather seat. When he was ready to pull out, he glanced over at me. "How do you feel about Thai food?"

"I love Thai."

"Good." He checked his mirrors and pulled into traffic.

"So what made you come see me?" I asked over the noise of the engine.

He didn't look at me because he was changing lanes. "You remember Nalla? She asked about you."

My stomach knotted up. "What did you tell her?"

"I told her what you told me," he said simply.

"And?"

"She said I was wrong. She said I owed you an apology. I thought about it, and she was right."

"So I guess I should thank Nalla," I said.

"Do you mind that I told her?"

"Normally I would say yes, but I'm glad you did. You came back."

He smiled, laid his hand on mine, and squeezed it.

***

Decorated in dark teak and gold, the restaurant was small and nearly full. Apparently people liked it, which was a good sign. We sat at table against the wall and squinted at the menu in the low light of a candle burning in a gold vase.

After we ordered, Manish stared into my eyes. It wasn't as awkward as it sounds. We needed to reconnect, assure ourselves that we were okay.

He had a sophisticated manner that made him look far more comfortable with himself than I felt. He rested his arms on the table and leaned in. "What are you thinking?"

"I was thinking how glad I am that you wanted to see me again." I played with my teacup and wondered how open he was going to be.

He sat back and looked a little embarrassed. "I'm glad I did. I like being with you. Did you like the hike? You seemed to enjoy yourself."

I chuckled. "Yeah. I haven't done a lot of hiking, but I liked it. It was nice being out in the trees. It was really pretty."

"It is. You seemed to get along with everyone, too. Nalla was very taken with you."

"Really?" I didn't know why I was so surprised.

He took a sip of tea and set it down. "Tell me more about yourself."

"Like what?"

"Like where you grew up."

Before I could answer, the food came and we spent some time dishing out curry and noodles and commenting on how everything tasted. Then we talked. I told him about my family in Northern California, and he told me about his family in Mumbai. I told him about my old plans to go to SFU. He told me about going to the Indian Institute of Technology and working in Silicon Valley. Then we talked through another pot of tea about silly things, like monster movies and my grandmother's cure for hiccups. He laughed at my story about my first attempts to surf, and I listened in awe as he told me about India.

We walked back to the car hand in hand. Whatever anxiety we both felt before was in the past. But one thing we didn't talk about in all the talking skirted around my thoughts.

I waited for him to click his seat belt. "Manish, are you religious?"

He shrugged. "Not really. My parents are, but I never followed their religion. It's more cultural to me than anything. What about you? Are you religious?"

Good question. "I just became a Christian. I'm going to go to church on Sunday with a friend. Want to come?"

He grimaced. "Not really."

I smiled back. "It's okay. I'm not sure what it will be like myself."

"So why are you going?"

"I think it's going to help me," I said. "What I told you, about going to prison? That left me pretty beat-up. I met a guy who's helping me let God fix all that."

"Is it helping?"

"So far."

"Then good." He smiled and started the engine.

We drove through the city just to be together, because the evening was too perfect to end, because we knew those times of magic and romance were over too fast. We ended up near the Marina and parked. We got out and walked hand in hand over the grass and watched the lights on the Golden Gate Bridge. I'm pretty sure there were other people nearby, but I can't remember exactly. I only remember Manish, his voice, his laugh, his arm around my shoulders, his kiss when he stopped and turned me to face him.

All kinds of fireworks went off inside when Manish kissed me. He was smart, good looking, interesting, and he wanted to be with me. I leaned my head against his neck and realized I never ever remembered feeling so happy. It was only one date, but after all the hell I'd been through, it felt like answered prayer. It felt like something warming up my cold, cold heart that I thought I would never feel.

The wind from the bay whipped around us, and I shivered involuntarily.

"You're cold. We should go," he said as he pulled my jacket tight around me.

"I hate to leave though," I said. "It's been so great tonight."

"Who said we had to end it?" He looked evenly at me and I knew he wasn't really asking a question. "We can go someplace warmer." His voice was low and velvety.

I studied his eyes to confirm what he implied. Why not? How long had I been miserable? How long had I lived tortured and alone? I looked back at him and nodded. "Okay, let's do that."

Fifteen

Early light danced on the far wall as a breeze bounced the shadow of leaves against the shadow of a lattice. I watched it take on sharper and sharper clarity as the light grew stronger. I was amazed at how fast it changed. The sound of the shower stopped abruptly, and I knew I needed to get up. Manish said he would drop me off at my apartment on his way to work. I'd have time to shower and change before going to work myself.

I slid out of bed and pulled my clothes on quickly. I didn't want him to see me naked. Stupid, after what we did the night before. I pulled my T-shirt on and stood in front of a mirror in his room. My hair was bed-head on steroids. I ran my hands through it, but only managed to flatten it down a little. I needed a knit hat—one of those full face ones.

Manish walked out of the bathroom in a mist of warm shampoo with a towel wrapped around his waist. He stood behind me, put his arms around me, and kissed the top of my head. His body was warm from the shower and still a little damp. "You should have joined me."

I looked back at him in the mirror and shook my head. "I need clothes to change into anyway. I'll shower at home."

He turned me around to look in my face. "Are you okay? Any reservations about last night?"

I didn't answer right away because I wasn't sure I knew what the answer was.

He lifted my chin and studied my eyes.

"I'm not sure," I said. "Part of me says I'm okay, part of me says I don't know what I want."

He used both hands to sweep hair from my face with a look of concern. "I don't want you to feel bad about being with me. And just so you know, I don't feel bad at all about being with you." Then he leaned in and kissed me like he did at the Marina, and I thought the heat that rose up inside me would startle him, but he didn't seem to notice.

I pulled back and looked at the clock next to his bed. "We have to get going or we'll both be late."

He dropped his hands reluctantly and looked resigned. "You're right." He dressed while I wandered around his apartment looking at artifacts from India. "What about something to eat? Coffee?" he asked as he stood in the bedroom doorway and tucked his shirt into his pants.

I shrugged. "I'm good. I'll grab some coffee at my apartment."

"You sure? We can stop at Starbucks."

I put a carved elephant back in its place and looked at him. "It's okay."

We drove through the city quietly. I just wasn't up to conversation. I watched people out-and-about on the streets, and Manish stole glances at me. I know he was worried about what we did. So was I.

***

I pulled the key out of the door and closed it softly behind me.

Trish came out of her room, leaned against the doorframe in her pink robe, and folded her arms like she was waiting for juicy news. She gave me a sly smile and tilted her head. "Well?"

I tossed my keys on the floor of my room and turned to her. "Manish came to see me at work yesterday."

"Manish! Really?" Her eyes got big. "I thought he was history."

"So did I."

"Must have been a good night," she said. "Or not. Why do you look like that?"

"Like what?"

"Like you're not very happy about it at all." Her smile disappeared, and she bit her lip.

"I don't know," I said. I shoved my hands into my pockets and slumped against the hallway wall. "Manish is fantastic. He really is. But something doesn't feel right." I rubbed my stomach like the uneasiness I was feeling lived there.

"Maybe you weren't ready to sleep with him yet."

"Or at all," I said.

"Really?" She looked curious.

"I don't know, Trish. Wouldn't you think that a guy who knows about me and wants to be with me anyway, and who is as smart and good looking as he is would make me feel like a real person finally?"

She didn't answer.

"Instead, I feel like I'm getting away with something my parents wouldn't approve of. It's not what I thought it would be like."

She shook her head and shrugged. "Take your time. It'll work out one way or another. The shower's yours if you need it," she said and disappeared back into her room.

I stood under the warm water hitting my face with my eyes closed. *God, what am I getting myself into? What am I really doing with my life?* Was it wrong to be with Manish, or was it just wrong to have sex with Manish? Something definitely didn't feel right. As much as I wanted to be with him, I felt very uneasy when I thought of him.

I saw my Bible on the floor by my bed as I dressed and started thinking about Jesus. Jesus was awesome. Talk about confident. That man was in charge! I remembered John 3:16, "For God so loved the world that he gave his only begotten Son." God loves me. God loves me. I kept thinking about that as I swallowed coffee and smoked out on the back steps. Thinking about God made me feel better. I had to figure out how to deal with my life and not get any more screwed up.

Sixteen

I'd just started a big print job at work when Brenda yelled at me.

She nodded to the door. "Jenna! I think this one's for you,"

Bats sort of floated around the front door, looking a little lost. He doesn't usually come inside our shop, so he wasn't sure what to do.

"Hey, Bats!" I called to him. "Just a second." I made sure it was safe to walk away before the monster did anything that would bite me in the butt later.

We went out and leaned against the side of the building and lit up.

He looked down the street then back to me. "You got your Bible?"

"Not with me."

He looked nervous, edgier than usual.

"You okay?"

He shook his head again, but I couldn't tell what it meant.

"Look, Bats, is everything okay?"

He looked around like an informant in the movies then took a drag. I was suddenly shocked by how skinny he was. I wondered when he'd last had real food. He dipped his head and leaned close.

"Jenna, I did something stupid."

Oh, man. That could be real trouble. "What is it, Bats?" I blew out smoke and prepared myself.

"A guy came in for a tat. Some of that Chinese shi . . . um, words, whatever. So I was working on him and he was going on about how he was gonna impress the ladies and how he was gonna get laid. Crap. I wasn't listening. But when he got up, a bag of C drops out of his pocket. I picked it up real fast and he didn't know it was gone."

"Bats." I just shook my head.

"I know, I know, Jenna. But he dropped it, right in front of me. So my lady— Stitch. You remember? We partied. We . . ." He looked at me out of the corner of his eye and stopped and cleared his throat.

"Let me guess, tat man wants his coke back." I exhaled heavily.

"Yeah!" He started walking around in circles waving his arms like a lunatic. "He came in shouting and yelling that he was going to kill me for stealing his crap. He's a big guy, Jenna. I'm not gonna fight him. I didn't see a gun, but that don't mean nothin'. He was mad. Real mad."

He looked around again and took another drag.

"Is that why you asked about the Bible? You think God could fix it for you?"

He looked at me sheepishly and nodded. "Yeah. Would he do that, you think? If I promised not to do it again?"

Bats! He looked like a little kid confessing to stealing cookies. "Yeah, Bats. I think he'd do that."

Actually, I was pretty impressed Bats would think to turn to God for help. I had struggled with the decision myself. He seemed to take to it pretty easily.

He stood in front of me with his puppy-dog eyes. "So, how does it work? I'm afraid this guy is really going to kill me."

I had to think. I never had to explain God to anyone before because I was still trying to figure it all out myself.

"There's this place in the Bible called Psalms. Whoever wrote it talks a lot about God protecting him, like a shield. I have no idea how that works, but I think if it's in the Bible, it's real—like you should believe it."

"So, do I ask God to protect me like a shield? Is that what you do?" He spread his hands out in a helpless question. "Like a shield, really? This is serious, Jenna. I don't know what to do."

"That's what it says. If you want it to work, you have to believe. Just try it, Bats."

He looked down the street then froze. "That's him, Jenna. That's him. He's coming to kill me."

Sure enough, a pretty big dude was mowing down the street, with murder in his eyes. His look was locked onto Bats, and he kept opening and clenching his big hands.

"Talk to God, Bats! Ask him to protect you!"

"Um, God . . . " He started weakly, but didn't seem to know how to finish and froze up, staring down the street. I didn't think he could get another word out.

"God, please protect Bats." I finished for him. "Don't let him get hurt."

I was nervous. I didn't want to get caught up in the mess, but Bats was my friend. I backed against the wall and watched it all in slow motion.

Bats waited like a rabbit for the inevitable to rain down on him. I could see him shaking. He was taller than me, but skinny. I probably could've beaten him up.

Big Dude stormed up and stopped in front of Bats and started swearing at him. "Where's my C! I know you took it, you miserable piece of —" Then he just stopped and screwed up his face. "You're pathetic. You're not even worth a fart."

He swung his big fist back, and Bats flung his arms up to cover his face, but Big Dude stopped. "I don't know why I don't turn you into peanut butter." He stood staring at Bats with a confused look on his face, then turned around and walked off.

Bats stood with his arms over his face for a long time, then practically cried in relief. He wiped his face with the bottom of his T-shirt and turned to me. "Jenna," he said in a shaky voice. "He did it. God protected me. That guy was going to kill me but he stopped. Did God make him stop?"

I was shocked. Honestly, truly shocked. I had thought Bats was dead too. "Wow, Bats. It's the real thing. I think God *did* make him stop."

"Yeah." He looked back down the street where Big Dude disappeared around the corner then back to me. "So now what, Jenna?"

"What do you mean?"

"I mean, God protected me. So now what I gotta do?"

"You want to change your life? I mean really change your life?" I wasn't sure he understood what that meant.

He looked back down the street and nodded. "Yeah."

"Okay. Meet me after I get off work and we'll talk about it," I said as I ground out my smoke.

His shoulders relaxed and he took a deep breath. "Okay. Thanks, Jenna. I knew you'd help. See you later." He started to leave but stopped and put his hand on my shoulder. "Thanks, Jenna. I mean it."

***

That evening, Bats walked with me to my apartment.

"Stitch isn't going to be upset about you coming over, is she?" I asked as I unlocked the street door.

"Naw," he said. "She's cool. I told her all about how you teach me stuff from the Bible. She thinks you're a good influence on me."

I shook my head. "I never had anyone say that about me before." I unlocked the apartment door and let him in. Normally I'd think of somewhere else to talk to him, but he looked so thin. I wanted to feed him, and I couldn't afford to take him out because I had no idea how much he'd eat.

He walked in and looked around at the long hallway as I moved past him.

"Back here. Have a seat." I pointed to the kitchen table. I opened a cupboard and pulled out a can of chicken soup. "I'm going to make you some soup and a sandwich. Okay?" I looked over my shoulder at him settling into a chair.

"Oh, you don't have to do that," he said, waving me off.

"No, I think you need to eat." I grabbed the can opener and opened the soup. He didn't argue anymore so I guessed he agreed with me. I poured the soup into a pan and turned on the burner.

I opened the fridge and leaned in. "You like baloney?"

He shrugged. "Yeah, okay."

"You like it fried?"

He looked up and grinned. "You fry baloney?"

"Yeah."

"Okay," he said. "I'll try it."

I stirred the soup and made a couple sandwiches. Then Trish came in.

"Hello!" she said, looking at Bats. She turned to me and lifted an eyebrow.

"Trish, this is Bats. Bats, this is Trish." I pointed from one to the other.

"Hey!" Bats jumped up and held out his hand.

"Nice to meet you," said Trish, shaking his hand like she was holding onto a wet fish.

"Bats works down the street from me at the tattoo parlor. He's the one that did my tat." I pointed to my ankle.

"I see." She looked at all the ink on his neck and arms then turned to me. "Are you planning to have something else done?"

"No. He wants to hear about God. I thought I'd feed him while I was at it."

"Oh! Mind if I listen?"

I shook my head. "No." I looked at Bats.

"I don't mind," he said.

Trish went to the fridge and took out a takeout box of something Indian and heated it while I put Bats' soup and sandwich on the table. He picked up the sandwich, sniffed it, then took a bite.

He smiled with approval. "Not bad."

I sat down with my own sandwich and took a bite before I remembered something.

"Water?"

He nodded with a mouthful.

I set down two glasses of water, and Trish joined us with her spicy dinner. We made small talk while I watched Bats inhale his food. Dude needed to eat more often.

He set his spoon down in his empty bowl and looked at me smiling. "Thanks, Jenna. You're a good cook."

I started to laugh as Trish and I exchanged looks. "You're welcome," I said. I picked up empty dishes and put them in the sink, then sat down again. I pulled over the Bible that I brought in and tapped it. I stopped to think about what I should tell him.

"Okay, well, there's two things you need to do. One, ask God to forgive you of your sins and stuff. And two, ask Jesus to come into your life." I glanced at Bats staring at me. I could tell he was listening hard. "So, the thing I learned is that God will forgive you for anything that you've done."

"Anything?" He screwed up his face. "But not everything."

"No, I'm pretty sure he'll forgive you for everything," I said.

Trish cleared away her leftovers and sat with her arms crossed to listen.

"Okay, so here's the way it works," I said as confidently as I could. "If you confess your sins, right? God will forgive you, then you have like *no* sins. And we all have to confess our sins because we all have them."

Bats leaned in and concentrated.

"Then God says that if we trust him, he'll take care of us. But here's the thing, you have to be serious about it. You can't say

'God please forgive me for stealing the jerk's coke' and then keep doing stupid stuff like that all the time. If you want God to help you, you've got to clean up your life. Okay?"

He nodded yes, but he said, "No."

"Seriously, Dude! If you want God to help you, you've got to do what he says. You can't steal and lie about it, stuff like that."

"'Kay, but I don't know if I can do that, Jenna." He looked worried.

I nodded. I worried about him, too.

"So, my friend Jess says we have to ask Jesus into our heart, and when we do, he makes us cleaned up inside, so we don't want to do the bad stuff anymore."

"Yeah? So I should do that?" He asked like he was hoping not to have to.

"Yeah, you should do that. If you want to be real about this—and God *did* save your life today—you should do it."

He looked down at the table for a long time then nodded. "Okay. I'll do it."

"Okay!" I was amazed that I said it all clear enough for him to understand. "So, I'm going to pray a prayer, and you should repeat it after me."

"Got it." He watched me expectantly. "What, should I close my eyes?"

"Yeah, close your eyes." I told him, like I knew.

Then I prayed like Jess prayed with me, and Bats and Trish both repeated it!

She peeked up at me and Bats 'cause we both stopped and looked at her.

"Okay," I said. "Good."

I finished the prayer and they both did it. Then they sat back and looked at me like baby birds, like I was supposed to know what to do next.

"So, I gotta go to church and all?" asked Bats when I didn't say anything.

"I guess so," I said. "I'm going to go on Sunday. You want to come?"

He looked away to think about it then nodded. "Yeah, okay. I'll bring Stitch. She'll want to come too."

"Can I come?" asked Trish.

"Yeah, come, Trish. It'll be good. We can all sit together and scare everyone!"

Bats laughed and sat back, suddenly more relaxed. "Yeah, I bet we'd look like a real crew."

"Do you know where it is?" asked Trish.

"No. I never asked," I said.

Bats pushed his chair back and stood up. "What time?"

I stopped to think. "Be here by 9:30, and we can all go together."

"Got it. Thanks for the fried baloney." He grinned.

"No problem. We have to get you a Bible so you can start reading it. It will help you figure all this out better," I said.

He looked a little worried at that, but he didn't say anything and nodded.

"You can take it slow," I told him. "There's no rush."

He relaxed a little and gave me a weak smile. "'Kay. Thanks, Jenna."

I walked him out to the front and said good-bye. I came back and Trish had her arms crossed, and she grinned at me like I just pulled a heist.

"Look at you, telling everyone about God." She teased.

I rolled my eyes. "Not everyone, trust me. Bats smokes with me outside of work, so I was just talking to him."

"You want to call Jess so he knows you're bringing your crew?" She tweaked her fingers with air quotes. "He might show up with a motorcycle."

"Oh, I'm sure we could manage." I laughed. "Yeah, you're right." I held out my hand and she gave me her phone.

I went to my room and thought about Jess. After having spent the night with Manish, I kind of thought about Jess differently now. He was so handsome that I couldn't deny I liked seeing him, but Manish was straightforward about wanting to date me. Yet Jess definitely knew stuff that I needed to know. Ahh!

"Hey, Jenna," Jess answered brightly. He always sounded like he didn't have anything else to do but talk to me, and I was pretty sure he had a business or something.

I sat on the edge of my bed with my legs stretched out and bounced my feet together. "Hey, Jess. Listen, I've got some friends who want to come to church on Sunday. Is that okay?"

"Sure it's okay! Who's coming? Your roommate?"

"Yeah, and a guy I know and his girlfriend."

"Okay. Are they all like you?" he asked.

I frowned. "What's that supposed to mean?"

"Sorry. I meant are they all newbies, learning about God?"

"Yeah. I'm actually the one who knows something this time. This guy Bats, he's been in some trouble with drugs, so I think God needs to straighten him out. I think his girlfriend needs help too."

"Gotcha," said Jess. "What about your roommate?"

"Oh, she's not into that. She's just curious. And guess what."

"What?"

"Bats and Trish prayed with me to ask Jesus into their hearts."

"What? Holy cow, Jenna. You're really the evangelist aren't you?"

"I don't know what that means, so I don't know."

"It's a good thing," said Jess. He chuckled then asked, "Will they all be at your place, or do they need directions?"

"I told them to be here by 9:30. Is that okay? Can we all go together?"

"Oh yeah. I have room in my car, or they can follow me. See you then," he said, then hung up, still chuckling.

Seventeen

Sunday morning I walked out of the bathroom and stopped in front of Trish for approval. I could tell she didn't think my jeans and the paisley shirt I got from Goodwill were what one wore when one went to church. She was wearing a short skirt with black leggings. I didn't even own a skirt. If I couldn't wear jeans or cargo pants, then church might be a problem.

"What?" I turned and checked myself out in the mirror.

She shook her head. "Nothing." She pushed me back into the bathroom and started fingering my hair. "Sit." She pointed to the edge of the bathtub then sprayed some of her stuff on my hair. She worked it in with her hands, fluffing and pulling. She finally seemed satisfied then stepped back to check it out.

"What do you think?" She nodded to the mirror.

I stood and looked at myself and smiled. She made it kind of punkish, like it was a mess but it was supposed to look like that. "I like it. Is this okay for church?"

She shrugged. "Heck if I know."

The door buzzer sent me out to let in Bats and Stitch, just as Jess walked up the street. Stitch was a cute blonde, slightly ditzy I thought, but she was happy to meet everyone. Jess glanced at my hair, but he didn't say anything.

"It's nice to meet you." Jess shook hands with everyone and stood there grinning.

I was afraid he'd start talking about me being an evangelist again so I nudged him. "Shouldn't we go?"

"Right." He looked at the other three. "Do you want to come with me or follow?"

"If you have room for us," said Trish.

Jess nodded. "There's room."

Jess drove us across town and chatted like a taxi driver. Everyone made me sit in the front seat because I was Jess' friend, but it felt weird. I looked back at Trish and she winked at me. Girl! Like she totally thought Jess was hot and we should be a couple. He did look kinda hot. He caught me looking at him and smiled. It made me feel a little melty inside, but I knew he was just being nice. Then I thought of Manish and sighed to myself. I wished he had come with us.

We pulled into the parking lot of a big, blocky looking building. Didn't look like a church at all. The church I remember going to when I was younger looked like a church—anyone would think so. This looked like a department store. It might have been one, once.

We got inside and I was a little surprised to see that most people were dressed more or less like I was. I only saw a couple of women wearing skirts, so that made me feel better. Plus, it seemed to be a pretty young crowd. Not that it would have mattered, but I liked so many people being around my age.

"Come in here, guys." Jess opened a big door and waved us in.

A big biker-looking guy with tats, bald head, and a goatee shook my hand. "Glad to see you," he said in a gravely voice and handed us a folded paper with times and dates for different meetings.

"Thanks," I said. I wondered what *his* story was. It never occurred to me that I might meet people with shady histories at church.

"These are friends of mine," Jess told him, then introduced us. "This is Bill. If you have any questions about how to come to know Jesus, Bill's the guy to talk to."

"Nice to meet you," said Bats, nodding. He walked into the big auditorium and looked around like he expected to see friends in there.

Jess hesitated then pointed to the back section of seats. "Let's sit back here. You might like it better further back your first time."

We filed into a back row and sat in some pretty comfortable chairs and watched everyone. There was a band warming up on the stage, and people were chatting and hugging each other. It seemed like everyone who went past had to stop and chat with Jess, so he had to introduce us every time. I just smiled and nodded because there was no way I was going to remember anyone.

I leaned over to Trish. "What do you think?"

She was watching some kind of commercial that rotated meetings and announcements on the front wall. "I don't know," she said, still watching the slideshow. "It looks all right." She turned to me quickly. "Do you feel uncomfortable?"

"No. I just have no idea what to expect."

"Me neither. Just go with it." She shrugged and turned to watch people.

I looked down the row at Bats and Stitch. They stared like they were watching aliens—really interesting aliens.

Pretty soon the band started playing. Not really my style, but it wasn't bad. Everyone was on their feet, so we stood up too. I liked that the words to the songs were on a big screen. I liked what they said: God is awesome and big and he loves us so much. It made my heart feel warm. I clapped with the music and got into it.

Jess leaned over to me. "Not your quiet church service here."

"Not really," I said. "Not what I remember."

"You like it?"

I looked around at the people. Yeah, there were some just standing there, but most looked like they couldn't care less what anyone thought of them as they raised their hands or clapped. There was a girl kind of dancing to the music in the corner. She *really* didn't care what people thought of her. I liked that. I nodded. "Yeah, I do."

Then the music slowed down, and people stopped clapping. Most of them had their eyes closed whether they were singing or not. So I closed my eyes and listened. At first I just felt silly, but then I started listening to the words about how great God was and how much we loved him. Did I love him? I thought about the prayer I prayed to Jesus to ask him into my heart. That was a prayer of desperation when I needed him to do something for me. I listened to the music and felt a flutter in my stomach. Yes, I did love him. I really did. I was so grateful that he forgave me and made me feel peace. I started crying. I couldn't even say why. Emotion just welled up inside me and spilled out and I couldn't stop it. Someone put tissues in my hands, and I wiped my eyes and blew my nose as quietly as I could.

I looked up at Jess but couldn't say anything. He put his arm around my shoulders and gave me a hug. I looked over at Trish, and she was wiping tears from her eyes kind of fast, like she didn't want anyone to see her do it.

We sat the rest of the time after the music stopped, and the pastor talked. I tried to listen and pay attention, but really I was thinking about how I felt. There was definitely something very peaceful going on inside. It felt like I'd been running in circles my whole life and finally got to stop and rest. Every so often, I caught myself taking deep cleansing breaths, like they tell you to do in those yoga classes. I felt calmer. And then I thought about Jesus. It felt like he was giving me a big bear hug. How was that possible?

'Cause he was in heaven, right? I had to remember to ask Jess about that later.

At the end of the service, the pastor asked anyone who didn't know Jesus to raise their hand. I already prayed that prayer, so I didn't do anything, but Bats did. Then Stitch raised her hand, and Trish raised hers. So the pastor asked everyone who raised their hand to go up to the front.

Jess leaned down and whispered. "You should go with them."

"Really? Why?"

"I know you already prayed to ask Jesus in your heart, but it will be good to really settle it. And it might make your friends feel better. I can go with you, too." He nodded encouragement at me like he was waiting for me to agree.

"Yeah, okay," I said.

So we went up with three other people who raised their hands, and were all herded into a room off to the side. They had us all pray a prayer more or less like what Jess prayed with me, but Bats interrupted them.

"We already prayed like that," he said, pointing to Trish and himself.

The young guy leading the prayer grinned. "That's cool, man. You know, you can pray it again now. It's all right. Then you'll totally know that you're saved."

Bats thought about it and nodded. "Yeah, okay."

After everyone prayed, the church people handed out Bibles. I showed them mine, so I didn't take one. Then they went around and prayed with everyone. A girl about my age put her hand on my head. She didn't pray with her eyes closed, she looked off, sort of dreamy like.

"Whoa!" she said. "You're like David. You're about to kill a giant. And God wants to tell you that he's put everything you need in your hands and not to be afraid."

Jess stood next to me with his hand on my shoulder and nodded. "I agree. You've got a sword, Jenna. You don't even realize that you have it, but God is going to show you how to use it to kill giants."

Then they prayed over me and went to the others. I had no idea what they were talking about, but hey, killing giants? Why not! I just hoped that someday I'd figure out what that meant.

When they went to pray for Bats, he started laughing. I mean, really laughing. Every time anyone touched him, he laughed harder. It was hysterical and made us all laugh. We all took turns poking him and watching him lose it even more. He'd try to stop and breathe and would suddenly erupt into more laughing. Stitch was crying, she laughed so much watching him. He finally had to walk away with his hands on his hips and take deep breaths all bent over.

When Bats got his breath back and calmed down, we stood around wondering what to do next.

"Want to go to lunch?" asked Jess, looking at the four of us.

We all nodded and said yes, but it took a while to get out of the church, with everyone shaking hands and stopping Jess to have a "quick word." We finally collected outside and started for the car, but Jess stopped us.

"You know, there's a hamburger place just down the street, if you don't mind walking. We won't have to fight for a parking spot."

"Works for me," I said.

Everyone agreed, so we walked a few blocks to a little dive hamburger joint. I was surprised Jess would suggest the place, actually. I don't know why I thought he was more highbrow than that.

We crammed into a booth, and suddenly I was starving. Everything on the menu looked perfect, but I controlled myself and just ordered a cheeseburger and diet coke.

When all the orders had been taken, Jess folded his hands on the table and smiled, like he was utterly pleased with himself for arranging a meeting of Christian newbies.

109

"So, how do you feel?" he asked, looking around the table.

We gave each other the sideways look, hoping someone else would speak up.

Stitch tilted her head and blinked a few times. With her big blue eyes and blond curls, she could actually be the blond from all the blond jokes, but she was really sweet. "I feel like I got a shower, from the inside," she cooed.

Bats looked at her and nodded. "Yeah, that's good. Like a shower from the inside." He looked at Jess like Stitch had said it all.

Jess smiled and looked at Trish. "What about you, Trish?"

She gazed up at the ceiling and smiled and stretched a little. "I feel good. Feels peaceful."

Bats nodded. "Yeah, that's good. Peaceful."

"What about you, Jenna?" Jess asked.

"I feel like I'm starting to get it," I said. "I mean, I prayed that prayer before, but today I *felt* it. You know what I mean?"

Bats nodded again. "Yeah, that's good."

He made me laugh. "Bats, you're so funny."

He made a silly grin and grabbed his water glass.

"So now what?" asked Jess.

"What do you mean?" Trish looked confused.

"Do you want to say 'that was nice' and leave it at that? Or do you want to hold onto what you just got and go deeper?" He sat back and glanced at each of us to let his questions sink in.

"What does that mean?" asked Stitch, looking worried.

"Do you want to learn more about what it means to be a Christian? Really get into who God is and what he can do in your life?" asked Jess, tapping the edge of the table with his finger.

We all got quiet and thought about it.

"I want to learn more," said Trish. "I mean, if I'm going to do this, I guess I'd better learn what I'm into."

"Me too," said the rest of us.

"Good." Jess leaned forward and smiled. "Very good."

The waitress brought our orders, and suddenly we were all focused on eating.

When we finished our hamburgers, I got to wondering about what Jess meant. "So what *is* the next thing?"

He wiped his mouth with his napkin then took a drink and looked around at everyone. "You all got new Bibles, right? You need to read them. It's your owner's manual, your handbook for what God wants to do in your life."

We all pulled our Bibles out and started flipping through pages. Bats closed his and set it down, looking deflated. I knew what was going through his head—*how am I supposed to understand this?*

Apparently Jess realized the same thing. "It's okay. You're not on your own here. I don't mean you have to study this and memorize it front to back. I'd like to set up a Bible study once a week so we go through it so you have a way to ask questions, and you'll learn some of the basics that are important to get down."

Bats looked only slightly relieved and glanced at Stitch. She was reading with her nose right down into the book then looked up with a wild expression.

"Wow! There's some scary shi—sorry. I mean, there's some scary stuff in here!"

Jess nodded. "That's why we need a Bible study. You need to understand what's in there, in context."

"'In context,' what's that mean?" Stitch looked from Bats to Jess.

"It means understanding what was going on when that scripture was written and what it means to us," said Jess. "While you're learning this for the first time, it's important that you get what God is trying to say, what he's trying to do. Yeah, some of the stories are pretty wild."

Stitch looked satisfied and closed her book. "Okay. 'Cause that's going to be interesting to understand, in context."

Trish smiled at me and looked away quickly.

Jess turned to me. "So Jenna, where's a good place for them to start reading?"

Ha! Put me on the spot. But it was okay, because I knew where he had me start. "John. There's a place called John where it's all about Jesus." I raised an eyebrow at him to prove I knew where he was going with this.

"John it is then," he said. "Why don't you find it for them?"

"Oh, okay." I took Trish's Bible and flipped around until I found it. She stuck a napkin there and closed it. Then I did the same thing for Bats and Stitch.

Jess smiled around the table, fully enjoying what was going on.

"So, Tuesdays?" Trish asked. "Is that a good night?"

We all nodded and agreed.

"Sure. Tuesdays are good," Stitch said. "Except when I have to work." Then she got a worried look and turned to Jess. "Is it okay to be a cocktail waitress and go to church? 'Cause I don't think we get a lot of church folks in the bar. At least not that I'm aware of." She rolled her eyes. "We see all kinds."

"Don't worry about it," said Jess. "If God wants you to be somewhere else, he'll open another door for you. I mean, you'll find something else."

"Okay," said Stitch. She looked relieved at Bats.

"So Tuesdays it is," said Jess. "7:00?"

We all agreed 7:00 would be fine. Everyone had this happy look because we were suddenly a team of some kind. None of us had any idea what we were into, but it felt good being together and having hope for the first time.

Eighteen

When we got home after church, I took my Bible to the park and found an empty bench. It was a warm, short-sleeve day. The kind that people moved to California for. A couple of winos stretched out under a tree, talking about God-knew-what, and teenagers in their grunge outfits sprawled on the grass. I didn't think the winos would care, but the kids might if they knew about all the dogs that use that park.

I thought about church and the way I felt like I'd connected with God. What would Manish think of it? Did it matter to me if he never understood what I was learning? What if he did believe in his parents' religion? Would that matter? I wished he were interested in Jesus. Who wouldn't be happy once they invited him into their heart?

I thought about talking to Jess about Manish, but I knew it would be an awkward conversation. I played with the binding on my Bible and decided to ignore the issue for now. Maybe it was best to let it work itself out and hope it didn't come back to bite me later on.

Our first Bible study was going to be about John, but I already read it, so I wanted to read something else. I'd already read through all the Psalms, so I opened up pages randomly. Then I found a story about David! The girl from the church said I was like David.

I backed up until I found the beginning of the story and read about this kid who killed a giant! That's what she'd said. I had no idea she was talking about something from the Bible. David and Goliath—of course. My Mom made me go to Sunday school when I was a kid, but I never paid attention to anything. Cassie and I were more interested in getting Bret Wilson to look at us. Stumbling across something I recognized made me want to start from the beginning of the book to see what else I'd be familiar with.

I was so amazed by the whole David killing Goliath part. What a brave kid. He really was. I couldn't do that. I didn't care what that girl said. With a slingshot? I didn't think so. What was she talking about anyway? And Jess agreed with her, though he said I had a sword. Could I take down a giant like Goliath with a sword? Get real.

I closed the book and shook my head. I didn't get it. There was so much I didn't understand. I wondered if I ever would. Would I ever get to the place where people would say stuff like that to me and I'd know what they meant? What would understanding what they said do for me anyway? I just didn't get it.

And then, wham! Small boy, blond, curly hair. He might have been the same one from the last time. Who knew? He walked in front of two adults, with his hands in his pockets, looking as innocent as ever, like he had no idea how devastating he could be. He went past me looking alive and healthy, not like the one I remembered lying in a pool of blood. I felt throbbing behind my eyes as I watched the three make their way down the path. I tried to look away. I tried so hard. I could see that curly head for a long, long time before he was lost behind other bodies far down the path.

The headache slammed inside my head so hard it felt like I got wacked with a baseball bat. It was worse than I ever remembered having before. Ever. Pounding pain all but blinded me. In fact, I honestly couldn't see straight.

I stood up and immediately threw up. I probably grossed out anyone around me, but I didn't have the energy to care. Someone came running up and tried to look in my face to see what I needed, but I couldn't look at them. I couldn't focus.

"Should I call 911?"

I had my palms on my temples with my eyes closed. "No. I need to go home."

"Where? Do you live nearby?"

"Yes," I said. "Broderick."

So whoever it was walked me down to Broderick and kept asking if I needed to go to the hospital, but I couldn't talk. It was as much as I could manage walking. When I recognized that I was close to home, I made the person leave me. I never figured out if it was a man or woman. He or she put my Bible in my hand before going. I was grateful for that later on.

Trish yelled when she saw me come in.

"Jenna! What happened?" She launched herself out of the couch in the living room and ran over to look at my eyes.

"My head," I whispered.

"Right," she said.

She ran down the hall and came back with her purse and keys in hand.

"Come on." She pulled me out the door. We got down the steps to the sidewalk and she stopped. "You wait right here. I'm going to get my car." She stooped to look in my face. "Got it?"

"Yes," I said weakly.

Pound, pound, pound. I could feel veins splitting open, blood spewing internally. Any second and it would burst out my ears and mouth like in those horrible monster movies. Trish had to be fast because I was going to die right there on the sidewalk. *Oh, please God, please let me die. Let me be done with this forever.* I couldn't stand it.

About a week later, Trish pulled up and double-parked in front of me. She jumped out and manhandled me into her car. I didn't know what she was saying. I was crying. No, I'm pretty sure I was screaming. I don't remember much.

I vaguely remember getting to the hospital. Trish pulling me along. Bright lights that burned the tissue from my eyes. Insurance. They needed to know about insurance. Trish pulled my wallet from my pocket. The pounding got worse. Finally a doctor looked me over and asked questions. I'm not sure what I answered, if I answered. He gave me a shot and told Trish to get me home to sleep it off. I remember stumbling up the steps to the apartment, but the world was pretty woozy then.

Nineteen

I woke up feeling like I had definitely been drugged. I was awake, but my brain felt cloudy. I blinked, rubbed my eyes, and realized that the headache was gone. Oh, thank you, Jesus! The absence of pain was a gift. I wanted to live like that forever. I rolled over to see what time it was. The clock on the floor said 10:00. 10:00? But it was light outside. I rolled back to stare at the ceiling. I went to the park Sunday after church. That's when my head blew up. That's when Trish took me to the hospital. It had to be Monday morning! Oh, God!

I jumped up and ran out to see if by some miracle Trish was still home. I had to call work. I ran past a piece of notepaper on the floor outside my room, then stopped and picked it up.

Jenna,

I called your work and talked to Brenda. She said not to worry and to take the day off. Rest well.

Trish

Wow. Suddenly I could relax. I felt a little guilty about staying home now that I felt better, but I decided to do it anyway. I'd feel it in my paycheck, but I'd try to get some overtime later to make up for it. Besides, my brain was still fuzzy.

I took the kind of long, hot shower you can't enjoy on a workday. I made some toast and spread it with peanut butter and honey then poured a cup of coffee. The coffee was getting on the old side, but if you add enough sugar, you can drink anything and anything is better than prison coffee. I took my breakfast and my Bible out to the front room.

Our windows were about head high to anyone walking past on the sidewalk, but if you turned the blinds slats facing up, you still got light in without too many looky-loos. It was foggy outside and the room felt cold and damp, so I grabbed a throw, kicked off my slippers, and settled into the couch with my legs pulled up.

I had something on my mind as I ate my toast. Could God make those headaches go away forever? I thought about all the people that Jesus healed in the Bible. He even raised some from the dead. Like, completely dead. He could still do that couldn't he? I mean, if he was alive now, like it says, why couldn't he do that?

I wiped my fingers on a napkin and took a drink of the hot coffee. I opened my Bible again to where I had the bulletin from the church stuck in as a bookmark and read the part about David killing Goliath. Jess said that God had put a sword in my hand and I would kill giants. What the heck did that mean? I got that he probably didn't mean a real sword. I doubted God wanted me to go around killing anyone for real, so I understood that it meant something else, but what?

I looked back at the story, and then I got it! I really got it. It read, "David said to Goliath, 'You are coming to fight against me with a sword, a spear and a javelin. But I'm coming against you in the name of the Lord who rules over all. He is the God of the armies of Israel. He's the one you have dared to fight against.'"

That was it. Goliath's sword was a real sword. David's sword was the name of the Lord who rules over all. Yeah, he still used his slingshot, but I thought what the girl at church meant was what David said about the name of the Lord—he used it like a sword. David threw the stone, but he said "the battle belongs to the Lord."

I set the book down on my lap and sat back to think it through. I got the headaches because I killed a child. Did I just walk away from that? That boy should be walking around, playing, like the kid in the park. It was so wrong that a child was dead and not alive and happy. I blinked back tears and closed my eyes. I was so sick of living with the pain. Was it okay to let that go? Was it okay to put the guilt behind me?

If I really had a sword that was the name of the Lord, I wanted to swing it and see what I could hit. I sat up and stared across the room. People prayed in Jesus' name at church. Jesus did all those miracles and brought people back from the dead. That was the key, wasn't it?

"In the name of the Jesus who rules over all, I kill these headaches!" I said it out loud, and I said it like I meant it. "I will have no more headaches, ever!"

I could've been wrong, but it felt like something shifted in my head, ever so slightly, almost like a faint shadow crossing my vision, then it was gone. I stared at the wall above the fireplace while I checked to see what happened. Did I feel any different? I guessed I'd find out as time went on.

Psalms. The word drifted through my mind.

I took a deep breath and wiped my eyes. Psalms? I flipped pages until I found Psalms. I didn't know what to look for. I turned several pages and stopped when my eyes landed on "Lord, you are good. You are forgiving. You are full of love for all who call out to you."

Oh, man! Thank you Lord for forgiving me. I knew I didn't deserve it. I wiped some stray tears on my sleeve and thought about how good God was.

Now forgive yourself.

No way. In my mind, all I could see was the image of a small, broken body.

Forgive yourself.

119

It seemed wrong to forgive myself. It was all fine and good for God to. He could do whatever he wanted. But I still remembered that mother's face and how full of rage she was. I laid my head back against the couch and closed my eyes. I killed that boy. He was dead because of me.

Forgive yourself.

I knew I heard it as clear as day. God was telling me to do it. I had to try.

"I forgive myself for killing that little boy. It was an accident. I didn't mean to do it. I'm letting it go, in Jesus' name."

Suddenly, a wave of emotion welled up, and I started crying loud, wrenching sobs. I pulled my knees up and hugged them as I wailed. Wave after wave of sobs spilled out as I sniffed and wiped my eyes. I didn't know how long I cried, but I was exhausted and drained when I ran out of tears. I got up and went to the bathroom to blow my nose. I ran a washcloth under cold water and pressed it against my face. I looked in the mirror and saw puffy eyes and a red nose. Good thing I was home alone. I sniffed and went back into the living room. I threw the blanket over myself and leaned back against the cushions.

I was tired from the crying, like all my energy leaked out through my tears. I exhaled and realized something was missing. Something that used to hang around my neck, like a dead cat tied around the neck of a dog that killed cats. I felt free. It was like what I felt in church when everyone was singing. It seemed powerful, but peaceful. I think God was happy. I think he was letting me know that I was on the right track. I killed a giant. In Jesus' name, in the name of the Lord who rules over all, I killed a giant and his name was Unforgiveness. I blew out a long breath as I thought about it. Not forgiving myself was killing me. I had no idea.

I looked up and laughed out loud. It felt awesome! In the name of the Lord! In the name of the Lord! There was something big behind that! Like a real sword. I realized there were layers to all of it—coming against an evil that terrorized me with pain, and the freedom of forgiveness. I somehow stumbled on something powerful and profound that was going to change my life.

I felt of rush of excitement and got up and started walking around the room pumping my fists. I stopped and shadow boxed the air, then paced some more. Ha! Stupid giants that would come against the armies of the living God! Take that! I punched the air with a fist. That's what I'm talking about!

For the first time, I really wished I had a cell phone. I wanted to call Jess and tell him what happened. He'd understand about killing the giant, better than Trish. Too bad. I'd have to wait.

Twenty

I dropped the burner plates I'd pulled off the stove into soapy water to soak and had started cleaning the stove when the door buzzed. I felt so good all day that I was cleaning everything in sight. Trish would be majorly impressed. But Trish didn't use the doorbell.

I went out to the lobby and saw Manish through the glass street door.

"Ooooooh . . . my goodness," I said as I let him in. "I'm such a mess. I've been cleaning."

He leaned down and kissed me lightly. "You look beautiful."

I raised an eyebrow at him but didn't argue. Never stop people from saying something that nice, even if it wasn't true.

He followed me into the living room and we sat facing each other on the couch. I pulled my feet up and crossed my legs and beamed.

"You look good," he said. "I mean, you look good, but someone from your work said you were home sick today." He got a mischievous look. "Are you playing hooky?"

I shook my head. "No, not really. I had a massive headache yesterday. Trish, my roommate, took me to the hospital. They gave me a shot that knocked me out until this morning, so my boss said to stay home."

He suddenly looked concerned. "So, how do you feel now?"

"I feel fine!" I looked in his eyes and decided to tell him. I told him how the attacks came when I saw small blond boys. I told him how I asked God to forgive me and how I forgave myself. I told him how good I felt.

He listened quietly until I was done. I couldn't tell if he thought I was a nut job or charmingly eccentric.

He looked me over like he needed to check for cooties. "You said you were going to church. I didn't realize you were this serious about it."

"Does that bother you?" I took a deep breath to prepare myself.

He got a kind look in his eyes and took my hand. "I like that you are honest about everything, and this is something that you feel strongly about. No, it doesn't bother me."

I exhaled and relaxed. "I guess meeting me in a club didn't prepare you for church lady."

He laughed. "True."

I looked down at my hand resting in my lap. It was red and nasty looking.

"Oh, geez." I rubbed grease from my knuckles. "I was cleaning the stove."

"Want me to help?" he asked.

I think my jaw dropped. "What?"

"Come on." He got up and pulled me to my feet. I followed him down the hall, and he stopped to survey the mess. "You can't leave it like that," he said, pushing up the sleeves of his pullover. He picked up the scrubber and started cleaning the burner.

"Seriously? You came over to clean my stove?" I just stood and watched him.

"Don't be a slouch." He opened the oven to check it out. "Get to work!"

I laughed and started cleaning the knobs in the sink. Pretty soon we had the stove put back together and looking nice and shiny.

Manish dried his hands on a towel and nodded approvingly. "Now we should cook something!"

"What, and get it dirty again? And anyway, you remember what I told you about my cooking?"

"Oh yes, that's right." He hung the towel over the oven handle. "You seem so efficient about everything. I can't believe you can't cook."

"I do a mean fried baloney I'll have you know," I said with fake pretention.

"Right, I forgot about the baloney sandwich. Well then, I guess we'll have to go find real food. I'm getting hungry."

"I'm serious about the baloney." I was pretty sure that wasn't going to fly, so I headed down the hall to get my jacket from my room on the way out. "There's a good pizza place on Haight."

He nodded. "Okay. Pizza sounds good."

I snuggled down into the leather seat of his car and buckled up. "What is that?" I asked, pointing to his keychain. It was a figure of an elephant head on a human body with four arms. I'd seen it before and wondered about it.

He looked down to see what I was pointing at. "The charm? It's called Ganesh. It's the god that removes obstacles. My mother gave it to me when I moved to America."

"I thought you didn't believe in that," I said. Something started to tighten in the pit of my stomach.

"I don't, not really."

I watched his face. "I think you do, at least a little."

He shrugged. "Maybe. It's so much a part of my culture. Does that bother you? It doesn't bother me that you go to church."

"Hmm. I don't know." I looked at the charm again and cringed a little. I got the creepy feeling that it was watching me. "It just looks so strange."

He checked his mirrors and changed lanes. "The gods aren't like us. They're not supposed to be."

"I guess not." The thing in my stomach twinged as the charm swung and clinked lightly against his keys.

We drove around for a while before finding parking and walked down to the pizza place. The menu was incredibly complicated, with dozens of choices.

Manish sighed as he read it over. "So many different kinds. What do you like?"

"I like the simple one. Mozzarella, tomato, basil."

"Margarita." He nodded. "Sounds good to me."

We found a booth and settled in with our drinks.

There was an awkward pause, the kind you knew you should break by saying something, but I couldn't think of what that would be. I decided to let him do it.

He stared at the paper cover from his straw while he twisted it into a string. "So, Jenna, tell me what it was like in prison."

"Oh." Not what I expected. I shoved my soda aside and leaned on the table. "It was no picnic," I said slowly. "It was humiliating, and I don't want to tell you all the reasons why. It was only a two-year sentence, but it felt like a lifetime. Like, once you went there, you'd never really get out." I looked up at him. "But that was before God forgave me. I don't feel that any more. I really feel finally free."

Manish nodded his head slowly and looked down at the paper string he was rolling up. "I don't understand that really. I never learned about Christianity when I moved here. I never knew anyone who believed in it." He looked up at me. "I'm sorry for what happened. You seem amazing to me. For what you've been through, you seem so full of life, so positive."

I rolled my eyes. "You have no idea. I've had a very bad, very dark time adjusting to my life since then."

"That's even more amazing then," he said. "Some people would fall apart, do drugs, alcohol, whatever."

I dipped my head. "You're right. I don't do those things. I dealt with my demons through massive headaches and self-condemnation. It hasn't been easy. That's why I'm so happy to be a Christian now, I guess. I don't think about killing myself anymore."

Manish's eyes bugged a bit. "Really?"

"Yeah. I used to think about it a lot. I always tried to figure out how to make myself do it."

"Did you ever go to counseling?"

I shook my head. "Everyone said I should, but I just couldn't make myself. It's really hard to talk about, and a counselor wants to poke at all the open wounds in your life."

"Maybe at your church," he suggested.

I started to pick up my drink and stopped. "Maybe."

A server set our pizza down on a tall rack between us and broke the awkward tension I'd been feeling. We made small talk about nothing while we ate, but something unsettled me. It might have been the Indian charm on his keychain. It bothered me more than I wanted to admit, and I felt bad that it did. He was so accepting of my faith. Why should I fuss about his?

We sat in the car after dinner, both of us knowing the question that hung in the air between us.

I reached over and rubbed his hand resting on the small center console. "Were you wondering if I wanted to go to your place?"

He raised his eyebrows and nodded. "Yeah. You want to?"

I squeezed his arm then pulled my hand away. "Not this time. I'd like to go home."

"Is everything all right?"

I nodded vaguely. "Yeah, sure. There's some reading I want to do, and tomorrow is a work day. You know."

He looked like he was reading between the lines because he seemed to tightened up. He started the car and didn't speak again while he drove me home.

"Thanks for helping me clean the stove, and for dinner," I said as the engine idled. I knew I needed to get out, but I didn't want to leave him feeling rejected. I eyed the elephant charm swinging slightly from the key chain.

He picked up my hand and kissed it. "Have a good night." There was something melancholy about the way he said it that tore at my heart.

I leaned over and kissed him quickly. "Thanks, Manish." I got out and watched him pull away. Unsettled, unsettled. It just didn't feel right.

Twenty-one

Trish was in her room when I got home. She opened her door and watched me come down the hall.

"So how are you?" she asked.

"I'm okay." I stopped and leaned against the wall. "Thanks for calling Brenda for me."

"She was fine. She was pretty worried about you going to the hospital. Did you still have the headache when you woke up?"

"No. It was all gone. I was a little fuzzy, but the pain was gone."

"The doctor did say he was giving you some pretty strong stuff." She looked at a nail file she had in her hand and started scratching at her nails.

Suddenly something hit me. "Trish!"

She looked up in alarm. "What?"

"I haven't had a cigarette all day!" I hadn't even thought about it until just then.

"Really? But how?"

"Oh man! I have to tell you what happened." I followed her into her room, sat on the end of her bed, and started talking nonstop. I kind of jumbled it up, talking about David and Goliath, then what that girl at church had said, then how I figured out what David's sword was. She listened hard and kept nodding, and I

128

think I finally made some sense of it because she sat back with big eyes and this amazed look.

"Wow, Jenna! That's awesome! What if you never have those headaches again?"

"Yeah! That's what I'm talking about! I killed it!" I did a sword thrust in the air for effect, but she wasn't really looking at me.

"Yeah," she said a little weakly as she looked off to think about it. She turned back to me and shrugged a little. "I'm not sure I get exactly how that works, but I believe you did something. Hey! No cigarettes! You must have killed more giants than you thought."

"No kidding!" I just shook my head. "Even now, as I think about it, I don't feel like having a smoke."

She laughed. "Just think of the money you're going to save now!"

"Yeah! There's that, too. Winner, winner, chicken dinner!"

"So where were you?" she asked.

"Oh, Manish came by. Get this, I was cleaning the stove when he came so he helped me finish it. He scrubbed all the burners."

"I thought so," she said. "The whole kitchen looked like it got cleaned."

"I was just so excited by what God did that I had to burn it off. Then we went out for pizza."

She fingered her nail file and looked up at me. "What do you think of this guy I haven't met yet?"

I looked up at the corner of the ceiling and wondered that myself. "He's super cute. Really nice. He asked me about prison."

"He did?"

"Yeah. I don't think he knows another woman who did that, so he was curious."

"I can understand that," she said.

"But . . . I think there's this thing about him being kinda-sorta Hindu."

"What's that mean?"

"Well, he says he doesn't believe in it, but he has this keychain with an elephant god on it, and he says it's part of his culture."

Trish shrugged. "Maybe something you can talk to Jess about."

"Yeah, maybe."

Trish yawned and I took the hint. "'Kay. See you in the morning."

***

Bats came over for his smoke break the next day and loitered outside the door until I saw him. I went out to visit even though I wasn't going to light up.

"'Sup, Bats?" I asked and squatted down next to him.

He gave me a worried look then took a drag. He waited until he blew it all out before answering me.

"I don't know if I can do this, Jenna," he said, flicking ash on the sidewalk.

"Do what?"

"The whole church thing." He looked down and shook his head. "I tried reading the Bible like he said to, and I can't get it. It's too hard." He looked up, pleading me to let him off the hook.

"Bats." I reached over and patted his knee. "Don't give up, okay? I know how it is. It didn't make sense at first for me either."

"Yeah, but Jenna—" He looked like he was going to cry. "I did a lot of crap that messed up my head. I don't think I *can* do it."

He had a point. I knew he'd done a lot of bad stuff. Didn't surprise me if it messed him up. I thought about it for a second.

"Do you think that your head being messed up is any worse than being blind or dead?"

"What?" He squinted at me.

"Well, Jesus took care of some pretty bad cases in the Bible. I don't think that your head is any worse than some guy who died. Jesus yelled at him and he came back alive. I bet he can fix your head. It can't be any harder."

He stared down the street and thought about it. "Yeah, can't be any harder." He looked back at me with big eyes. "So how do you get Jesus to yell at my head?"

I laughed and thought for a second. "I think we pray and ask him."

"Okay," he nodded. "Can you do that, Jenna?"

"Okay, let's try it," I said. I didn't really know what to do, so I stood up and took a deep breath. I put my hand on Bats' head and closed my eyes like I saw people do in church.

"Jesus, please fix Bats' head like you fixed the people in the Bible so he can read without any problems, in Jesus' name." Then I thought about how God took away smoking for me. "And take away any desire Bats might have to do drugs again and fix all the issues that drugs ever did to him. Amen."

I took my hand off him, and he looked up at me and smiled.

"Thanks, Jenna. I'll see you tonight at your place, right?"

I nodded. "Yep. 7:00."

I thought a lot about killing giants while I worked. I wondered what other ones might be lurking in my head that I'd have to deal with eventually. I figured there were still some to face, because at one point I did want to disembowel the monster for breaking down again. I could actually see myself with a light saber, ripping the thing open like a dead Ton-Ton. Man, the things they got to do in the movies.

The good new was that by the end of the day I was excited about our Bible study. It was going to be awesome learning about Jesus. I actually ran home and hopped up the stairs, panting. I raced through the apartment, picking up things and tried to think of what Trish would want me to do.

Fortunately she got home and started making coffee.

Coffee. I didn't think of that. I was pacing around the living room when the door buzzed. It was Jess.

"Hey, mighty warrior of God," he said as he walked in.

"Hey." I moved past him and closed the door. "You know, I have stuff to talk to you about."

"Okay," he said brightly.

He followed me into the living room and sat in the overstuffed chair. Trish brought in two kitchen chairs and sat in one while I leaned on the other.

"I prayed for Bats today," I said.

"You did?" asked Jess. "What about?"

"You know he did drugs for years, right? Well, it messed him up pretty bad. He doesn't read very well anymore. In fact, he was really discouraged because he couldn't read the Bible. So I prayed and asked Jesus to fix his head so he wouldn't have any problem and take away any desire to do drugs again."

"Did it work?" asked Trish.

"I don't know. We'll see." I looked at Jess. "Did I tell you about praying for him when the guy from the tattoo parlor tried to kill him?"

"Um, no," said Jess. His eyes got big, and he leaned in to listen.

"Well, Bats stole this guy's coke for some stupid reason and was scared he was going to get his lights punched out, for good, you know? And then the guy came after him, so I prayed for God to protect him."

"And? What happened?" asked Jess, clearly enjoying the story.

"The guy looked like he was going to beat the crap out of Bats, but he stopped. He just stopped. He was mad, but he walked away."

"Awesome!" said Jess. "I told you, mighty warrior of God!"

I was about to tell him about killing the giants in my life when Bats and Stitch came. We got all our hugs and everyone sat down, then Trish jumped up.

"Who wants coffee?" she asked. "I have cookies." She smiled slyly.

"Um, yeah." Bats raised his hand weakly, like he didn't think he had permission.

"Me too," said Stitch.

"Jess?" Trish asked.

He nodded so I went in to help. When everyone was coffeed up and cookies passed, Trish sat down looking smug, like we were finally ready to start.

"Bats, Jenna told me how she prayed for you today. How do you feel now?" asked Jess.

Bats swallowed and looked off while he took inventory in his head. He nodded and looked back. "I feel okay."

"Great!" said Jess. "Why don't you read the beginning of John for us?"

Bats shot me a panicked look but I nodded to him and he opened his Bible to where he had a piece of paper sticking out and read slowly. "In the beginning was the Word, and the Word was with God, and the Word was God. He was in the beginning with God."

He stopped and stared at the page for a long time while we waited, because none of us knew what was going on. Finally he looked up with a dead serious look. Then tears started running down his face.

Stitch stared at Jess in alarm and started rubbing Bats' back.

"What is it, Bats?" asked Jess.

Bats gulped and wiped his face. "I can read that."

"That's great, Bats!" said Trish.

"No, you don't understand," he said. "I've haven't been able to really read since—" He looked down and shook his head. "I've been so messed up. Stitch reads everything for me if I have to," he said, pointing to her. "But this." He held the Bible open in his hand and tapped it. "I read it. And the *Word* was with God." He looked up at us. "And now the Word is with me."

Suddenly I couldn't swallow. I felt the force of what he said, like watching a dying man come back to life. God really did do a miracle in him. It wasn't until later that it hit me that he did it after my own prayer. That God would do that because I prayed a little prayer . . . I had so much to learn.

Jess teared up too. We all did. Bats totally lost it and cried. I could see his whole world had opened up for him. He'd always felt stupid. He never had to say it, but I knew. Jesus gave him back something that the drugs took away. I had no idea that becoming a Christian and the whole church thing would be so—so life changing. I just thought it was something you were supposed to do so you didn't go to hell.

"Bats, what's you real name?" I asked.

He looked up, surprised, then embarrassed. "Leonard," he said sheepishly. He sniffed and took the tissue Trish handed him.

"What would you like us to call you?" asked Trish.

He shook his head and looked away. "I don't care."

"Can we call you Lenny?" she asked.

He grinned. "My Mom called me Lenny when I was little." He nodded. "Yeah, okay, Lenny." He blew his nose and sniffed again.

Stitch smiled and dug her thumbs into his shoulders. "Lenny. I have to get used to that."

"What about you, Stitch?" asked Trish.

She rolled her eyes, her blond curls bouncing around her head. "Wendy. My real name is Wendy."

"Why do they call you Stitch?" asked Trish.

Wendy looked at Lenny and pinched his shoulders. "From that kids' movie. Bats, I mean Lenny, said I reminded him of that little alien guy."

We all had to laugh at that because there was nothing of the little alien guy that any of us could see in her. Lenny must have been high at the time.

I took a sip of my coffee, but it was already getting cold so I set it aside. I was going to like this group a lot.

Jess had Lenny read more and then he told us about the Word being Jesus and that what Lenny said about the Word being with him was true. I was impressed with how Jess could explain everything and answer our questions. He was so smart.

After our Bible study, none of us jumped up right away. It was kind of nice having friends sitting around, sharing stuff.

"So Trish," said Wendy. "Where's your shop? I could use a haircut." She ran her fingers through her hair and pulled a curl out to see how long it was.

Trish told her where she worked, then tilted her head as she studied Wendy. "I don't think you want to cut it too much shorter. I think it looks good at that length."

"Really?" Wendy looked pleased. "Okay, but then you have to tell me when I really need it."

"You got it," said Trish. "Now Lenny, on the other hand."

"What!" He looked alarmed. "Leave my hair alone. I like it." He ran his hand through the shaggy mess at the back of his head.

Trish shrugged. "Just saying."

"Come on *Lenny*," said Wendy, standing up. "We should go."

I walked them out to the door and came back as Jess started helping Trish pick up coffee cups, but she shooed him away.

"I think Jenna wants to talk to you," she said, and went down the hall to the kitchen.

We sat back down and I wondered how to tell him about my breakthrough without having to go into the gory details. I told him how emotional I got about feeling forgiven for my sins, that God told me to forgive myself and that I killed a giant like David did.

"Wow," he said. "What God did in you can sometimes take years to do. I love how full of faith you are." He sat back and smile. "That's awesome, Jenna."

"And I think I'm not a smoker anymore," I said.

"How did that happen?"

"I don't know, but ever since I killed that giant of unforgiveness, I haven't wanted to smoke."

"Yea, God!" He closed his eyes for a moment and grinned. "God is so good!" He looked at me and sighed. "Your life is going to be so different now. If you keep trusting him to do things like that, you're going to be so amazed."

"Yeah, I guess so. Listen, Jess. I wanted to ask you about something else."

"Yeah?" He leaned forward a little and looked serious.

"Well, I started dating this guy."

He didn't say anything, but his eyebrow dropped a little.

"He's Indian." I went on. "I told him about how I started reading the Bible and going to church, and he's totally fine with it, I think. But the thing is, he has this Hindu god charm on his keychain. He says he doesn't really believe in it, but keeps it because his mother gave it to him and it's part of his culture. I think he actually does believe in it a little." I shrugged. "I'm not sure what to think about that."

Jess sat back and looked thoughtful. "It's not really a good idea to develop a relationship with someone who doesn't believe the same way you do." He paused. "For one thing, the Hindu god is an idol. God hates idols. It's pretty serious. What you carry in your spirit now is light. What the idol carries is darkness. You can't join together with that."

"I'm not talking about marrying him," I said a little too fast.

"Who knows?" he said. "You don't know how far things can get. I'm just saying that you're off to such a good start now with your faith, I hate to see you do anything that would sidetrack you."

"You think it would sidetrack me? I still believe in God and what he did for me."

"Jenna, the enemy can be so subtle. You could start making small compromises you're not even aware of."

"So what about if he didn't have anything to do with idols?"

"If he's not saved, it's the same issue. Your light and his darkness."

I leaned back. "Yeah. I guess I knew that. Something didn't feel right inside." I rubbed my stomach and stared at the floor.

"That's actually a good thing," he said.

"What is?"

"That you feel uncomfortable if the situation isn't right with God. It'll be a barometer for you. Pay attention to it."

"Okay. There's so much stuff I don't know yet."

"You're doing fine." He sat back with his hands on the arms of the chair and smiled. "You're doing great in fact. You have a pretty sensitive spirit, so you hear God. That's so good. The 'stuff,'" he made air quotes, "will come. You'll learn as you go, like we all do."

"Wouldn't it be nice if God just fixed us so we were perfect?" I asked. "Or gave us an electronic voice that would tell what we're supposed to be doing."

"Yeah, it would be awesome. But he didn't do that. This way, we have to trust him with our lives, and that's exactly what he wants us to do." He bounced his hand on the arm of the chair. "You're doing good, warrior."

"Warrior." I knew what he meant, but it still sounded weird.

"You are, whether you feel it or not," he said. "And if you keep believing it, you'll see even more stuff happening." He stood up and looked down at me. "Let me pray for you before I go."

"Okay." I looked down and closed my eyes.

He put his hand on my head and asked God to keep speaking to me and to give me more faith and blessing.

"Thanks, Jess," I said as I walked him out.

He turned back and smiled at me. "Have a good night, Jenna."

Twenty-two

I didn't have a great night like Jess said to have. I kept thinking of Manish. I was really starting to like him. I really I freaked him out when I told him about prison, but he came back. He wanted to get to know me, despite my past or my present. He didn't care about me being in prison or being a Christian. No, that's not true. I think he did care, but it didn't stop him from wanting to be with me. It didn't seem right to tell him that I couldn't date him if he wasn't a Christian, when he was being so accepting. I didn't even want to ask Jess about sleeping with Manish. That would have been too weird.

I picked up the phone in the break room at work then sat at the little table. I stared at Manish's business card for a minute while I worked up some courage. My stomach tightened up as I dialed his number.

"Hello?"

"Hi. This is Jenna."

"Hi, Jenna." He sounded guarded. "What's up?"

"I was just wondering if I was going to see you tonight."

He paused. "What's the matter? You sound upset."

"No, I'm not upset." I was actually a little upset.

"Okay . . . I'll see you tonight. I have to work a little late today, but I'll be there as soon as I can."

"Okay, I'll see you later."

I hung up feeling like Brutus arranging to meet Cesar.

It was really hard to get through the rest of the day. It was like I completely forgot all the joy I had dancing around my living room because I felt forgiven. Instead, I felt dread. I knew I was going to hurt someone I liked. How would he understand?

I went to the park at Alamo Square instead of going straight home. I sat on a bench looking down at the row of fancy Victorian houses called the Painted Ladies that show up all the time in San Francisco post cards. I didn't actually feel like smoking, but I wanted to. It was something I used to do when I was broody and miserable. It was a bad habit and it was good that I let it go, but I still wanted a cigarette.

I pulled out my Bible from my inside jacket pocket. I carried it with me all the time. I liked dipping into it when I needed help. I opened it randomly to 2 Corinthians and looked down at chapter six. "And what agreement has the temple of God with idols? For you are the temple of the living God." I sat back and stared. It was almost exactly like what Jess said. I really did have to break it off with Manish, whether it felt bad or not.

I thought about me being light and the idol being dark. It was a good way to put it. I wondered if my light would make the dark light, but Jess had made it pretty clear that wasn't a good idea. I sighed and felt my stomach roll over when I thought about telling Manish. I wanted to throw up.

***

Manish stood on the doorstep looking sweeter than I'd ever seen him. How was that possible?

"Hey. Come in," I said.

He pecked my cheek as he passed me in the doorway, and suddenly I was afraid I was going to lose my resolve. I sat in the living room, and he sat across from me, leaning his arms against his thighs.

"So, what's going on?" he asked.

I took a deep breath and let it out hard. "I . . . can't really date you anymore."

He looked like he expected it.

"Why not?" he asked flatly.

"I shouldn't be with someone who doesn't believe the same why I do. I know it doesn't bother you, but it's kind of a big deal to a Christian." Oh, God! I felt so bad.

He didn't say anything. He just looked down at the floor while my stomach did flip flops.

"Otherwise, there wouldn't be any reason to not be with you, Manish," I said. "You're wonderful. I really like you."

He looked so hurt, I knew I wasn't making him feel any better with my it's-not-you-it's-me speech.

"I'm sorry," I said finally.

It took a while for him to look up at me. "I understand. I actually respect that you feel so strongly about your faith that you would do this. I don't have that."

We stood up, looking at each other, both knowing it was going to be for the last time. I felt miserable.

He reached out and hugged me. I felt his arms holding me tighter than he ever had before. I didn't want to let him go. I didn't want to let go of this precious gift of friendship, or like, or love. I didn't have it before and I didn't want to lose it.

I pulled back from him. "Manish . . . " I started thinking of some way to make it work. There had to be a way. Then I remembered Jess sitting in the same room only a day earlier warning me against compromise. "I'm going to miss you."

"I'm going to miss you, too," he said. He leaned down and kissed my hair and walked out.

I didn't walk him to the door. I sat down and cried.

***

"I did it," I said.

Trish looked up from her rice bowl. "What did you do?"

I dropped my forehead to the back of the kitchen chair I was straddling. "I broke up with Manish."

"Oh. Is that what Jess said to do?" Chopsticks in midair.

"Yeah." I rested my chin on the chair back. "He said my light and his darkness didn't go together, and God hates idols."

She gave me a sympathetic look. "I'm sorry, Honey. Probably still hurts like the dickens."

"It sure hurt telling him."

"How did he take it?"

"He took it pretty well. Better than I expected."

"Maybe he saw it coming," she said and fished out a thin strip of beef out of her bowl and ate it.

"Maybe. If so, he was smarter about it than I was. I felt this thing in my stomach, like it knew I had to break up with him, so I thought I would feel better now, but I don't."

Trish poked at her bowl. "What do you think about Jess?"

"What do you mean?" I asked, sitting up straight.

"He's pretty cute, don't you think?"

I nodded. "Yeah, he is, but . . ."

"So? He definitely believes the same way you do, and more." She pointed her chopsticks at me. "And I think he likes you."

I frowned. Was I so dense that I wouldn't see that?

"I've seen him watch you, Jenna. He's been so patient, praying for you and leading you to God. I really think there's something more going on."

I shook my head. "He's never said anything."

"Not when you were seeing someone else."

"But he didn't know that. I just told him yesterday."

"Still, I'm just saying." She went back to her bowl like the conversation was closed.

I smiled at her. The last time she had ideas about Jess, she was pretty off base. Then I thought about the look on his face when I told him about Manish. Maybe she was right.

Twenty-three

Laurel drew circles on the table with the small plastic stick she used to stir her coffee. She looked a lot better than the last time I saw her. The bruising was all but gone, and she seemed to move easier, though her arm was still in a sling.

"Are you at least enjoying your time off?" I asked.

"Not really." She rolled her eyes and lifted her cast slightly. "This thing gets in the way and I'm right handed, so everything is harder."

"But you don't have to deal with box loads of paper and messing with those posters and stuff you usually have to print. And you can sleep in, right?"

She didn't look encouraged.

I reached down and picked up my jacket that fell on the floor and set it on the back of my chair. "Are you seeing a counselor?"

"Yeah." She went back to drawing circles and looking glum.

"Is it helping?"

She stopped the circle and stared at nothing. "I don't know."

"Oh, Laurel. I'm so sorry." I sighed and wondered how to be helpful. "You want a refill?"

She shook her head no.

"Okay. I'll be right back." I got up and refilled my cup at the coffee counter and brought it back with extra packets of sugar.

"Bats has been asking about you," I said, shaking two packets together.

"Who?" She looked up, wrinkling her forehead.

"Bats. The guy who works in the tattoo parlor down the street."

"You mean inked-up scrounge?" She looked surprised.

"He's not a scrounge." I poured sugar and gave her a pretend glare.

"That's what Brenda calls him."

"He's really very sweet," I said stirring. "He's a Christian now and getting himself pulled together."

She took a sip of her coffee and looked me over. "So how's that working out? I mean for you?"

"I like it. Becoming a Christian saved my life, for real."

She frowned. "What do you mean?"

I told her how I wanted to kill myself because of the pain I was living with. I told her about being free and hearing God talk to me.

She listened but she looked like I was telling her bedtime stories. She shifted in her chair and wouldn't look at me. "Wow. I never thought I'd hear that stuff from you."

"Yeah, I know. I never thought I would either. But it's changed my life, Laurel. I'm telling you, I was seriously working out how I was going to kill myself."

She finally looked up at me. "I didn't know about that. You always seemed to have it together. I mean, except those times when you were kicking and swearing at your monster," she said with a grin.

"Yeah, well, some of that hasn't changed."

I watched her eyes go to the door and flinch. I looked around to see a good looking guy walk in and go to the counter. I looked back at Laurel. Her head was down and she was hugging herself.

"Is that the . . . " I asked, not sure how to finish. I looked at the guy again.

She shook her head no but wouldn't look up.

"Laurel, Jesus can take it all away," I said quietly.

She glanced up at the guy then back to the floor.

"I'm serious, Laurel." I leaned across the table and touched her good arm. "You don't have to live with it. He can take it away and you can be happy again."

She looked up at me slowly. "If it was anyone else telling me that," she said softly. She studied my eyes and cringed as the guy walked past her.

"Come to church with me. What's it going to hurt? At least give it a shot."

She winced. "Jenna, I'm not . . ."

"I wasn't either," I said. "I didn't believe anything. But guess what? Just 'cause you don't believe something doesn't make it not true. Come with me. If you don't like it, you don't have to go back."

She sighed heavily and stared across the room for a while. "Okay."

Twenty-four

I got off the bus at the far end of the Panhandle and walked down through the park. I was thinking about Laurel. I wondered what to do now that she agreed to go to church. What could I say that would convince her that Jesus could fix her inside? Jess would know. I got a happy feeling just knowing that I could talk to him about her.

I tucked my hands into my jacket pockets and walked along the path, suddenly aware of a crazy guy following me. He was obviously homeless and loony, not one of the regulars I had names for. He shouted obscenities and waved his arms around over his head. He looked at me and shouted some more, but I don't think he really saw me, I just happened to be in his line of vision. I stopped and let him walk past.

When he got even with me I said, "Hey! Jesus loves you."

He stopped and stared at me, really focusing for the first time. Then he walked off, mumbling to himself about Jesus.

That's when I heard chuckling. I looked around and Jess was sitting on a bench with a small stack of folders on his lap and his cell phone in his hand.

I went over and sat next to him. "So, what? Are you locked into my park-walking mojo or something?"

He laughed and shrugged. "I don't know. I guess so. I like how you talked to your friend there." He pointed to the homeless guy.

"Yeah, well, I'm not sure you ever get through to them." I turned and watched the homeless guy stop and yell at a tree.

"I wouldn't be so sure," said Jess. "Your words carry power."

"What do you mean?"

"Life and death are in the power of the tongue."

"Seriously?"

He nodded. "Very seriously. Watch what you say."

"Okay, I will use my powers for good and not evil." I sat back with my hands in my pockets and looked across the park. "So, I broke up with Manish."

"You did?" His hand, resting on the top of the bench, started tapping lightly.

"Yeah."

"What did you tell him?"

"I said that I needed to be with someone who believes like I do."

"How did he take it?" he asked casually.

I looked around at him. "He took it pretty well. At least I think so."

Jess moved the stack of folders and crossed his leg to face me better. "I'm sorry. Really. What you did was pretty hard, I know, but I have to tell you that it's the best thing for you."

"I know. It's just that he was so nice, and he didn't care what I believed."

"Yeah," he sighed. "I'm really sorry."

"I asked a friend of mine to come to church on Sunday," I said.

"Is he . . . Indian?"

"No!" I gave him an annoyed look. "A girl friend. She was raped and beat up by a guy she met at a club a while back. She needs help."

"Whoa. I'm sorry to hear that."

"Could you, could we pick her up?"

"Sure."

"I don't know what to tell her." I swung my feet under the bench and shrugged.

"About what?"

"About God. I mean, she's agreed to come to church, but only just. She doesn't really believe what I tell her. She only agreed to go to church because I asked her."

Jess watched a young couple walk past holding hands, then looked back at me. "Sometimes you just have to let God do what he does. If you try to help him, you can get in the way."

"So what does that mean? What do I do?"

"Let her come to church then see what she has to say. We can talk to her together later if you want."

"That would be great. Thanks, Jess." Suddenly I felt better. I knew he'd know what to do.

"Good." He leaned back and put his arm across the back of the bench again. "Jenna, how would you feel about going out with me?"

Whoa! Trish was right! I made lines on the ground with the heel of my shoe then looked at him. "I guess I'd be okay with that. You already know I have issues to work through, so I guess that doesn't freak you out."

He pressed his lips together and waved his hand like he was swatting a fly from his face. "Past is past. We don't need to go there. I know your heart for God and it's beautiful. I love how you dive into the Word and come up with gems. To be honest, I want to hang out with you to see what God is going to do next."

"What do you mean?"

"Oh, Jenna—" He leaned toward me. "You've got destiny written all over you. Your life is just beginning."

I smiled at him. "Yeah, I guess so. It feels like it."

"Where do you think God wants to take you?"

I shook my head and shrugged. "I have no idea. It just feels like I'm starting over. I really don't know where that's going to go."

"Don't worry about it," he said. "Give it time. The things in your heart that you really want to do are from God anyway, so you should get to do what you love."

I stared at the ground. "I'm not sure what that is now."

"That's okay. Hey, I want to check out a house in the Marina district. Want to come?"

"Well, I don't know," I said. "I have so many appointments on my calendar. It's all rush, rush, rush with me."

He looked serious. "Yes, I can see that. Any chance you can fit me in?"

I sighed heavily. "It could take some work."

"There might be ice cream."

"Ice cream?"

"Could be." He looked at me with his head cocked to side.

"As it turns out I always have an open space for ice cream. When did you say?"

"Um, now?"

"Okay," I said, standing up. "Lead on."

"Wow," he said, picking up his stuff. "Found your weakness button."

"That and . . . I'm not telling you any more," I said.

He tucked his folders under his arm and grinned. "I have my ways."

"I bet," I said, following him through the park.

We found an ice cream parlor on the way to the Marina, and I suggested we eat our cones inside. I didn't like the idea of dripping ice cream in his fancy car, and I didn't want him to have to tell me not to. We sat at a small table by the window, and I watched him devour his ice cream faster than anyone I've ever seen.

"So, how was it?" I asked in disbelief.

"Good," he said, looking satisfied.

"How do you know? You barely had time to taste it."

He leaned back against his chair. "Some things are so good you just have to go for it." He stared at my cone. "You going to finish that?"

"Yes!" I pulled my cone away from him. "Don't get any ideas. I have a tiny plastic spoon and I know how to use it."

"Okay, okay." He raised his hands, palms out. "Don't hurt me."

"How do you not get an ice cream headache when you eat it so fast?"

"I don't get them."

"Ever?"

"No." He looked apologetic.

"Wow." I slurped up a drip. "So tell me how long you've been a Christian." I didn't want him to just sit there and watch me eat.

He seemed pleased with the question and leaned on the table. "Since high school. I went to a revival meeting with a friend. I got saved that night."

"What was it like?"

"I never went to church before that, so I didn't know what to expect. But when I heard the message I knew it was truth. You know how you feel it inside? I prayed and felt the love of God on me for the first time. You never forget that, your first love." He looked reminiscent, then looked at me evenly. "Don't ever lose that. If you let your love get cold, you stop hearing from God the way you do now."

I stopped licking my ice cream. I'd never thought about my new life being any other way than trusting God completely. "I guess it's like married people, isn't it? They grow apart."

"That's only because the enemy wants you to grow apart from God, so he works at it all the time. If you keep your heart humble and grateful, he can't do anything."

Good to know. I finished off my cone and wiped my face.

"Not that you won't have ups and downs," he said. "You'll always go through those, but you can go through them with God and get stronger and stronger."

I folded up my napkin and squeezed it in my hand. "That's what I want."

He smiled broadly. "I know. That's what I love about you." He stood up and let me pass him as we went outside.

Twenty-five

I felt a little guilty about hanging out with Jess so soon after breaking it off with Manish. But then, it wasn't like we had spent that much time together. Better to end it sooner than later if you had to. Manish was such a nice guy. I hoped he was happy.

I dropped a ream of paper on one end to even out the sheets before feeding them to the monster. I could see things working out with Jess and I. He knew so much that I needed to learn, and he was so excited by what God was doing in me.

I needed a cell phone.

I thought about my old cell phone and what it did to me and felt my stomach start to knot up. I thought that giant was dead. Jess told me to keep claiming a victory over it, so I closed my eyes and saw myself holding up the giant's head like David did. The thing was dead. He was dead in the name of the Lord. Thank you, Jesus! I took a deep breath and let it out. I felt better, peaceful. Victory. I could do it.

I asked Brenda if Lenny could have lunch with me in the break room sometimes. She said yes, though I could tell she didn't go for the tats. But she'd seen Lenny enough to know that he was okay.

Right at noon, I saw him come into the store and I waved him over. I'd told him before that he had to bring lunch with him. He said he didn't eat lunch, but I said yes, he did, and he had to bring it. He held up a brown paper bag and grinned at me as I led him back.

We sat down at the little table in the break room and he dumped his bag out.

"Look, food," he said, like he was proving his point.

"A stick of jerky, a bag of chips, and cookies. Where did you shop, a gas station?"

"You said bring my own food, so I did." He tore open the jerky and ripped off a bite with his teeth.

"Nice try. Next time think of real food." I pulled out my baloney sandwich and started eating it. "So Lenny, what do you think of Jess?" Lenny might not have been the brightest bulb in the pack, but he did have street sense. I knew he could read people.

He gnawed at the jerky and bounced his head. "I like him. The guy knows stuff. And he likes you." He looked at me smugly.

"Why do you say that?"

"I seen the way he looks at you. He doesn't look at the rest of us like that. You like him?"

I smiled and nodded. "Yeah, I do. He asked me out."

"Yeah? Good for you. Hey, you think he'd like a tat? I'd do one for him for free. Maybe a cross or something?"

I laughed. "I don't know. I'll ask him. I don't see him as a tat kind of guy though."

He reached for the cookies. "Yeah, I know. Just asking."

"How are things going with you and Wendy?"

He bobbed his head. "Good. I mean, you know, this Christian stuff is kinda hard. It's kinda hard, Jenna." He started to eat a cookie then dropped his hand. "I keep thinking of all the bad stuff I used to do, and part of me still wants to keep doing it."

"You know what Jess says? God can fix anything," I wiped mustard off my mouth and looked him in the eye. "I believe it's hard for you. It's hard for me too, but I prayed about it and God took a lot away for me. I feel so much better now."

"Yeah?" He looked like he wasn't entirely sure he believed me.

Sherman, the part time guy, came in and hesitated, then grabbed something from the refrigerator and left.

I waited until we were alone again. "Let's pray about it."

"Right now?"

"Yeah." I reached over and put my hand on his and closed my eyes. "God, you did so much for me, killing old giants that used to give me so much pain. Please be with Lenny and help him be the man you want him to be. Help him not want to go back to his old life and old ways. Take away those thoughts and give him new thoughts, about you. In Jesus' name. Amen."

Lenny was quiet. He looked up and sighed deeply. "Thanks, Jenna. You help me so much. I'd be dead now if it wasn't for you."

"Well, now it's your turn," I said, going back to my sandwich. "You can help someone else. Just think if everyone did that, helped someone else find God, wouldn't the world be better?"

"Yeah!" His eyes got big. "Like universal love!"

***

Trish was banging around in the kitchen when I got home.

"Hey, you're home early," I said.

"My last two appointments canceled on me." She set a salad on the table. "Want some? I made enough. There's chicken in it."

"Yeah, okay." I set the table quickly and we both sat down.

"Soooo, Jess asked me out," I said, handing her the salad bowl.

She took it and looked up with bright eyes. "Really? I knew it!" She giggled.

I just laughed. I knew it would make her day.

"So what did you guys do?" she asked as she filled her plate.

153

"We got ice cream. Then I went with him to see a house for sale in the Marina district."

She handed the bowl back to me. "Not much of a first date, but that's okay."

"I think it was fine. I like that it didn't feel like a date."

"He's so handsome, Jenna. He's smart, seems like a good business man. What a good catch." She bounced her eyebrows at me and took a bite.

"I know! I'm not quite sure how that happened. I mean, really, he should be going after you. You're the pretty one. You run your own business."

She smiled and shrugged. "Not everyone is comfortable with the cross-cultural thing."

"It's not like you don't speak English," I said sarcastically.

"Still . . . it's okay," she said. "I like him liking you. You deserve a good relationship. It's probably better going out with Jess than the other guy who's not a Christian anyway. So when are you seeing him again?"

"Jess? I think tonight." I stabbed a crouton and crunched into it.

"Guess I'll have to get used to seeing him around here for a while."

"For a while?"

"Well, then you know, you two will start making big plans. You'll get engaged, get married, have kids, move to a big house that he's been saving for you in Marin County, and raise goats or something. You know." She took a bite and her look dared me to argue about it.

"Oh, that's what you mean." I gave her an exaggerated look of agreement. "Are you moving in with us? 'Cause, I just want to be sure there's room, with the goats and all."

"Not with the goats!" she said dramatically. "In the guest house."

"Yes of course, the guest house. How many kids?"

"Two. Girls. Jess has his heart set on two boys, but you have girls instead and he loves them so much that he builds them their own little castle in a field of poppies."

"Wow." I took a drink and wondered what my roommate did in her room at night. "I think you should be a writer."

"No. But I think I could be a good life-consultant. I could tell people who don't know what to do with themselves how to live, and they could pay me for it. Of course, I do that now."

"I bet you do. A good hairdresser or bartender—what do you need a therapist for?"

"Exactly. But I think therapists make more than I do."

"So, what about you?" I asked. "You got everyone else's life planned out. When are you going to settle down with Romeo? I'm sure you've met lots of great guys."

"Someday. I'm not in a hurry."

"Is he going to be Japanese?"

"Not necessarily. My parents would prefer it, but I don't care. Just let him be smart, and handsome, and well off, and a Christian, and like sushi, and be able to reach the top shelves, and give amazing neck rubs."

"Amen!" I said.

Twenty-six

I made Trish go do something while I cleaned up after dinner. For one, I wanted to thank her for making it. And two, I didn't want her to see me looking at the clock every thirty seconds. It was silly how giddy I felt knowing Jess was coming over just to see me. He'd asked me if he should call Trish to let me know when to expect him, but I didn't want to start that. I really did need my own phone.

I finished washing the dishes and took my time wiping down the counter and table because it gave me something to do. I even cleaned the sink. Finally the door buzzed.

"I'll get it!" shouted Trish from inside her room.

She didn't come out.

"Just kidding," she yelled.

I gave her door a bang when I ran past, and I could hear her laugh.

Jess leaned in when I opened the street door and kissed me on the cheek before I could say anything. I felt relief that he still liked me. He hadn't changed his mind.

"For you," he said and pulled a mixed bouquet out from behind his back. Must have been cute watching him from the street.

"Thanks, Jess," I said, taking them. "I never got flowers before." I held them gingerly, like they would break if you breathed on them.

"I don't know why not," he said, coming into the apartment. "It was the first thing I thought of this morning."

That stopped me. I turned and looked up at him in amazement.

"Really?"

"Uh-huh." He started to kiss me again then looked up and smiled at Trish coming out of her room. "Hi, Trish."

"Hi, Jess. Oh, pretty! You should put them in water. There's a vase in the cupboard up there." She pointed back to the kitchen. Then she passed us in the hallway, smiling like a goofball.

Jess got the vase down for me, and I filled it with water. I didn't know what you were supposed to do with flowers, so I just dropped them in. Jess lifted them out and pulled the rubber band off the stems then set them back in the vase and kind of fluffed them a little.

"Oh." I felt embarrassed.

"It's okay," he said. "I don't know what to do with them either."

I put the vase on the table and turned to him. "How was your day?"

He rubbed my arms and smiled down at me. "Wonderful. How was yours?"

"Slow . . . and wonderful!"

He laughed and hugged me then kissed the top of my head.

"Hey, guess what?" I asked as I pulled back from him a little. "What?"

I told him about praying for Bats. I mean Lenny. I waited for him to say something but he just stared at me.

"Was that okay to do?"

He nodded with a stunned look. "Yes, it's okay. You really don't need my help in this do you?"

"What do you mean?"

"I mean it's great, Jenna. You're doing everything I would tell you to do, but you're doing it on your own. Like God is giving you wisdom exactly when you need it."

"He is?" That surprised me. It didn't feel like it.

He cupped his hands around my face and kissed me. "I'm so proud of you."

My heart went wild and I'm pretty sure I blushed. He was proud of me! My Mom used to say that when I was a kid when I brought home report cards. But you watch your kid sit in a courtroom and go off to prison, and you stop saying stuff like that. I didn't expect how loved it made me feel.

He must have watched all that emotion flow over my face, because he looked more serious and held my face up by my chin.

"I mean it, Jenna. I'm really proud of you. You've gone from a place of real pain to letting God work miracles in you. And you're doing it all by yourself, just you and him."

I wasn't getting the big deal. "I prayed like you said to, that's all."

He smiled like you do when a kid says something sweet. Kind of bugged me for a second.

"But most people, a lot of people, need so much hand-holding when they first come to Christ. And a lot of them will need it forever. They want to be told what to do all the time. They don't trust their own faith. You do! You believe everything God tells you, so it's easy for him to work through you." He held my eyes and I wanted to melt. No one ever looked at me like that before.

"Thanks for helping me, Jess. You're the one who kept following me around until I caved."

He pulled me into a big hug and sighed. "God knew."

Right about then I wanted time to stop forever. I wondered if God had a special app that could freeze a moment in time, so you could carry it around in your pocket, and pull it out whenever you wanted to step into it again. I'd buy that app, and I didn't even have a phone.

Jess pushed me back so he could look in my face. "You had dinner?"

"Yep."

"How about dessert?"

"Dessert? Keep going."

"Well, I was thinking of this little place in North Beach that makes a pretty awesome crème brûlée."

"Crème brûlée? Is that like ice cream?"

He just smiled. "You'll have to find out for yourself."

"Yeah, okay."

I went to my room and grabbed my jacket. Jess waited at the door while I poked my head into the living room.

"We're going out for dessert."

Trish looked up and winked. "Have a good time."

"What's crème brûlée?" I whispered.

She smiled and waved me off.

It was awesome driving through the city with Jess. For all the downside of living in a big city—the urine in front of the house, the homeless guys sleeping everywhere, the gangs—there was another cleaner, upbeat energy. With my world narrowed down to about six blocks, I rarely got out in my own town. Maybe that would change now. Somehow it felt different with Jess.

I watched the lights in the tall buildings and the people crowded at the corners waiting to cross the streets. I didn't know why being out in the city at night felt so special. Maybe because I only ever went out when there was something special to do. I glanced at Jess and he smiled at me and made my heart dance a little.

We drove into a parking garage and had to hunt around for a space. It was cold out, but Jess put his arm around me, and I didn't care if we walked through a blizzard. I felt a little under-dressed, going into the restaurant wearing my army jacket over my Bugs

Bunny T-shirt. I glanced at a few women dolled up for the runway and hoped Jess didn't mind.

We were seated in a booth with a white tablecloth and a small candle glowing in a round, red vase. It looked cozy and romantic. The waitress handed us menus and took our coffee orders. I looked at the dessert list, but had already decided to try the brulu, bruly thing.

Jess looked from the menu to me. "Want to try it?"

I nodded and he ordered for both of us.

He drummed his fingers on the table and raised an eyebrow. "So when are you going to get a cell phone? You have no idea how many times I wanted to call you today."

"You mean if I got a cell phone you'd be calling me all day and get me fired?" I asked like a smart aleck.

"I didn't say I *would* call you all day, I just wanted to."

"To be honest, I'm thinking about it. I should get one."

"Good." He had that relieved look, like he checked something off his list of things to do.

The coffee came and smelled delicious. I stirred in sugar and took a sip.

"Mmm! Hot! But good." I set the cup down. "I love good coffee."

"You sound like my friend Erick. I think he mainlines coffee when he sleeps at night because that's the only time he's not actually drinking it."

He sat back and stretched his arm out along the top of the booth and fingered the stitching. "So, Jenna, I know I asked you the other day, but what do you really want to do with your life?"

His question took me by surprise. "I don't know. Doing what I'm doing, I guess."

He looked at me skeptically. "Come on now. I doubt that when you were a kid, you told everyone you wanted to grow up to work in Copyland. What did you really say?"

I looked down at the crease in the tablecloth and smoothed it out. "Geology. I was going to school to learn geology."

"Really?" I wasn't sure if he was impressed or only surprised. "What happened?"

I studied him, trying to decide if I should tell him. I couldn't do it. He looked so handsome in the candlelight, and the way he looked at me—I didn't want to ruin it. Manish's reaction was so shocking.

"Things happened. I had a car accident." Was all I could say.

"So." He shrugged. "Go back and do it."

Go back and do it. I hadn't ever thought I could. It was like that horrible moment in time erased all my plans and dreams. I never thought I deserved to pick them up again.

I was still staring at the tablecloth when the bruly thing appeared in front of me. I looked up at Jess in surprise.

He was watching me and grinning. "Go ahead. Try it!"

"It's not ice cream."

"I never said it was."

I picked up my spoon hesitantly and was a little shocked to find such a hard crust on the top.

"That's the fun part, breaking up the crust." He jabbed at his and broke it open to show the custard underneath.

I followed his lead and mashed into mine. It tasted divine. So sweet. My eyes must have lit up because he laughed out loud when I took my first bite. "That's good," I said, pointing at the shallow bowl with my spoon.

"I thought you'd like it. I'm sorry though. Any crème brûlée you have anywhere else will pale by comparison. You're going to have to come back here every time."

"Good to know," I said, scraping up a spoonful.

I all but licked the bowl clean, much to Jess' entertainment. The coffee was good, perfect with the sweet dessert. The background music and the low light all ganged up on me. It felt like one of those sappy love story moments. I loved it.

Jess watched me with his chin in his hand. "You look so happy."

I blushed. I'm sure I blushed. Hopefully he didn't notice in the candlelight. "Thank you. This has been really nice." I looked around the restaurant then back to him.

He was still watching me. "Well, that was the plan. You deserve a really nice night out. I doubt that you've had enough of those."

"Not like this. It feels like prom night." I giggled.

He picked up his coffee. "It's way better than my prom night."

"Oh? What happened?"

He shook his head. "Just two teenagers getting drunk and throwing up in the parking lot. You don't want to know."

"Okay." I laughed. "You're right, I don't want to know."

"Want to go for a drive?" he asked.

"A drive?" I didn't expect that. "Okay."

We left the parking garage and he still didn't tell me where he wanted to drive to, but I didn't care. It felt like a night of adventure, like good things could happen. I leaned back in the seat and watched the lights and the buildings and the night drift by like a bruly brûlée dream.

Suddenly I sat up. "We're going over the Golden Gate Bridge?"

He just looked over at me and smiled. "That okay?"

"Sure." It had been years since I'd been over the bridge at night. I felt kind of giddy, like a kid playing grownup. Everything felt so dramatic, like in the movies when they run off on stupid, wild adventures that all end well.

I looked up at the tall orange support towers and watched the heavy coils of steel slide past. It's fun on the bridge during the day, especially walking, if you bundle up, but at night, there's something magical about it. We finally crossed to the Marin side and pulled off to an exit that crossed the highway.

"You ever been to the Marin headlands at night?" he asked.

"No," I said, looking around, kid again.

We pulled into the parking lot along with a dozen other cars and got out. He grabbed a jacket from his backseat and pulled it on. "It gets cold up here."

He took my hand and walked me up the hill along a narrow path. With the lights from the bridge and a half moon, we could see fairly well. Actually, I wasn't paying attention to anything. He was holding my hand. I walked where he led. I loved that he was holding my hand.

When we made it to the top of the hill, San Francisco spread out before us across the bay like a fairy city connected to a dazzling bridge as party boats glided slowly by. Shadowy couples wandered around the hill, clinging to each other in the chilly wind and pointing to various spots in the city.

"Well, what do you think?" he asked.

"It's beautiful. Really beautiful. I didn't even know about coming here at night."

He squeezed my hand then moved in front of me. He put his hands on my face and kissed me before I had time to think. He pulled his face back and I could just make out that he was looking into my eyes. He smiled and kissed me again. "You look so beautiful tonight, Jenna."

I had a hard time being called beautiful. I always thought of myself as plain. Trish was the pretty one. I didn't argue though, because I didn't want to ruin the moment. It was a Cinderella moment. I even wondered if it was too good to be real.

"Jenna," he whispered and held me tightly.

I closed my eyes and felt his arms around me. It felt so safe. When was the last time I felt so safe? I thought of Manish holding me, but this was different. This time held no uneasy feeling about it being wrong. Then my mind flashed back to my high school boyfriend, Dustin Barns. Dustin really only wanted sex. He definitely didn't make me feel safe. I didn't want to think about

Dustin Barns. A real man was holding me, and I wanted to soak in every second of it.

Suddenly, despite Jess's arms around me, I started shivering. It was really cold, and the wind blew across the headlands like the freezer door was open.

Jess rubbed my arms briskly. "You're cold aren't you?" he said with his face against my ear.

"Um . . . " I didn't want to admit it, but the moment was quickly freezing up. Any minute and my nose would start dripping icicles, and it wouldn't be pretty. "Um, yes."

"Okay." He put his arm around my shoulder and walked me away. "I'm cold too." He hugged me to him, and I stumbled along trying to act like it was just fine to walk at an angle down the hill.

We got back to the car, and he started it up and turned the heater on high. We both sat there warming up and looked at each other in the dim light, feeling wonderful.

"Is this really okay?" he asked.

I knew what he meant. It was fast. We were just getting to know each other. Would it change things, mess things up? I didn't know. I looked at his amazing eyes and that silver hair shining in the moonlight. He was so handsome. "It's okay with me."

"Good." He smiled then leaned over and kissed me again. This time deeper, longer, like we'd been separated for months, and I just got off the ship from Southampton after the war. People were getting into their car next to us and made us self-conscious, so we sat back and looked at each other, knowing that we were really into something now. He reached over and touched the back of my head then put the car in gear and backed out.

He couldn't find parking in front of my apartment, so we walked from three blocks away. He had his arm around my shoulder, and I had my arm around his waist. It felt like it was the most natural thing in the world.

We stood in the lobby outside my apartment, and he kissed me goodnight. He held my hands against his chest and looked into my eyes. "Sleep well," he said.

"You too." You too! How lame was that? I relived the evening over and over later and never understood why he was attracted to me. It certainly wasn't for my stunning command of language.

Twenty-seven

The next few days floated by in a fog. You know—the dreamy, lovey kind of fog where everything you think of is sweet and mushy and revolting to everyone else. This felt so right, no uneasiness in my stomach like with Manish. I was happy. I tried not to talk about Jess in every single conversation, but it took work. I thought Laurel was going to whack me in the head after a while, so I had to just stop talking. Then I just sighed a lot.

I was also reading my Bible. I wanted to learn so much, and it was awesome that when I had questions Jess could usually answer them for me.

I sat on my bed, leaning against the wall one night, and realized my neck was stiff from sitting there so long. I closed my Bible, rolled my head to stretch out the kinks, and looked at the clock. It was one in the morning. Sometimes I got so absorbed in reading, I let time fly by without seeing it. But my body definitely felt it.

I decided to get a drink before I turned in. I was surprised to see the kitchen light on. I didn't realize that Trish was still up. I walked down the hall and stopped in the doorway. She was sitting at the table with her head in her hands, crying.

"Trish? Are you okay? What's wrong?" I pulled a chair out and sat down.

She continued to cry for a while so I just let her, but my mind was racing, trying to think of what in the world would upset her so badly. Trish was a rock. She handled everything. She was always the one there for me when I fell apart. Sitting there watching her cry kind of tore at my foundations a little. I didn't realize how much I depended on her being strong. I handed her a napkin and waited.

Finally she wiped her eyes and blew her nose. She still didn't look at me. She took another napkin from me and wiped her eyes again and started breathing normally. She leaned her face in her hands again then shook her head.

I thought back to earlier. Jess was at a client meeting all evening, so I fixed myself dinner and went to my room. I heard Trish come home later, but I hadn't actually seen her all evening. What could have happened?

She looked up, rested her chin on her clasped hands, and sighed. "I'm fine," she said, clearly lying.

"You don't look like you're fine."

"No, I am, really," she said a little shakily. She sat back and brushed her hair from her face. "Boy, God really knows how to get to you sometimes."

"What? What does that mean?"

She let out another deep breath. "One of my customers gave me this book." She reached over and touched a paperback sitting on the table. It was turned over so I couldn't see the title. "It's about a kid who dies and goes to heaven. Then he comes back and tells everyone stuff that he shouldn't know unless what he said happened really happened."

"Wow. That upset you?"

"What he said." She looked down at the table for a long time, like she was trying to decide something. She tilted her head but continued to look down. "He said that the unborn babies are in heaven, babies that have been miscarried or aborted. He told his

Mom about a baby she lost before he was born. He said he played with her in heaven."

"Really? That's cool. That's really cool."

Trish kept looking down at the table and started crying again. I handed her another napkin. "You have a baby in heaven?"

She nodded and wiped her nose. "I had an abortion, years ago," she waved like it was a long time ago. "I never knew if it was a boy or a girl."

"Now you know you'll see your baby in heaven."

"The boy in the book said the babies are not angry. They're waiting to see their moms." She looked at me and sniffed.

"Oh man, Trish." I scooted my chair over next to her and leaned in to hug her. She held on tight and cried some more. It was a bit awkward, hugging from that position, but still good. She cried for a while then pulled away to blow her nose some more.

I didn't say anything. What can you say? I just sat there and let her talk if she wanted to.

"I was in high school," she said quietly. She seemed pretty composed, but she sounded bitter. "I had this boyfriend, Keith. You know how when you're in high school you think you know everything?"

I didn't answer. Didn't need to.

"I thought I was in love. Geesh! Why can't you tell the difference between love and hormones when you're sixteen? It would make things so much easier to deal with. Keith and I thought we were together forever. Then I got pregnant and he got out. I've never seen anyone so truly terrified in my life. I'm not sure if he ever spoke to me again. I had to go to the clinic by myself."

"Did you're parents know?"

"No. I didn't tell anyone. You're the first person, besides Keith. I was so stupid." She closed her eyes and rubbed her eyelids.

"Not stupid. Young and naive."

"Yeah, that's what I said, stupid."

"But now, how do you feel, after reading the book?"

She actually made a tiny smile. "I feel like I've been forgiven. When I became a Christian, I asked God to forgive me about this. I just never said anything to anyone. But after reading this, I feel like God knows how much it's hurt all these years. And now I know my baby is with him. I want to see him, her. I want to know what kind of baby I have." She wadded up her mess of napkins. "Even though I know God forgives us when we go to him, I never thought I would feel forgiven for this."

"You killed a giant, Trish! Think about how many women are carrying that pain and guilt. You have something to share with them now. You can give them hope and forgiveness."

She looked across the room in thought. "Yeah. I think I'll keep this book at my station so it can start conversations. Thanks, Jenna."

"You be awesome, girl." I squeezed her hand.

She looked around at the clock on the stove. "I know it's late, but I'm going to make some hot chocolate. Want some?"

"You betcha."

Twenty-eight

Laurel stood in her doorway, looking nervous.

"You ready to go to church?" I asked.

"No."

"Come on." I turned from her apartment to go down the stairs and had to glance back to make sure she was following me.

"I'm having second thoughts about this I'll have you know," she said.

I glanced at her over my shoulder. "I know, but I'll be there with you. I won't let anyone hurt you."

I made introductions in the car for Trish and Jess.

"How's your poor arm?" asked Trish.

"It's better. I get the cast off in a couple of weeks," said Laurel, settling in next to her.

"Is it itchy?" Jess looked at her in the rearview mirror.

"Sometimes," she said. "Not too bad."

"Have you ever been to church before?" asked Jess.

She shook her head. "No."

He gave her another look in the mirror then pulled out.

"You don't have to do anything you're not comfortable with," he said. "We just like to get together and meet with God."

Her face scrunched up like that wasn't something she was looking forward to.

Trish smiled at her. "I know that sounds weird, but it's really pretty awesome."

Laurel caught my eye for a moment, and I could see the question she wasn't asking, so I nodded at her encouragingly. She looked out the window and didn't talk any more.

When we got to church, Laurel stayed next to me and watched everyone with suspicion. We took some seats in the back and she sat like her name was about to be called for execution.

"I don't know about this, Jenna." She frowned at the bulletin like it had cooties.

I turned to face her better. "Listen, it's going to be fine. I want you to listen to everything and believe it 'cause it's going to be true. When they say God is good, it really means that God is good. He loves you more than you can possibly imagine."

"Oh yeah. So why do I have this?" she said, lifting her casted arm.

"You weren't listening to him when that happened were you?"

She glared at me. "He let it happen."

"No, Laurel. You let it happen." I glanced around to see where Jess was, but he was talking to someone in the aisle. "God has better plans for you than that." I pointed to her arm.

She let out a hard sigh and watched a group of teenagers make their way to the front.

"Just be open and let God tell you himself," I said.

"Hey, Jenna." Lenny waved at me from the aisle.

"Hey, Lenny. Where's Wendy?"

He turned and pointed to a small knot of people in the back.

"Lenny, this is Laurel, from Copyland."

"I thought you said his name was Bats," she said.

I shrugged. "Lenny's his real name. I keep forgetting."

"Hey." Lenny waved. He pointed to her arm. "Hope you get out of that soon."

She nodded grudgingly. "Me too."

I tried not to watch her too much during the service, but I wanted to see how she was taking it. She didn't look like she was taking it very well. In fact, I was so concerned about her not being open to what God was doing that I didn't feel anything myself.

At the end of the service, they had people pray to ask Jesus into their hearts, but Laurel didn't do anything. She stared at the seat in front of her with a stone face.

I glanced at Jess and he nodded knowingly.

"Give her time," he whispered in my ear.

She didn't want to go to lunch. She wanted to go home.

I followed her out of the car trying desperately to think of what to say.

"Laurel, listen . . . ."

"Save it, Jenna." She looked angry, then turned and walked into her building.

I watched her walk away and felt my heart break. I got in the car and leaned my elbow on the window and my head on my fist.

"Did she say anything?" asked Trish.

"No. She just looked mad. Like I dragged her there and she knew it was going to be a useless waste of time." I rubbed my fist against my head. "I don't get it."

"People are different," said Jess. "You have to let them get to where they need to go. She's just not ready to hear it yet."

I looked at him. "But, she *needs* to. She really needs to."

"I know. We all do," he said softly. "You can't make her believe, but you can pray. Don't underestimate how powerful prayer can be."

"Really? Like killing giants and stuff?"

He grinned. "Exactly like killing giants and stuff."

"I'm in," said Trish from the back seat.

I looked around at her.

"Seriously," she said. "Let's pray and kill us some giants."

"Okay." Suddenly I felt like picking up that sword. I weighed it in my hands and thought about what it could do. I really wanted Laurel to know God.

Twenty-nine

The next few weeks flew by. You heard people say that when you were a kid, but you just didn't believe it—especially when you ran out of summer so fast. But you got older, and days started bumping into each other. You looked back and wondered where the month went. My days were going by like that.

Jess and I saw each other every day. Well, almost every day. A couple times he had a men's thing at church in the evening or client appointments when he was showing property he wanted to sell. But at least we could talk to each other, because I finally got a cell phone.

Jess went with me. I walked into the store like I was entering enemy territory. I actually felt a little jumpy, like one of the little monsters was going to leap off the wall and bite me.

Jess, however, was like a kid in a candy store. He kept picking up phones, playing with them, and ooing over functionality. He'd call me over to look at this one and that one. I could tell he was bummed that his contract wasn't close to allowing him to get a new one.

In the end I got a phone, nothing fancy, but something I could afford. We took it back to my place and started playing with it. I made my first call to Jess sitting next to me on the couch. I knew it should be okay. There was no reason why I couldn't have a cell phone, but it had been so long that it didn't feel right. My self-imposed restriction was harder to let go of than I thought, and that bothered me, because I knew that God had forgiven me.

Jess left early because he had work to do. He stood at the door and kissed me then whispered in my ear, "I'm going to call you later. Don't put me into voicemail."

He made me laugh. He was so happy with my new toy.

I sat on my bed and looked down at the cell phone in my hands. I could almost see it making faces at me. I had to know if it was really, truly okay. I could talk myself into stuff, and other people could say it was okay, but did God say it was okay?

I picked up my Bible and just flipped through it. I scanned down a page and stopped when I read, "To people who are pure, all things are pure." Was I pure? Yes, I believed that God saved my life, and I believed what I read in the Bible. Did that make me pure? I remembered something Jess said, that once we are saved, Jesus' blood covers us. It still kind of grossed me out to think like that, but that covering was what did it. It really did make me pure, at least to God. I just had to accept it. He forgave me and a cell phone wasn't evil. It was what you did with it that could be.

I looked down at the shiny, black gadget in my hand. It didn't seem to be mocking me anymore, it was just a phone.

And then it rang.

I punched the answer button. "Hello."

"Is this the party to whom I am speaking?"

"Um, maybe," I said. "Are you the party to whom I am listening?"

"Yes. Yes, it is," Jess said.

"Oh, good. Are you getting your work done?"

"Just got home."

"So get to work!"

"I will. I just wanted to hear your voice. I'm so glad I can finally call you."

"I know. Me too." I didn't know what else to say. It was so odd. When we were together, we could talk forever. Now I felt awkward and self-conscious.

"Okay, I'll get back to work," he said. "Sleep well. Dream of me."

I laughed. "I'll try."

"Good-bye," he said softly.

"Bye."

I hung up and thought about how my nightmares had turned to dreams, dreams of Jess and I. Well, daydreams really. I thought about our house and two girls and the goats. I liked Trish's version. It made me giddy. How completely the opposite of the horror my life had been.

***

"Hello?"

"Hi Laurel, it's me Jenna." I found walking home was a good time to chat. I used to find that obnoxious in other people, but really, it was a good use of time if you didn't talk so loud that you got evil stares from people passing by.

"Hey Jenna."

"Got a new cell phone, so now you have my number."

"Wow. What's next? Buying a car?" she asked like a snark.

"One step at a time," I said. "I still have to get used to this thing."

"Still, I bet you'll use it more than you think you will."

"Yeah, probably. How are you doing?" I hurried across the street to make the light and avoid a bike messenger.

"I got my cast off yesterday."

"Really? How does it feel?"

"I can't believe how good it feels. I have to lift weights because my arm is pretty weak, but it's so much easier to do everything. It's like I was missing a limb and now I got it back."

"Awesome," I said. "What do you think about coming to church on Sunday? Jess and I could pick you up."

176

She didn't say anything.

"Laurel?" I waited for a mom and a stroller to pass in front of me and wondered if the line dropped.

I heard her sigh. "Jenna, I'm sorry. I know you want me to, but it's just not something I want to do."

"Okay," I said. "I just wanted you to know that you're invited, any time. When are you coming back to work?"

"Tomorrow, actually."

"Oh, good. Okay. I'll see you then."

"'Kay. See you."

I punched the end button and slid the phone into my pocket. Why was she acting like that about going to church? Why had I acted like that? Like anyone talking about God wasn't worth listening to? *God, what would it take to get inside Laurel's head?*

When I got home, I found Wendy and Trish in deep conversation in the living room. They both turned and looked up at me when I came in and dropped into a chair.

"What's up, guys?" I asked.

Wendy looked at Trish knowingly, like they had some kind of understanding that I was interrupting.

I started to get up. "Sorry."

"No, it's okay," said Wendy. "You don't have to leave. I just came over to ask Trish what she thought about a few things."

I nodded like I understood, but I wondered what was going on.

Wendy looked embarrassed and pulled at her mini skirt. "It's just, I'm not sure that Bats . . . Lenny and I should, you know . . . ."

"Get high?" I guessed. "I thought he stopped that."

Wendy looked at me with big eyes then turned to Trish.

Trish raised an eyebrow and shrugged.

"Well." Wendy turned back to me. "What I meant was, should we still sleep together. Trish said the Bible says not too. Does that mean we shouldn't get high either? I mean, it has been a while, but. . . "

177

I looked at Trish. Suddenly I was feeling guilty about sleeping with Manish, but felt glad that I wasn't anymore.

Trish started sifting through a small stack of books and magazines by her chair. She pulled out a small pamphlet and flipped through it then folded a page back. "I picked this up from the lobby of the church. It talks about how our body is God's temple and we need to honor it. I mean, think about it. When we ask Jesus to live in our heart, he really does move in. We have to live like we're taking him with us everywhere, because we actually are."

"Wow," Wendy nodded slowly, letting it all sink in. "I never thought about it like that. This Christian stuff is pretty deep." She spread her hands over her knees and stared at the floor. She looked up worried. "You know, I don't know if I can do this."

"Sure you can," said Trish. She moved over and put her arm around Wendy's shoulders. "We're here for you and God is here for you. You're not on your own."

"But what about when I go home and Bats. . . *Lenny* comes over and we still want to, you know."

"You make a decision now," I said. "Don't wait until you have to decide what to do. Decide now."

Both girls looked up at me in surprise.

"That sounds pretty profound," said Trish. "But it's good."

"Yeah," said Wendy, hesitantly.

"You want to do the right thing?" I asked her. "For real?"

"Yeah, I do," said Wendy. She sat up and looked determined.

"Then you decide right now that you *will* do the right thing." I didn't know where that came from, but it seemed the right thing to say.

"Okay. I am deciding right now to do the right thing!" She looked rather pleased at Trish and I. "That's it? Is that all I have to do?"

"Well, and then do the right thing when you're supposed to," I said.

"Oh, okay." She nodded. "Wow! You're pretty smart." She smiled at me. "Thanks."

"So, you and Lenny go back a ways?" asked Trish.

"Yeah," said Wendy. "We been together for a long time." She spread her hands on her lap and looked thoughtful. "My Dad always called me his little angel." She said it almost sarcastically. "That really confused me because you see angels at Christmas time in the baby Jesus pictures. They have that halo and you know they're holy and all. But I don't think people would do to angels what my Dad did to me."

Trish and I gave each other a horrified look.

Wendy didn't seem to notice. She was looking down and far away. "I got sick of it when I was fifteen. I ran away. I came to San Francisco and stayed in a youth shelter for a while. The pimps were always trying to get me to work the streets, but I wouldn't do it. So I started waitressing. Been doing that ever since. When I met Bats, I mean Lenny, he was so nice. He was the first guy I ever met who wasn't trying to . . . you know. He just wanted to be nice to me."

"I'm not surprised," I said. "I always thought he was a good guy, underneath all the ink."

She smiled. "Yeah, at first I thought he was all tough and stuff, because he had so much ink, you know? But now, it's like he's just a little kid who likes to draw on himself."

Trish giggled. "I can see that."

"So, Wendy," I said. "Have you ever forgiven your father?"

She lost her smile and pressed her lips together for a moment. "No. I mainly try not to think about him."

"I think it will help *you* if you forgive him," I said. "God had me forgive myself for stuff I did. I feel so much better now."

"Yeah?" Her eyes got big as she thought about it.

"Yeah. We can pray with you if you want," I said. "What about your mom? Was she there back then?"

She rolled her eyes. "Yeah, she was there. And she didn't stop it either."

"Then you should forgive her too," I said.

She sighed and thought about it. "Okay. You're probably right. Lenny always said for years I should get counseling about this, but I didn't want to." She looked over at me. "So what do I do?"

I had to think about that. "You know how we prayed to accept Jesus in our hearts? We repeated what that guy was praying?"

She nodded. "Uh-huh."

"So, I'll start and you repeat it as we go. How's that?" I asked.

"Okay." She closed her eyes and settled into her seat.

I wasn't sure if I was saying the right words, but I think we did okay. Wendy followed everything I said and told God she forgave both her father and mother. Then, for good measure, I had her forgive the pimps for trying to take advantage of her. She looked at me a little surprised but closed her eyes and said it anyway.

When she said "amen," she sat back and looked pleased.

"Feel better?" asked Trish.

Wendy looked thoughtful and nodded. "Yeah, I do."

"Well, that's a pretty big issue to deal with," said Trish. "I'm glad you let go of it."

Wendy nodded again. "Yeah. My dad always said there was only one thing I was good for." She looked a little defiant. "But not anymore."

"That was never true," said Trish.

"I know, but when you're a kid and that's all you hear, it's hard to not believe it."

"You are so beautiful," I told her. "Especially now that you have Jesus shining in you. Jess says that my whole life is just beginning. That's true for you too, Wendy. All that old stuff is just history now."

She did look beautiful, and it looked like she was starting to believe it. Her face changed from timid to confident.

"Thanks, you guys." She gushed at us. "You really help. I'm so happy you made friends with Ba—Lenny so we could be friends too," she said, leaning toward me.

"Me too," I said.

"About that thing we were talking about earlier, the sleeping together and getting high?" said Trish.

"Yeah?" said Wendy.

"I know you made a decision to do the right thing, but let's pray about it anyway," said Trish. "If we try to do too much on our own, we might not get as far as when we ask God for help."

"That sounded like something Jess would say," I said. "Can we pray for Laurel too?"

"Of course!" said Trish.

We settled down close to each other and prayed. We were awesome.

Thirty

Jess and I walked along Fisherman's Wharf, holding hands and trying not to get bumped into the street by tourists and waffle cones. We went past rows of gift shops hocking anything and everything with San Francisco stamped on it. In between the gift shops were restaurants with street-side counters where Dungeness crab was cooked and sold. Every vendor display had sourdough bowls with clam chowder, or rows of whole cooked crab, while big pots boiled and filled the air with steam. We stopped and watched a kitchen worker drop wriggling crabs into a giant pot. I love crab, but seeing them meet their death was hard to watch. I looked away and Jess laughed.

"No crab for you?" he asked.

"I didn't say that." I looked down the ice-filled counter stacked with crab sandwiches and shrimp cocktails. "I'll take one of those sandwiches."

He smiled and ordered two and some drinks.

We took our sandwiches around the back side of the buildings and out along the small marina where sailboats were tied up. We found a spot in the sun and sat on the edge of the dock with our legs hanging over the side and ate. Several seagulls landed immediately and began pacing behind us, but I wasn't temped to feed them. Crab is not something you waste on seagulls. A harbor seal popped its head up between the boats then disappeared. We never did see where it went. We could hear sea lions barking from the big distant floating platforms where they lounged and posed for pictures.

I looked over at the man who made my heart go thumpy and wanted to know everything about him.

"When you were a kid, what did you want to do when you grew up? I'm guessing it wasn't bumping into weird women in the park all the time."

I thought it was an innocent question, kind of easy, but Jess didn't answer. He swallowed his bite and stared at the sun glinting on the water. I wasn't sure why it seemed like I crossed the line somehow.

He cleared his throat and kept looking at the water. "I was going to be a lawyer. My uncle was a lawyer, and I always admired him. He made a lot of money and lived pretty well. I was sure I could do that. The thing is, I was cocky."

"That's not bad in a lawyer." I brushed crumbs off my lap and watched him stare at the ripple of water a gull made as it swam past.

"But I didn't get there," he said. "I finished my business degree at Berkeley, but I screwed up my chances to get into law school."

"What happened?"

"I cheated on my entrance exam." He turned away from me and threw a piece of bread to a seagull advancing on him on the dock. "I had a friend who sold me the answers. I got caught."

"Wow! That just doesn't sound like you."

He shrugged. "It's true. I even called myself a Christian at the time." He shook his head in disgust. "I can't believe I did that. It wasn't until later that I realized what my salvation in Christ really meant to me. There's no way I would think of doing something that stupid now." He looked at me evenly. "Thank God he's forgiving and lets us start over wherever we find him. I mean, where we really find him."

"So, that's when you started the real estate thing?"

"Yeah. It was a lot easier back then, of course, but it didn't take me long to figure out how to set up a good business for myself."

I swung my feet and looked at him out of the corner of my eye. "I sorta think you would do good at anything."

He smirked. "Well, thanks for your confidence. Sometimes I think about what my life would be like now if I was that lawyer with the big income." He turned to me and smiled. "I don't think I'd be any happier." He gulped a drink, set the bottle down carefully, and looked out over the boats. "So Jenna, after you grow up and finish your geology degree, what do you think about having kids?"

I swallowed hard and took a drink to give myself a moment to think. That was a change of subject! "Well, if you go by Trish's plan for my life, I'll have two. Girls. And you will build them a small castle in a field of poppies."

He hesitated and stared at the boats for a moment then turned to me. "Really? And what do you think about this plan of Trish's?"

I knew he wasn't really asking about kids. He was asking about our future together. It was that gentle probing to see if we wanted the same things, if we could see ourselves getting married. "I kind of like it." I looked in his eyes, those amazing blue eyes, and saw him smile just a teeny bit. "Still, it scares me to think about being responsible for kids. I've been so messed up, Jess. I'm afraid I don't really have what it takes to raise kids the way they should be. I mean, who wants a mom who's been as messed up as I've been?"

He reached over with his napkin and wiped mayo off the side of my mouth and smiled. "That was before. That's the old you talking. The new you tells me amazing stories of praying over your friends and letting God deliver you from all that old stuff. The new you is perfect for raising kids."

"Perfect? I'm not sure that's the right word."

He shrugged and looked down at his half eaten sandwich. "Okay, maybe not perfect. No one is really perfect for being a parent." He handed me another napkin because I was making a mess. "But you've got a good heart. You'd make a great mom."

"Still a scary thought. I think I need more God-time to get cleaned up."

"Don't we all?" He somehow finished the rest of his sandwich in two bites.

I took a bite and thought about being married. "You've been married before, right? I think you said that once."

He nodded and wadded up his sandwich wrapper. "Yeah, after I started my business."

"What happened?"

He shook his head slowly. "You know, when bad things happen in life, not everyone trusts God for help. My ex-wife didn't. She left."

"Did she start out trusting God?"

"Yeah, she did."

"Wow." I looked down at the water where a seagull floated by. I didn't like to know that people could turn away from God like that. I looked back at him. "I never want to do that."

He took my hand and kissed it. "As long as you feel like that, you never will."

I smiled back at him, but I couldn't let go of what he said. "I just don't get how someone could stop loving God. I mean, God! He's totally perfect, and he helps us so much. Why would anyone walk away from that?"

He pulled one leg up and leaned against his knee. "Jenna, when you got saved, it was almost like you were living in a third world country. Nothing was easy for you before. Jesus brought you out of darkness into light. Your life has changed dramatically. For some people, life isn't as hard as it was for you. They don't need to depend on God to get through the day. They can take care of themselves. Their salvation isn't dramatic at all. And then when bad things happen, when tragedy hits them, they don't have a real foundation to stand on, like that story about the man who built his house on sand instead of rock. If your focus isn't completely on God, you'll crumble at the slightest problem."

I felt a little tingling inside as I thought about Jesus in my life. "I can't imagine not trusting God completely."

"We really need each other. I mean, as Christians, we need other people."

"Really? Why? I like having friends, but do I *need* them?"

"Yes, actually." He shifted his weight as he leaned on his knee. "You want people who will talk to you honestly if you start drifting away from God. Friends can see that in each other. And you want friends who listen to the Holy Spirit and inspire you to go after him more. It's why we're called a body. We need each other."

"What about your ex-wife? Did she have friends?"

He looked down and nodded his head. "She did, but she didn't want to listen to anyone. And the further she got from God, the angrier she got."

"That's sad."

He looked off above the masts of the boats rocking gently along the pier. "Forgiveness is a treasure we may never fully understand."

Thirty-one

I couldn't wait to get off work. I loved our Tuesday night Bible studies. Laurel and I waited for Brenda to lock up, and I flew home. I mean I skipped. I mean I walked really fast. I couldn't wait to get to our little group of baby ducks gobbling down the word and asking questions and praying for each other. We had each other's backs. And when we prayed, we felt God himself come and sit with us. Sometimes the hours flew past because the atmosphere was so amazing. By the end of the night, I could almost feel my spirit swelling, in a good way.

Jess was sitting on the steps to my apartment doing paperwork when I got home. I liked watching him when he didn't know it. I liked seeing him absorbed in thought and thinking things through. And then he saw me and his face lit up like the sun coming out from behind clouds. He looked at me like that.

"Hi, handsome," I said as I walked up to him.

"Hi, gorgeous." He gave me a quick kiss and collected his stuff and followed me inside. "I brought dinner." He held up a bag from the grocery store down the street.

"What?" I turned around in shock. "You're going to turn down my specialty?"

"Yeeeeah," he said slowly. "I thought we should save that for special occasions. I mean, special *kinds* of occasions."

"Hmph!" I took his bag and went into the kitchen. "So what's in here?" I pulled out a roasted chicken, a loaf of artisan bread, two different cheeses, and pickles.

He looked expectantly. "Okay?"

I grinned. "I could be okay with this. Looks delish."

By the time we had everything on the table, Trish came home.

"Dinner," I yelled to her as she entered.

"Wow!" She stood with her hands on her hips looking at the spread. She turned to Jess and smiled broadly. "It's so good to have you around. Jenna needs real food."

"Hey!" I said. "Soup is real food."

"Yeah, you should actually make it some time." She picked up the bread and pulled out a cutting board.

I mumbled under my breath. "I make it. I know how to open a can."

Jess didn't say anything but kissed the back of my head and grabbed a plate, wisely deciding to stay out of it.

We sat at the table with our makeshift picnic and talked about our day, then realized what time it was and hurried to clean up.

Wendy practically bounced in later. She grabbed each of us and gave us big hugs. "Guess what?" She glanced at Lenny, then back at us like she was holding her breath and ready to explode.

"What?" I asked. I had to let her out of her tension before she blew up.

"I quit the bar." She said it so fast I had to stop and think what she said.

"Really?" said Trish.

"Yes!" Wendy bounced on her toes and clapped like a little kid.

"How did that happen?" asked Jess.

"Well, you know I wasn't too sure about working there anymore, so I prayed about it. I asked God, if he wanted me to work somewhere else, could he get me a new job, and he did. One of my customers came in last night and asked if I wanted to work in his restaurant."

"As a waitress?" asked Trish.

"Yeah, as a waitress," said Wendy. "But it's a really nice place."

"That's awesome," I said.

"Yeah. He said I should give it a try and we'll see. So I said yes and I quit at the bar."

"Wow," said Trish. "Congratulations."

"Thanks," said Wendy, clapping her hands like an excited kid.

We had been standing in the living room, so I told everyone to sit down, but Lenny kept standing and shifting from foot to foot like he was nervous about something. He caught my eye and nodded to the hallway.

"What's up?" I asked him as we moved away from the door.

He hunched over a little, like he was trying to hide the fact that we were talking. "I think I know who hurt your friend." He looked up and stared in my eyes.

"You know who hurt Laurel?"

"Yeah," he said in a low voice. "A bunch of guys came in to get tats. Thought they were tough, know what I mean? And one of them kept talking like he was a ladies' man and all that and started bragging about letting some girl have it." He looked uncomfortable and his gaze shifted around on the floor. "And they kept talking, and someone asked where he met her, and he said at the club at the warehouse. And another guy said yeah he was there, and he'd seen the girl, and she was hot. And another guy asked which one was she, and the one guy said she was kind of short and had long blond hair. Just like Laurel." He finished and looked down at his shoulder. I was squeezing it.

I pulled my hand back when I realized what I was doing. "This guy, the one you think did it, do you know his name?"

He smiled a gruesome smile. "Yeah. Paid by credit card."

Thirty-two

Laurel sat in her living room with her hands folded and her expression blank. She hadn't moved since we came in. I knew what she was thinking. Ever since she found out the police had brought the guy in for questioning, she knew she'd have to ID him. She'd have to look at him again.

I looked up at Jess and sat down across from her. We had a little time. I remembered when I had to go to court and see the mom of the kid I hit. I never did see the dad. I don't know why. I was on the other end of spectrum from Laurel though. I was the one who created the pain and horror. But I was sorry for what I did. The guy Laurel had to see was bragging. Scumbag.

Jess cleared his throat, and Laurel looked up, startled. She was scared.

"Laurel, we're going with you," I said. "We're not sending you off alone. And we'll be here for you tomorrow, and the day after that, and the day after that."

She gave me a weak smile. "Thanks."

I could barely hear her. I looked up at Jess and he nodded toward the door, so I stood. "Let's go, girl."

As it turned out, we didn't get to stay with her the whole time. We had to wait while she went in to look at a lineup. I paced the waiting area like a parent hoping my kid's dangerous operation was going okay.

"Hey, hey, hey," said Jess. He pulled my arm as I walked past and sat me down next to him. "Relax. Don't make yourself sick over this."

"I can't help it. She's my friend."

"I know, but this is when you trust God to do what he does best." He put his arm across my shoulders. "He's way better at it than you are."

He was teasing me, but he was right. "Yeah, okay. It just must be so hard for her."

"I know." He gave my shoulders a squeeze. "That's why we're here." He put his head down on mine. "But Jenna, you can't control the universe. That's God's job. He just needs you to show his love."

I sat back and leaned against him. "Easier said than done."

He kissed the side of my face. "I know."

Laurel finally came out, hugging her coat and staring at the floor in front of her. Her stare wasn't scared. She looked mad.

"You got him?" I asked.

She didn't look up, but she nodded.

"Was it hard to pick him out?" I stood and wanted to hug her, but she didn't seem in the mood for a hug.

"No, I knew him as soon as I saw him. That's the guy."

"Just so you know, guys that beat up on women don't do well in prison," I said.

She continued to look hard at the floor, but her eyebrows made a quick flick.

Jess came up and put his arm around both of us. "Let's go."

After we got in the car, I turned in my seat to look at her. "Trish and I want you to come over now for dinner. Are you okay with that?" I fully expected her to blow me off but she didn't.

"Really?" she said.

"Yeah. Be with people. Hang out. Eat."

She gave me a half smile. "Okay."

Jess had been waiting to hear her answer, then pulled out of the parking lot.

***

The apartment smelled awesome when we walked in.

"Wow, whatever that is, I'm ready to eat it now," said Jess. He followed his nose to the kitchen.

The table was set extra long with the expansion leaf put in. It was beautiful, with a light yellow tablecloth and a low vase of flowers in the middle. I'd never seen our table set like that before. I was a little amazed.

"Hi, Laurel," said Trish drying her hands on a towel.

Laurel smiled shyly. "Hi." She looked around the room and I realized she'd never been over before.

I watched Trish clean up the counter. "What should I do?" I asked.

She glanced over her shoulder. "Get Laurel something to drink."

"Here, let me take that." Jess reached for Laurel's coat, then took mine and disappeared.

"Drinks. Right." I went to the fridge and opened the door. "We have orange juice. We have water. We have soda."

"We have wine," said Trish.

Laurel's head bobbed. "I'll have that."

"Red or white?" asked Trish.

"Whatever," said Laurel.

"Red it is then." Trish had an open bottle she'd apparently been cooking with. She handed it to me, then pulled a lasagna out of the oven.

"Yes! Now that's what I'm talking about," said Jess, walking in with his eyes on the steaming dish.

I filled Laurel's glass and started to ask if Trish wanted one, when the door buzzed.

Jess went to answer it and came back with Wendy and Lenny carrying a covered bowl.

"Hi, everyone," said Wendy.

"What's that you got there?" asked Jess, with his nose down trying to smell whatever Lenny was carrying.

"Salad," said Wendy. She took the dish from Lenny and elbowed Jess out of the way. "It's to share, so back off."

"Laurel, you remember Wendy from church? And you know Lenny," I said.

Laurel turned to Lenny and stared at him. He looked up uncomfortably and just stood there as Laurel advanced on him and gave him a hug. She held him for a half a minute then let him go and turned away.

Lenny looked uncomfortable. "I wish I could have done more," he said. "He was in my shop. I wish I could have let him have it right there."

"You did the right thing," said Jess. "He's going to go to trial, and he's going to jail. He's not getting away with anything."

Laurel took a drink of her wine and stared across the kitchen.

"Got any more of that?" asked Wendy, pointing to Laurel's glass.

"Oh, sure," said Trish. "Sorry about that. Jenna, get some more glasses down."

The dinner was great, but Laurel didn't say much. Mostly she was quiet while we talked and laughed at Lenny's silly jokes. The kitchen was warm, the food was awesome, and there was a lot of love around the table. I wanted Laurel to feel that. I thought she would just play the wallflower all night, but then she surprised me.

She held up her glass to give a toast, and we all quickly grabbed our glasses of wine and water and soda and held them up. "To friends, and people who do the right thing."

I was ready to repeat her toast with a hardy *Hear! Hear!*, but I couldn't. I couldn't say anything. And nobody else could either.

We all just held our glasses up, feeling overwhelmed by her sentiment.

She solemnly looked around the table, still holding up her glass. "Thank you."

When she took a drink we all did. It was suddenly quiet after that. It didn't seem right to launch back into silly talk after feeling such an emotionally charged moment.

"You want a tattoo, Laurel?" asked Lenny. "I'll do you a good one."

I almost dropped my glass. Trish and I looked at each other and tried very hard to not laugh out loud.

"What?" asked Lenny, looking around at us.

"Nothing," I said. "It's a nice offer." I set my glass down carefully and looked at Laurel.

Laurel was grinning and tapping the stem of her glass. "I might. I might just do that. What do you think I should get?"

"I can do a rose or a butterfly," said Lenny. He looked up as he thought. "Dragonflies are hot now." He looked at her. "Unless you want something like barbed wire. I could do it around your arm, you know." He grinned and traced a circle around his bicep.

She wrinkled her nose. "I was thinking more of something like a dove or a cross."

We all just stared at her.

"Really?" I asked.

"Well," she shrugged. "Isn't that what you guys are all about? The Christian thing?"

I smiled at her. "Yeah, I guess so."

I glanced at Jess. He was taking a drink and bounced his eyebrows at me.

"How about something like this." Lenny pulled a pen out of his pocket and started drawing on his napkin, then he handed it to Laurel. "See, it's a cross and it's got a Celtic knot wrapped around the middle. That's for friendship. And the cross is in the middle of it."

I stretched my neck so I could see it. "Good job, Lenny. I like it."

"So do I," said Laurel. She set it on the table and patted it. "That's what I want."

"You got it," said Lenny. "You come in any time and I'll do it. No charge."

We finished dinner and talked forever, then Lenny and Wendy offered to take Laurel home. They all got their coats on and were moving to the door, but Laurel stopped and hugged me.

"Thank you," she whispered in my ear. "I needed this more than I realized."

I took her shoulders and held her. "We're here for you, you got it?"

She smiled. "Got it."

Thirty-three

I leaned back in my seat and watched the houses go by as Jess drove through the city. We turned onto a smaller road that twisted and turned, taking us higher and higher up to Twin Peaks. I'd never been there before and didn't realize how high up you felt over the city. We got out of the car and I zipped my jacket against the wind. Then I walked over to the low stone wall along the viewing area and leaned against it. It was an amazing panorama of the city and the bay. Sutro Tower, so close, looked like a discarded toy from a giant erector set. Kind of scary how big it was.

"Angel Island. Alcatraz." I pointed out to the bay then looked down on the city. "I can't see where I live. Is it over there?" I pointed to my left.

Jess moved my arm to the left and down. "I think more over there. With the hills in the way, it's hard to see all the neighborhoods."

"Where do you live?" I already knew he didn't live near me, but I hadn't been there yet.

He pointed across the city.

I looked back at him. "That's not very close at all. You sure hang out a lot in my neighborhood."

"Real estate, baby. You go where the houses are. I just happened to be working a lot in your area when I met you."

"So, where would you live if you could live anywhere you wanted?" I asked.

He turned and leaned against the wall to face me. "Oh, I was thinking of some place where we could a have a couple of kids and a field of poppies."

My heart started doing wobbly stuff. Every time I looked at him, I was dumbfounded that he wanted to be with me. I couldn't believe my luck, but in the back of my mind, something started to make me doubt.

"How about you?" he asked.

I kind of nodded and mumbled something that never turned into actual words.

"You, what?" he asked.

I turned back to the view and shook my head. "It's hard, Jess. I never believed that I deserved anything this good. I mean, being in a relationship with you, it's more than I ever dreamed. It's hard to ask for something better than the best thing that's ever happened to me."

"Are you saying you can't see yourself being married to me?"

"I'm afraid . . . that the balloon is going to pop. That all this is going to blow up in my face somehow." I squeezed the edge of the rock wall. It was real. My dreams might not be.

"What makes you think you can't be happy?" He turned my shoulders so I faced him. "Jenna, this is your decision. When you got saved, Jesus gave you a key that set you free. You can choose to stay in your cell, or you can come out and live. Which do you want?"

He chose his metaphor well. When I was in a cell, I knew why I was there. We all dreamed of the day we would get out. We thought we'd be able to get back to our lives and carry on, and now Jess was telling me that I was putting myself back in lock-up.

"Do you want to be with me?" he asked.

"Yes, I do," I said quickly. "I'm just afraid that I'm going to sabotage this somehow and it won't last."

He took my hands and held them against his chest. "Can you feel my heart?"

I looked at his chest and realized I could. I nodded and looked up at him.

"It's yours. I'm giving it to you. I want you to be happy and I'll do whatever it takes for that to happen. *You* have to believe that you deserve it." He looked into my eyes with such earnestness. "Will you just make the choice to accept that it's okay for you to be happy?"

I looked away. How could it be that simple?

"I can't make that choice for you," he said. "I can't make you happy if you won't accept it."

I leaned my head against his chest and stared at the blue water of the bay off in the distance, letting his words settle into my brain. This is exactly where I could sabotage everything.

"And you should also know that this isn't a one-way relationship," he said. "I get as much from you as you get from me. Why do you think I want you so much?"

I looked up at him. "That's the part I don't understand."

"I know," he said. "But it's true. I love you, Jenna. I want to be with you and I want you to receive being loved."

I looked at my hands, still pressed against his chest. "It just feels so fragile."

"Right now it is," he said. "But love, relationships, take work. Soon you get roots that go deep, so when times get hard, you don't fall apart. I'm not saying we won't have issues to deal with, but I want to go through them with you."

I sighed and looked in his eyes. "You amaze me. I don't know why you want me, but I sure want you. Okay." I patted his chest lightly and smiled up at him. "I choose to be happy, with you."

He pulled me to him in a big hug and held me tight. "That's my girl. Now we can face anything."

***

Jess dropped me off at my apartment and went home to get some work done. I was still walking on air, absolutely in awe of what was happening in my life. I let myself in and found Trish curled up on the couch doing paperwork and watching TV.

"Hey," she said, not looking away from her show.

"Hey." I sat down next to her. I don't know what she was watching. My mind was still up on Twin Peaks with a pair of gorgeous blue eyes.

"I guess you haven't called Tyrone to let him know you have a cell phone," she said. "He called today to remind you that you have an appointment tomorrow.

Tyrone was my parole officer.

Thirty-four

The next morning I called Brenda to let her know I'd be in late. She was cool with me seeing my parole officer, because I tried hard to do everything right. She said she'd say something to Tyrone about how good I worked if it would help. And she liked that I had my own phone now. I had been the only one of her employees without one.

After I downed the last of my coffee, I dashed out and caught a bus on Fell, then got off on Market. I had to hoof it a few blocks to get to Tyrone's office because a group of seniors needed help getting on the bus and made us stop for a long time. I was five minutes late, but he wasn't ready for me anyway. I sat in the hallway on a metal and plastic chair and watched people coming in and out—other parolees looking pretty scary, fresh from prison. You knew most of them were back to their old tricks already. That's why Tyrone liked me. I was actually trying. Those guys, they'd be back inside in a few months. I didn't like the look of them.

The door to Tyrone's office opened and *Jess* stepped out. He was obviously startled at seeing me. Then something dark swept over his eyes.

"Jess!" I jumped up and knocked over my chair. "What are you doing here?"

He looked down the hall for a few seconds and clinched his fist. His face hardened and he walked away without looking back.

My heart sank to my knees. Why was Jess there? Why? Was he checking on me? Did he find out what I'd done and to talk to my parole officer to confirm it? He looked upset. He looked angry, really angry.

I wanted to run after him, but Tyrone came out smiling and waving me into his office.

"Have a seat," he said pleasantly, like the world hadn't just ended outside his door. He sat and looked up at me, then frowned. "What's the matter?"

"That man that just came out." I choked. "Why was he here?"

"Oh," said Tyrone. He looked relieved, even pleased. "First things first." He folded his hands, put them on his desk, and smiled his big, toothy smile. "Jenna, I'm happy to tell you that you are officially done with parole." He waited for me to respond, to yell, jump up and down. It was a big deal. But I couldn't. I could barely breathe. His smile dropped and his eyebrows came together. "What's the matter with you? I just told you that your parole is over. You're free."

I nodded vaguely. "Thanks, Tyrone."

"Are you okay?" He looked over the top of his glasses and stared at me.

"What about that man that was in here?"

He sat back, pulled off his glasses, and dropped them on the desk. "That was Jesse Brown, father of David."

Jesse Brown! Jess Brown! Jess was David's father? Jess was married to that woman who wanted to see me dismembered in the courtroom? He hated me. I saw the look on his face. Now that he knew who I was, he hated me. We only just started a relationship, like baby chicks, so fragile in our feelings for each other. Now it was over, devastatingly over.

I think the blood must have drained from my face because Tyrone jumped up and ran over to me.

"Jenna, are you okay? Do you need some water?"

At least that's what I think he said. I could feel steel walls slamming down inside my head, shutting off access to actual brain activity. I felt like I was going into lizard mode, nothing working but instincts of hunger, sleep, fight, or flight.

Tyrone squatted down in front of me, looking into my eyes with his hands on my shoulders. "Look at me," he said. "Jenna!"

I struggled with the motor control to do that. Slowly, I got my gaze to pull up to his.

"What's going on? You sat in the courtroom with David's mother. You've been there before. What's wrong? This is why I told you—you need counseling! Now do you get it?"

I blinked a few times to get a sense of reality back. "I'm okay. I just didn't expect to see him here. Why *was* he here?"

Tyrone kept staring at me until I gave him the look, then he got up and went back to his chair. "He's been checking up on you. He told me he never went to the trial to see who you were, but that he always wanted to know how you were doing. He said he forgave you a long time ago. I didn't know he was stopping by. When I told him you were done with parole, he was happy. For what it's worth, Jenna, he's happy for you."

No, Jess was definitely not happy for me. He was the opposite of happy for me. I'd thought my life was finally turning into something good. Like God was really trying to help me.

"Here." Tyrone handed me a piece of paper. It looked official—seal of the state, signatures. "It's your copy, confirming the end of your parole. Hold on to it." He wouldn't let go until I met his eyes.

"*Okay!*" I took the paper and folded it then put it in my back pocket with my wallet.

Tyrone sat back quietly and watched me. "I'm happy for you Jenna," he said finally. "You've done a good job with parole. You did everything I told you. You've got a job and a good friend. I know Trish keeps an eye on you. You've got the world ahead of you. Get some help. I don't want to see you back here under former circumstances, but keep in touch. Let me know how you're doing."

He stood and held out his hand.

I stood and shook it. "Thanks Tyrone. You've been good." I had to say something—he *had* been good—but it was work to get it out.

He nodded but looked serious. "Take care of yourself."

I walked out in robot mode. Keep walking, I told myself. Just walk. Walk by these thugs pretending to obey the law. Just walk. Walk outside. Sit. Sit on that little cement wall along the landscaping. Breathe. Breathe.

I forgot about everything in my life that was good—Trish, Lenny, Wendy, God—all of it gone. My whole existence narrowed down to one tiny black point on a giant white canvass. Jess hated me now. Everything we thought we had was gone, blown up in a destructive moment of my selfishness, because I wouldn't listen to people telling me not to text and drive. In my twisted desperation, I refocused the accident, not as the loss of an innocent life, but the loss of a love I didn't know I could have. And then my misery worked to make me wallow in it. If the accident never happened, Jess would be happily married. We wouldn't be together anyway. It was never supposed to be. Never. The balloon had popped, just like I said it would, just like I knew it would.

I couldn't see anything in front of me. I was looking at the gaping hole in my heart where Jess used to be. How could I feel numbness and excruciating pain at the same time? Shouldn't numbness act like numbness? Shouldn't it stop you from feeling pain? Wasn't that the way it was supposed to work?

I closed my eyes and covered my face with my hand as tears started squeezing out. I'd screwed up my life so bad. Why couldn't someone else be in charge, so I didn't have to keep making mistakes that hurt people? What was Jess thinking? How could he ever look at me again? He said he'd forgiven me, but I knew in his heart he couldn't have. How could he? I killed his son. How do you forgive that? I wished I was back in prison where I belonged. I never complained about being there, because I knew I deserved it. I never deserved to be let out.

I wiped my eyes and sniffed. That was it, the last straw. Every ounce of my spirit poured out in misery. All my tears finally reached an end. And then I got it. Suddenly the end didn't seem so hard. I knew exactly what to do.

Thirty-five

I got on a bus like a normal person and went to work. My head was clear. I didn't feel anything. It was odd. My brain somehow blocked out all thoughts about Jess and dead five-year-olds and lost dreams, like it had all been surgically removed through very painless, efficient surgery. I was amazed I hadn't found this place a long time ago. It was so much easier to . . . live.

I got to work and pulled Laurel into the break room when I could see it was empty.

"What's going on?" she asked. "Where were you today?"

"I had a meeting with my parole officer."

"Oh yeah? How'd that go?"

"It was okay," I sighed. "Listen, you said you could get me anything I needed for my headaches." I glanced around to make sure we weren't being overheard.

She checked my eyes to see what was going on. "Yeah, what do you need?"

"Xanax. Can you get that?" I asked calmly, casually.

She nodded. "Do you need it now? How's your head?"

"Yeah, I need it. How soon can I get it?"

"I'll call and see if I can get it this afternoon. It's going to cost."

I asked her how much and knew I needed to go to an ATM. I didn't have much in there, but I could cover it.

"Okay. Thanks, Laurel."

I ran out later and got the money. Still calm. I had a strange feeling that I was watching myself in a movie, like it was someone else's life, even though I knew what was going to happen.

Laurel told Brenda she had to leave early, and I found her waiting for me in a nearby grocery store parking lot after I got off work.

"Here you go." She handed me something wadded up in a baggy.

"Thanks." I slipped it in my pocket and dug out the money she needed.

"Are you okay?" she asked, checking me out.

"I need this stuff. What does that tell you?"

"All right, just don't go crazy taking them."

"Okay." I looked her in the eye and smiled a little. "Thank you, Laurel. You're a good friend."

"Go on!" She gave my arm a push. "Go home and feel better."

I gave her a lingering look then walked away.

But I didn't go home. I took the bus down to Ocean Beach. I walked across the road and sat on the sand as the sun began to set low in the sky. It was windy, so the waves picked up white caps, and salt water sprayed in a fine mist at my face. I was glad the ocean didn't care about me. Even if it could, it was so big it would've ignored me anyway. But I liked how big it was—destructive and beautiful, terrifying and peaceful. It was good to feel overpowered when you couldn't get yourself under control. If you gave into something bigger than you, then you could let go of yourself and all your crap. You could surrender to something like that.

I reached in my pocket and pulled out the baggy and looked at the handful of pills. I had expected more, but it was enough. I pulled my legs up in front of me and rested my hand holding the baggy on my knee. Suddenly I fell out of the movie and into my own head. I really was sitting on the beach with a handful of depressants. Was this it? Was this really it? Was I really going to end it all, right there?

Without warning, all the emotion I had blocked off came rushing back. The wind stung my eyes and made them water, but I started to cry anyway. I had been so happy, so unbelievably happy. But it was so short—like that was all I got, all my share was used up already. I thought about how Jess looked at me on Twin Peaks. He loved me. He believed in our future. I squeezed my eyes against the image. I wanted to forget it and to remember it always. I had been loved.

I pressed my head against my arm and wept. This pain—wasn't this what being a Christian was supposed to help? Wasn't God supposed to keep the world from falling apart around you? What good was it to have David's sword if you wanted to use on yourself?

I sniffed and lifted the baggy to look at it. I let out a deep breath and thought about blank nothingness, an end. I wouldn't hurt anyone ever again, and I would be done. Swallow some pills, close my eyes and never wake up. Be done.

Suddenly, a seagull swooped down, grabbed the baggy out of my hand, and flew off. I was so shocked. For a few seconds I wasn't sure what had happened. I saw the bird fly far down the beach and drop the baggy. A small swarm of gulls descended upon it and tore it to pieces.

"No!" I stood and yelled. There wasn't anyone around to hear me or to see me drop down crying. I collapsed on the sand and hugged my knees with my head down. Wracking sobs shook my body. Why, why? Why couldn't I rid the world of one blight on humanity? Why? Was I so messed up that I couldn't even kill myself right? *God, why won't you let me do this! I'm tired of all the pain.*

I'm tired of hurting people. I sniffed and choked sobs until I could finally stop and breathe again.

I looked up, my face wet and cold in the wind, and watched the waves roll in, slap the shore, and slip out, like nothing else in the universe mattered. The waves came in. They rumbled. They released themselves on the sand. They slid away. I was so exhausted and emptied that the waves were hypnotic. I watched them flow in and out, rumble and splash.

A seagull landed near me and squawked, eyeing me for anything else to steal. I was too empty to feel any rage against it. Maybe it had come to mock me. I managed a small, vengeful smile at the thought of what would happen to the thieves. Served them right.

The shameless thought brought me back to reality. It was getting dark, and I was cold and hungry. Like it or not, I had to go home. Regretfully, I got to my feet and dusted off sand.

***

Trish came out of her room as soon as I opened the door. "There you are. How was your meeting with Tyrone today?"

I went down the hall to the kitchen.

Trish followed me but didn't say anything. She sat in a chair at the table and watched me.

I pulled baloney out of the fridge and heated up a pan. I didn't want to talk. I wanted Trish to know what happened with Tyrone, but I couldn't face it. I put the baloney in the pan and listened to it sizzle. I poked at it with a fork until it was ready to turn over. I was so distracted, I didn't pay attention to getting the dark sear on it that I liked.

When I sat down with my sandwich, Trish dipped her head to look me in the eye.

"What happened?" she asked quietly.

I took a bite and thought about answering her. I was afraid that once I started talking I would lose it, and I was actually afraid of choking on my food. I got halfway through my sandwich and was done with it, so I pushed my plate back and sighed with my head in my hand.

"Jess is David Brown's father," I said.

Trish looked blank. "Who's David Brown?"

"The little boy from the accident."

Her eyes went wide. "How do you know? What happened?"

"Jess was at Tyrone's office today. He's been checking up on me all this time. He told Tyrone he never wanted to meet me, but wanted to know how I was doing. I just happened to be there the same time he was leaving." Somehow I managed to say all that without choking at all.

Trish stared at me. "What did he do? What did he say when he found out who you were?"

"Nothing. He didn't say anything. He just walked out."

"Oh, Jenna." She sat back and put her hand to her mouth. "I'm so sorry."

"It's over, Trish. He really hates me now. I saw the look in his eyes." I tried not to remember it but it came back all by itself. "It was a really scary look."

"You don't know that he hates you," she said halfheartedly. "Just give him time. I'm sure it was a huge shock to him."

"Yeah." I got up and threw the rest of my sandwich in the trash and walked down the hall to my room. I closed the door and lay on my bed in the dark with my arms over my face. At least she knew. I didn't have to go into it any more. There wasn't any way I was going to tell her about the pills though. I let out a sigh. Seagulls! Really! I was actually disappointed that I was going to have to deal with my life again. I thought I was going to be free.

I heard Trish walk past and go into her room. A minute later I heard her muffled voice. She was on the phone with someone. I didn't care. My headache, my old attacker, danced around the perimeter of my brain. I could feel the vice setting into place. I squeezed my eyes closed, but my they felt hot. The vice tightened and pain shot through my head.

"No!" I yelled out through burning tears. It wasn't supposed to come back. It was supposed to be dead.

"What is it?" Trish stood in the doorway, a dark silhouette against the hallway light. "Are you okay?"

"My head," I said with my arms still over my face.

"Oh, Jenna." She sat on the mattress next to me and put her hand on my head. "Jesus, we believe that these headaches are gone for good. We believe that you are bigger than they are. Make this pain stop now. Help Jenna find peace again."

Yes, that's right. Jesus could make it go away. He did before. I felt light open up in my spirit. I hadn't realized it was dark from all the horrible thoughts I'd had all day. I felt faith start to rise up. I agreed with her prayer. I wanted God to kill the enemy for me, like he said he would, like it said in the Bible.

Immediately, I felt the vice disappear. The pain dropped away like an old cloth. I sniffed and pulled my arms down.

"It's gone," I said, partly to confirm to myself.

"Yes! We believe, so it has to work."

"Yeah." I sat up and wiped my eyes. "Thanks, Trish."

I could see her trying to look at me in the dim light.

"Listen, Jenna, I called someone."

"Who?" I was terrified that she might have called Jess. I felt my stomach turn over just thinking about it.

"Remember the big guy from church? Bill? I found his number in the church bulletin."

"Why did you call him?"

"Because you need to talk to someone who knows what to do about Jess. Bill knows him. And he's a Christian. He'll know what to do." She patted my arm then squeezed it.

"Well, what did he say?"

"He's coming over."

"Now?"

"Yes. You should go get yourself washed up. You look like a mess," she said, standing up with a halfhearted smile.

"Thanks," I said sarcastically. Trish was so practical, and usually right. Sometimes I hated that about her. I got up and flipped on the light in the bathroom. Yep, she was right. I buried my face in a cold cloth and sighed. I needed to find God in this mess. What was Bill going to say?

Thirty-six

Bill filled the doorway, almost completely. I was glad he was friendly. He smiled, held out his big hand, and shook mine with the gentleness of someone who knew his strength.

"Come in," said Trish. She stepped back and waved him over to a chair in the living room.

"Thank you," he said, sitting down heavily.

I sat in the corner of the couch and pulled a pillow onto my lap. I didn't know what I was supposed to say. Trish settled on the other end of the couch and watched.

Bill sat back in his chair and eyed me. He watched me like he was sizing me up. He made me think that whatever he said would be worth listening to. I wasn't sure what I expected him to do though. How do you take a broken, torn-up mess and fix it?

"Trish told me about you and Jess," he said. He took a deep breath and let it out while he shook his head. "For the two of you to find each other like that is just God." He locked onto my eyes with the look of authority. "So it's going to be God who will get you through it." He pointed a meaty finger at me and held my eye.

"Okay," I said weakly.

"What you're feeling now is guilt, isn't it?" he asked.

Was it guilt? Pain, loss, terror, guilt. I shrugged my shoulders. "I don't know. Maybe."

"Jess's son died when you hit him. At the very least, you have to be feeling guilty about that."

I let out a breath. "Yeah. It's been bad for years." I told him about killing the giants and how the headaches were gone.

He listened quietly and nodded. "That's good. You've dealt with that, now you have to deal with what you've done to Jess."

I must have looked blank as I tried to think that through.

"You need to ask him to forgive you."

My stomach clenched. How could I face him? Why would he forgive me? How could he?

Apparently, Bill was reading my mind. "And he needs to forgive you. We're going to pray, but I want you to ask God to show you what to do. You know how to hear from him, you just told me, but you both need healing. There's a reason that God brought you together, so you'd both get healed." He closed his eyes and shook his head. "Just like God."

"Jess seems to be handling all this pretty well," said Trish. "At least, before today."

"His reaction today says different," said Bill. "He's done a good job coping, but now God wants to heal the real pain he's covered up." He looked at me and tilted his head. "What do you say?"

I shrugged. "I don't know how to face him. I mean, I see what you're saying, but I don't know how to do it. To be honest, I don't know if I *can* do it."

"Let me talk to Jess," he said. "If he agrees to forgive you, or at least listen to you, would you be okay with me bringing the two of you together to work it out?"

Suddenly my eyes filled up. "He hates me. I saw the look in his eyes. I don't think he'll want to see me."

Bill leaned forward on his knee while I wiped my eyes. "Listen to me, you've both been through hell, but you're going to be okay because we're going to pray you through this." He nodded at Trish as he said that. "And I know what I'm talking about." He sat back and rolled up his sleeve to show a tattoo of a cross and a tear dripping from it. He tapped it with his big finger. "That's so I never forget what I did. Before I met Jesus, I was bad. I put a man in the hospital for making me mad. He's never been the same since." He shook his head. "I almost killed him."

Not the same, I thought.

He looked hard at me, reading me perfectly. "You think ruining a man's life isn't as bad as killing him? I carried that guilt for a long time, until Jesus finally got me to go to that man and ask for forgiveness. He didn't want to hear it so I live with that, but I asked and I know that Jesus forgave me. Now you have to ask, too."

"But, what if Jess won't forgive me?" I asked. Even though I didn't think he ever would, I was suddenly afraid that he wouldn't.

"Doesn't matter," said Bill pulling his sleeve down. "You still need to do it. God will deal with Jess."

I played with the edging on the couch cushion. "Do you think he could ever like me again?" I had to ask.

"That part will work itself out," he said. "First thing is to deal with forgiveness and healing." He smiled a sweet smile for a big bald guy. "You okay?"

"I guess." It felt good to have someone so formidable on my side. I felt like I had a bodyguard.

"Good. Let's pray." He leaned forward and closed his eyes and prayed for God to heal Jess and me and give us wisdom. Wisdom! That was an awesome thing to ask for. He waited, I guess to see if Trish or I wanted to pray too, but neither of us knew how to do that, so he said "amen." He got up, patted my head, and grinned. "We'll get you through this, and then you'll feel like a new person. Trust me."

Trust him. That was going to be hard, really hard.

***

I spent the next few days freaking out. I forced myself to let go of the attempted suicide. It was stupid to even think of, and I

214

was ashamed I got as close as I did. Like it or not, I had reality to deal with. I just couldn't get over the fact that Jess was David's father. *God, was that really nice to do? I mean, did you really have to have us meet each other like that?* There are lots and lots of other people who live in San Francisco that I could have met who would have helped me become a Christian. Why him?

Then I started feeling guilty about messing with Jess's faith. What if he stopped trusting God? What if this totally broke him so he couldn't believe any more? Just knowing me had ruined his life. He was fine before. I managed to mess up his whole family all by myself. I took his son, made his wife divorce him, and destroyed a relationship with me he thought was safe. I wouldn't have been a bit surprised if he didn't want to have anything to do with me, ever.

Thirty-seven

Laurel and I waited out on the sidewalk for Brenda to lock up as usual.

"Want to go out somewhere?" asked Laurel. "We'll get drunk or something. You need to forget about stuff, at least for tonight." She kept her eyes on me to gauge my reaction. She didn't ask about using the pills, and I didn't tell her.

Brenda came out with her big key ring and locked the door then looked up at the two of us. "Something going on?"

"No," I said shaking my head. "Just leaving."

"Okay then," she said. "See you tomorrow."

I looked at Laurel and shook my head again. I knew she was trying to help. "I can't, but thanks for asking."

She sighed and shrugged. "Call me if you need to talk." She pulled her keys out and patted my shoulder before she walked away.

Getting drunk actually did sound like a good idea, but also like a really bad idea at the same time. I understood why people did it when it was just too hard to deal with stuff.

I turned to leave and saw Manish standing halfway down the block, watching me. My brain did a jog. Manish!

"Hi," I said as I got closer.

He smiled slightly. "Hi."

I didn't say anything. I wanted to hear what he was up to, to readjust my head to seeing him.

"I've been thinking about you so much." He leaned against a parking meter with his arms across his chest. "How are you?"

Such a harmless question. I sighed. "You have no idea."

"Come, tell me about it." He put his arm across my shoulder and walked me down the block.

I didn't know where he was taking me. I was still a little in shock at seeing him again. He walked me to the diner where Jess and I used to meet. Of course.

"You want something to eat?" he asked.

"Not really. I haven't had much of an appetite lately."

"Coffee at least?"

"Yeah, okay, coffee."

He ordered coffee and juice and leaned against the table. "So tell me."

So I told him. He already knew why I went to prison so it was easier to tell him about Jess. I could tell he was shocked when I said Jess was the boy's father, but he didn't say anything. When I was done he stared down at the table for a while, then looked up at me. "You really like this guy."

I stirred sugar into my cup after the waitress refilled it and nodded. "It's just so complicated."

"So, is it over?" he asked hopefully. "I mean, what if he doesn't want to get back together again?" He looked at me with his dark, kind eyes. So different from . . .

"I don't know." I shrugged. I felt emotion start to rise up at the thought. Man, I was such a mess.

"Let me just say that I think about you all the time." He looked away, like he was embarrassed. "I think about you at work when I'm supposed to be working. I think about you in bed. I think about the night we spent together, and I wish I had you with me." He reached out and took my hand. "Maybe this thing with Jess is for the better. It could give us time to work things out."

My heart flip-flopped all over the place. I looked into his adorable face and melted. The pain in my heart numbed. I was overcome by the smoothness of his words and the gentleness of his eyes. It was all too much to work out—what was right, what was wrong. I surrendered.

On the way to his apartment, I kept thinking maybe he was right. Maybe this was the best thing. Was it really that hard to decide between someone who hated me and someone who clearly wanted to be with me? There was probably a morality question about what we were going to do, but I couldn't allow anything to interfere with the patch job I was making for my wounds. Manish made me feel better. I wanted him to make me feel better. I needed it so badly.

We stood in the middle of his bedroom and held each other. It was a hug of desperation. Both of us knew how tenuous the relationship was. He lifted my chin and kissed me hard. I tensed up. If we were in the middle of wild sex it would have been the perfect kiss. If he was leaving on a dangerous military mission with a sketchy chance of coming back alive, it would have been the perfect kiss. But it was too hard, too desperate for our precarious bond. My emotions were too fragile.

He sensed my change of heart immediately. He stepped back and looked at me in the dim light from the hall. "It's not going to work, is it?"

I turned and hugged myself. My hopeless attempt at self-medicating my heart was going up in smoke. What did I expect? I sighed and rubbed my eyes.

"Jenna. Why? I want to be with you. We can do this." He held my shoulders, squeezing them harder than I think he realized.

My head whirled. Why was it so hard to get through life? Why? I liked Manish. He liked me. Jess didn't. Even I could work out that equation.

"Can you just hold me? Nothing else?" I asked in a quiet voice.

"Yes."

He pulled me over to the bed, and we laid down together with his arms around me. I leaned my head into his neck and closed my eyes. Suddenly I was back on Twin Peaks telling Jess that I wanted to be happy with him, and he said we could get through anything together. Clearly, he didn't mean that. A sob escaped unexpectedly.

Manish twisted to look at me in the low light. I couldn't look up at him, so he held me close and squeezed.

"I'll take you home," he said quietly.

Thirty-eight

Trish was folding laundry in front of the television when I came home and told her.

She looked worried and folded a towel on her lap. "Jenna, you better be careful about this. He could really mess things up for you."

My eyes bugged a little. "Seriously? I'm not sure he could mess things up more than I've done myself."

She reached for another towel. "I'm just saying, be careful."

I laid in bed that night thinking of Manish. He really wanted to be with me even after I told him everything. I was so amazed by him. I knew that Jess was over. He hated me, despite what Bill said. There was forgiveness, and then there was forgiveness. But even if he did forgive me, there wasn't going to be a relationship any more. How could there be?

And then there was Manish—gorgeous, kind, fantastic Manish. He was a good person. I liked him. I liked him a lot. But something in the back of my mind said that being with Manish would close to the door to everything I was learning about God. I could almost see a slippery slope in my head. Manish seemed to think it didn't matter. Couldn't I just be with someone who really wanted to be with me and still go to church? I thought about the elephant god on his keychain and felt my stomach knot up. That keychain gave me the creeps, I didn't care what Manish said about it.

I rolled over and wiped a tear from my face. I was going to end up without anyone in my life.

***

Lenny was sweet. I smoked a cigarette with him on a break a few days later and told him about Jess. He wasn't even fazed—by my smoking or what I told him.

"Jenna, I don't even want to tell you stuff that I've done," he said, flicking his cigarette. He looked at me knowingly. "I mean it."

"Thanks, Lenny." I took a drag and thought about the mess my life was in.

"Have you heard from Bill? Is he talking to Jess?"

I shook my head as I exhaled. "Haven't heard."

He shrugged. "Probably takes time to get your head around, know what I mean?"

I rolled my eyes. I couldn't even answer that.

"You been praying?" He looked up at me with puppy dog eyes.

I sighed. "Yeah." Then I shook my head in frustration. "But it seems like when I prayed before, I knew God was right there. Like I knew he was talking to me. But now, it's all . . . " I tried to think of the right words but ended up just waving my hand in the air.

"Hey, I know." He stood and shoved his free hand in his pocket. "Read your Bible! I bet there's all kinds of stuff in there to help." His face lit up like he came up with the perfect answer and waited for me to get it.

Maybe he did. "Okay, I will. I mean, I read it and all, but you're right, I need a real answer."

"You go, Jenna!" He punched me in the shoulder and walked back to work.

***

That night I leaned against the wall in my bedroom with my legs stretched on my bed and held my Bible on my lap. I didn't know where to look. The answer could be anywhere. I flipped through the pages and looked at verse after verse, but not really. I mean, I looked at them, but I was so lost, I couldn't actually understand what I was reading. I dropped my head back against the wall and sighed. *God, please, just show me what I'm supposed to know. It's got to be in here somewhere.*

I looked back at my Bible and opened it up. I read for a while then stopped. No way. *So admit your sins to each other, and pray for each other so that you will be healed.*

It really said that in there, just like Bill said. Jess and I had to admit our sins to each other. He didn't really do anything, but from what I learned, if he didn't forgive me, it would be a sin. I looked at the name of the verse, James 5:16. I said it to myself over and over so I would remember it.

I pushed up off the bed and bounced into the living room. Trish was watching TV and didn't pay attention to me coming in.

"I got it." I held up my Bible, like she would instinctively understand what in the world I was talking about.

She looked up, distracted by a young singer on TV. "Hmm?"

I dropped into the chair, excitement making me a little jumpy. "I've been praying, like Bill said, so I would know what God wanted me to do about Jess. I mean, I know Bill said we had to meet together so I could ask Jess for forgiveness, but I needed to know what God said."

She gave a slight nod. "And . . ."

"I found a verse, James 5:16: 'So admit your sins to each other, and pray for each other so that you will be healed.' Just like Bill said." I jabbed at the Bible, open in my hand.

She looked confused. "So, if it's just like Bill said, then what did you learn that's new?"

"Geez, Trish! I'm getting excited here." I didn't know why her question pissed me off.

"I'm sorry!" She grabbed the remote and muted the TV. "I didn't mean that . . . I don't know what I didn't mean."

I sighed. "It's okay. I guess I got excited because it wasn't Bill saying what to do, it was God, even though it was the same thing. And I found it!"

Her face lit up. "Well, that's good, Jenna. So, have you heard from Bill?"

"No." I shook my head.

"Give him a call. Find out what's going on."

I knew she was right, but I really didn't want to. I was working really hard to not make that call.

"Jenna, you have to deal with this. Just do it, then it will be done." She pulled her phone from her pocket, punched a few buttons, then held it up to me. "Bill's number."

I sighed heavily and entered the number into my own phone then blew out a deep breath.

"All right, here goes." I held my phone to my ear and wandered down the hall into my room and fell onto my bed.

Please don't pick up, please don't pick up, I prayed.

"Hello."

I looked up at the ceiling. Why did he pick up? *Why?*

"Hi, Bill? This is Jenna."

"Hey, Jenna. How are you?"

"I'm, um, I wanted to know what was going on with, you know."

"With Jess."

"Yeah, with Jess."

"Well, here's the thing, Jenna. I don't think Jess is ready yet."

My stomach dropped. I didn't know how it did that, but I definitely felt it drop. Even though I'd expected Jess to still be mad, I was devastated that he actually was. I sobbed involuntarily and covered my eyes with my free hand.

"I'm sorry," said Bill. "It's just going to take more time. Don't give up on him. God is in this, and he's got a plan. Don't rush it.

Don't try to make it work yourself. Just be patient and believe. Can you do that?"

I sobbed and sobbed and sobbed. I couldn't even try to talk. I leaned over and grabbed a tissue from a box on the floor and blew into it with one hand.

Bill waited quietly until I calmed down. "You okay?" he asked finally.

"I'm trying," I said shakily.

"You're going to get through this, and you're going to grow from it. This kind of thing changes you, if you allow it. You really have to believe the Word when it says fear not. You can't be afraid of what will or will not happen. It's not up to you anyway."

I glanced at my Bible next to my bed. "Easier said than done."

"I know it is, but it doesn't make it less true. I like you Jenna. You got spunk. Don't let the enemy kick it out of you. The reason this is so hard is because you got so much potential with God and the enemy can see it. Learn to rest in God through this and you'll end up stronger than when you started."

"Rest in God?" I rolled my eyes. "If only I could wake up and this would all be a bad dream."

"I know. There's a great verse in Psalms that says, 'return to your rest, o my soul, for the Lord has dealt bountifully with you.' You have to talk to yourself and make yourself be at peace with God."

"How? How do I do that?" It seemed too fantastic to be doable.

"Just try it. If David could do it, you can too."

"David did it?" David my hero?

"He was just a guy who trusted God." He waited a beat. "You going to be okay now?"

I still felt a bit shaky, but I knew I needed to let him go. "Yeah, I'm okay."

"Good. I'll let you know about Jess. In the meantime, you learn to find peace. That's your homework."

"Okay. Thanks, Bill."

"You take care now."

He hung up and left me alone in my room with a great big question hanging in the air. How did I find peace in this?

Thirty-nine

The next few days were full of frustration, cigarettes, and walks along the beach after work. A week went by. Another week went by. Trish, Lenny, and Wendy talked me into going to church with them. Thankfully Jess wasn't there. I didn't know where he was. No one talked to me about him. He was the topic of unspoken conversation.

I knew I had to get prayer at the end of the service. I'd been trying so hard to find the peace Bill said I needed, but I just felt like I was grasping at puff clouds. Saying I needed peace and feeling peace were two different things. I needed help. When the prayer team invited people to come up, I was the first one there.

A girl from the prayer team came over to me and stood calmly in front of me. "What do you want prayer for?" she asked.

I struggled to find where to begin. I put my hands on my chest and shook my head. "I'm so confused inside. I read what it says in the Bible about peace, and joy and all that, but I can't get it. I don't know how to get it."

She didn't say anything. She tilted her head and looked at me like she was checking me out. "What's going on?"

I dropped my hands and looked down. "I hurt someone. I can't even ask for forgiveness because he won't let me. I feel terrible. I don't know what to do." I looked at her, begging her to help.

"Have you confessed your sin to God?"

I nodded. "Yes."

"Good. For now then, you just have to give it to Jesus and let him deal with it."

"But that's the problem, I don't know how to do that." I waved my hands to make it completely clear that I was clueless.

"You know that Jesus said to cast your burdens on him. That means that he wants to carry them for us. And it's not a suggestion, it's a command. He doesn't expect you to carry this stuff yourself. It's part of the grace that he gave us."

"Okay, so . . . "

"So, close your eyes," she said.

I obeyed.

"Now hold out your hands like you're holding this thing that bothers you."

I cupped my hands and held them in front of me. I didn't care how stupid it looked, I was desperate.

"Now lift that up to Jesus and say, 'Jesus I'm giving you this thing that's so hard for me to carry.'"

I did what she said and held my hands up for him to take my mess. I opened my eyes and waited for the next thing.

"Good," she said. "You gave him your problems, now ask him what he wants to give you."

"What?"

"Just try it," she urged.

I closed my eyes and said, "Jesus, I give you this big problem, now what do you want to give me?" I listened. I wasn't sure what I was supposed to hear, so we both just waited. I strained in my spirit to hear anything, and then I heard it.

Peace.

"Peace! He said he would give me peace," I said quietly.

"That's awesome," she said, and prayed peace over me.

As she prayed, I began to feel it. I could see how I was holding onto fear so I let it go. I wanted that peace, and I soaked it in like a dry sponge. I stood with my hands on my heart and my eyes closed and felt the peace of God wrap around me. That's what Bill meant. I got it. When I opened my eyes, they were wet.

The girl hugged me and smiled. "Now you know how to do it. Give him your problems and receive whatever he wants to give you. Okay?"

I nodded, feeling relaxed and happy. Well, happier. I knew I still had Jess to face, maybe, if he was ever going to be willing, but now I felt better.

Bill stopped me on the way out. "How you doing?" he asked, looking down at me with a big hand on my shoulder.

"I got prayer today. I feel better." I smiled back at him.

"That's what I want to see," he said.

"Have you . . . talked to Jess recently?"

He dropped his hand off my shoulder. "Yeah I have. He's still having a hard time. Pray for him. He needs it to give this to the Lord to deal with."

Since I just did the same thing myself, I knew what he meant. "Okay. I'll do that."

He patted my back with a heavy thump. "I'm proud of you, Sis. You're doing good."

"You think so?"

He grinned. "I know so. You keep trusting God and keep his peace. This will all work out."

I nodded in agreement, though I wasn't as confident as he was.

Forty

I was just about to close the door to my room when I heard Trish yell from the kitchen.

"Garbage!"

It was a serious command. The next morning was garbage day, and taking the garbage out was one of the chores I agreed to. It wasn't like in the old days when you could just toss a bag into the big, metal garbage can. Now you had to divide all the recycled stuff into the appropriate containers. There were rules to garbage now.

I set the recycle bins and the actual garbage can on the curb and dusted my hands off on the back of my pants. Just as I started back up the steps to the building, my phone rang. I pulled it out of my pocket and looked at the number. It was the first call I'd gotten from my Mom on my new phone. I sat down on the steps and tapped the answer button.

"Hello."

"Hi, honey. It's me, your mother."

"I know, Mom. I guess Trish gave you my new number?"

"Yes. You don't mind do you?"

"Of course not. I'm sorry I haven't called earlier."

There was a pause that made me uneasy.

"Victoria, do you think you can you come home, for a visit?" There it was. She even called me Victoria. Her voice had that hopeful, pleading tone that went right to my guilt center.

I hesitated because the certainty that I could never face my parents again didn't rise up like it used to. Instead of dreading the pain a visit would cause, I realized how much I missed my Mom and Dad.

"Yeah, okay, I'd like to," I heard myself say. Suddenly I really wanted to.

"Oh, honey." She got quiet and I could guess that she was getting emotional. Finally she spoke again, but her voice was a little shaky. "I'm so glad. When can you come?"

"Let me see when I can get some time off and I'll let you know."

"I can't believe it. Your father will be so happy."

"Really?"

"Why do you say that?" She sounded hurt.

I sighed. "I know I've disappointed him. I wasn't sure I could face that before."

"What's changed now?" She didn't address my father's disappointment, confirming my thoughts.

"I became a Christian. I've been going to church and reading my Bible."

"But, you were a Christian. You were raised in church."

"That didn't make me a Christian, Mom. I didn't believe much back then. I believe it now. It's real to me."

"Well, good. Do you need help getting here? I can send money for a bus ticket."

"I can do it. I'll let you know when I can come."

"I'm so happy. I'm going to make a lemon meringue pie."

"Oh, wow. Thanks, Mom."

"Bye, honey."

"Bye."

I hung up and sat for a while thinking about seeing my parents and my hometown again. I'd been a different person when I lived there. So much water under the bridge. So many changes. What would it be like to see my old friends again? I didn't even know who was still living there.

I was going to need a lot of peace.

**

The bus pulled into town at precisely 7:30 a.m. It was a long ride by bus, but I'd learned to sleep through all kinds of discomfort and noise in prison, so I slept the whole way. Connerville hadn't changed at all. We passed a new McDonald's, and there was grocery store where there used to be a car dealership, but everything else looked just like it used to. I still counted only two stoplights all the way down Main Street.

I stepped off the bus and waited for the driver to retrieve the sports bag I used for my clothes. I looked across the street at the diner and saw a surprising number of people inside getting their morning coffee and eggs. I took a deep breath and tried to let go of the fear that I would see someone I knew. It was going to happen. I just wasn't sure I was really ready for it.

"Victoria!"

I wasn't used to anyone calling me that, but I knew my mother's voice.

She ran up and hugged me tightly before I could react to the changes in her face and hair. A gray swatch framed her face on one side. I was surprised she didn't color it. It seemed like all the women in the city colored their hair, so seeing gray in someone my mom's age was surprising. But the small wrinkles around her eyes were also new. I didn't know why I hadn't thought about her aging while I'd been gone.

She held my hands and smiled at me. "It's so good to see you." She was rounder than before, but still smartly dressed in her tan slacks and flowered blouse.

"It's good to see you too, Mom."

"Come on, let's get your things and get you home."

I picked up the bag the driver set at my feet and followed to her car.

"You got a new car!" I said, throwing my bag in the backseat.

"Yes. Your father insisted I would be safer in this. I don't know why. I never had an accident in the . . . old one." Her voice had regret all over it, like she wished she hadn't said anything about accidents.

"Still, must be nice to drive a new car," I said to let her know I was fine.

She relaxed a little and pulled out of the parking lot onto Main Street, obeying the law at twenty-five miles an hour. She held the steering wheel tightly and glanced at me with a pleased smile.

"It's so good to see you." Her expression hardened into worry. "You've lost weight. And your hair."

"What about my hair?" I touched my punky cut involuntarily.

"It's just so much shorter than I remember."

"Is Dad at work?" I asked to change the subject.

"Yes, but he's coming home early. He's so excited to see you."

"He is?"

"Of course! You think he wouldn't look forward to seeing his daughter after all this time?"

"I'm just . . . glad, that's all."

We turned onto Peach Street, and I watched a group of young kids troop down the sidewalk on their way to school. Nostalgia swept over me as I remembered walking the same way to school myself two or three lifetimes ago.

Mom crept through the dip in the road at Jackson Street, then passed our house to pull into the driveway around the corner.

I looked up at the two story white house, the trees, the flowers. It was the house where time stood still. I used to play in the yard and pull weeds in the flower bed with mom. I even had a lemonade stand on the corner when I was ten. I got out of the car in a haze of memory and displacement. Was it only yesterday I was cleaning pee off the apartment steps again?

Mom held the back door open for me, and I went into the kitchen and smiled. Exactly the same. This room I could count on never changing until the day the earth exploded, or whatever is supposed to happen.

"Go put your things in your room, and I'll make some breakfast. Do you want breakfast?"

"Sure." I really only wanted coffee, but I knew cooking for me would make her happy.

It was my room that shocked me the most. Not only was it unchanged, it hadn't been touched, except that mom must have dusted. Everything, every small thing was laying where I left it the day I went away to college. Two suitcases stood next to the dresser. Someone, probably mom, packed my things from my dorm and brought them home. The books I bought for my classes were stacked on my desk, never read. I glanced in the mirror above the dresser and couldn't join the image looking back at me with history of the room.

I dropped my bag on my bed and sat down. A stack of CDs next to my old stereo caught my eye, and I filed through them, remembering when I got each one. I opened the closet and saw all my clothes from high school—the leather boots I had to have and my cheerleader outfit from my junior year. I'd forgotten so much. I was amazed I'd blocked so many memories.

"Victoria," Mom called up the stairs.

"Coming."

The red Formica and metal table that had been Grandma's was set for just one.

"You're not eating anything?" I asked as I took a heavy mug from the cupboard and poured myself coffee.

She did a double-take watching me. "No, I ate with your father this morning. Do you still like it over easy?"

I glanced at the eggs cooking in the frying pan. "Yeah."

She dodged around me to get to the toaster. "Sit down. Sit down."

I obeyed and sat, stirred sugar into my coffee, and watched her. She was in her element, filling the room with the smell of bacon and sizzling eggs.

She set a plate in front of me, white with a scalloped edge from the set Dad bought for her birthday when I was thirteen. I salted my eggs and ate while she leaned her chin on her fist and watched every move I made.

"So, how are you, Mom?" I asked between bites.

She just sighed. "I'm so glad you're home. I just can't get over seeing you. All grown up. How are *you*?"

"I'm okay." I swept toast through egg yolk and ate it, then picked up the last piece of bacon with my fingers and crunched into it. But I could see she was waiting for more. "I told you on the phone, I'm better now. My life is completely changed."

"Uh-huh." She had that I'll-believe-it-when-I-see-it look.

I drank my coffee, then set it down carefully. "Do you know anything about Cassie?"

She fell back in her chair like she'd been jabbed with a cattle prod. I guess I didn't realize how fresh her pain was still. She picked up my plate and took it to the sink. "She's in town. She dropped out of college and works at the Save-U-Mart." She was quiet after that and started washing the dishes, scouring egg off the plate like it had been baked into porcelain.

I got up and put my arm across her shoulders. "I'm sorry, Mom."

"Nothing to be sorry about," she said curtly.

I took the plate from her as she rinsed it because I was afraid it wouldn't survive being slammed into the drainer.

"Mom, I let go of all that pain. I gave it to Jesus. I'm not carrying it any more. You need to do that."

She turned and stared at me with hard-set eyes. "I'm happy for you, but it's not that easy for the rest of us."

"You think it was easy for me? It wasn't. Mom, you have no idea how hard it was, but I'm so glad I did it. Not living with that guilt, not blaming myself every time I see a little blond boy walk by, not being tortured by nightmares, and plagued with headaches that put me in the hospital. I'm really glad I let go of it."

"You were in the hospital?" she looked concerned and hurt.

"Just the ER. I wasn't checked in."

"Victoria, why wouldn't you let us help?" Her question opened up the big can of worms I knew I wasn't going to manage very well.

I picked up the frying pan and poured bacon grease into the small crock that was always on the counter next to the stove. "Do you see how you react when I tell you about Jesus? That's how I reacted when anyone tried to help me." I sponged the rest of the grease out with a paper towel and tossed it into the garbage. "It just wasn't that easy, like you said."

We sat in the living room later, and mom grilled me about my job and my apartment and Trish.

She kept saying, "Your father will want to hear, but what about . . . ?"

I was a little horrified by how much she didn't know about me. I'd kept my secrets to myself. Suddenly, it didn't make sense to do that anymore.

I leaned back with my arm stretched out across the back of the couch and nearly jumped when a gray cat crawled out from underneath. I reached down and scratched its ear.

"Who's this? What happened to Rocky?"

"Rocky died about a year ago. This is Tuffy. We got him from one of your father's clients."

Tuffy leaned into my scratching and purred, then looked up at me and skittered back.

"He'll settle down when he sees more of you," said mom.

"Poor Rocky. What happened to him?"

"He had some kind of cat disease. Dr. Billings said there wasn't anything he could do."

"So you had him put down?"

She looked aside and nodded.

"That must have been hard, even if you knew there was nothing else to do."

She seemed thankful when she looked back at me. "It was very hard. Your father had to be the one to make the decision. I couldn't do it."

I thought about how hard it must have been for dad. He was as attached to that cat as mom and I. It must have been like losing another child. I knew better than to say anything.

"But Tuffy has been a great little kitty." She leaned over and picked up the cat and settled it in her lap. "He's very affectionate. Way more than Rocky ever was."

I smiled. It was good to see her enjoying her little friend.

Tuffy settled into her lap and glared at me, then closed his eyes and enjoyed the constant petting he was receiving. He looked up suddenly as the back door opened.

I looked around and watched my father walk into the room. My heart started to race as I wondered how this homecoming was going to go.

Forty-one

"So you made it," Dad said.

He'd put on quite a bit of weight and had a lot of gray at his temples. He looked me over as I stood to give him a hug. He patted me roughly on the back and moved to sit in his big armchair.

He had the same gruff exterior I remembered from growing up. He was never one to show softness, and I always wondered if he really did love me, until the day I left for college. He'd pulled me aside while we were packing the car and told me he was proud of me and knew I would be great doing anything I wanted. I remember I'd cried because I'd never heard him talk like that to me.

He sat in his chair as impassive as the sphinx. "I thought we'd never see you again."

"Dad!"

"What were we supposed to expect? You never called. You never came home."

"I know. I'm sorry. Why didn't you come with mom to see me when I was in prison?"

He flinched at the word and looked away.

I tried to envision my father walking into a prison to see his daughter in an orange jumpsuit. I wasn't surprised it never happened.

He crossed his legs and folded his hands on his lap, still not addressing the subject.

Mom sat quietly and held onto Tuffy, who apparently wanted down. Cats must pick up on tension in the air.

"I'm not the same as when I was in there. I became a Christian. Jesus helped me let go of all the—" I changed the word before it came out—"stuff I was carrying."

"Your mother said something about that. That apparently you were raised a heathen."

I shook my head. "Dad. I'm not saying I wasn't raised right. I'm just saying that I didn't believe it. I didn't believe God really loved me. I just heard stories."

"So what changed?" He asked it like he was talking to a client about modifying his insurance.

"I met a guy who told me that God can fix anything. And it turns out that he can. I just had to let him do it."

He exhaled dismissively and looked out the window.

"Anyone want pie?" My mother's voice startled me.

"Pie?" My father snapped. "I haven't even had my lunch yet."

"I know," she said, brushing cat hair off her slacks as Tuffy stood indignantly after being tossed to the floor. Mom looked at me with pleased, hopeful eyes.

"Pie always sounds good to me," I said.

She stood up faster than I would have expected and went to do what she did best, feed people.

"How's business?" I asked.

Dad grunted. "Everyone needs insurance. Are you working?" I understood the question. Prison was an unpleasant reality, but I'd better at least have a job.

I repeated everything I told mom earlier, while she brought pie out and poured coffee.

"And this boy, Jess. You really like him?" He tone had softened to what seemed like genuine interest.

"I do. But dad, he's so mad at me. Can you imagine?"

"The father of that little boy." He shook his head. "How is it possible that he should be the one you become friends with?"

I cut into meringue and crust. "God. There's no other way."

"And you haven't talked to him since you found out who he was?"

"Uh-uh." I said with a mouthful. "I'm afraid to."

"But you're going to," he said in a tone like I hadn't done my homework yet.

I sighed. "I guess so. This guy from my church is trying to work it out. I know it's never going to be like it was. Can you imagine him wanting to marry me now?"

Both my parents looked up, startled.

"Were you engaged?" my mother asked, looking shocked.

"No, but I think it was getting there."

They eyed each other but didn't say anything.

"Does he have a job?" asked dad, holding his pie on his knee.

"Dad, it's not like it's going to turn into anything now."

"You don't know that. What's he do for a living?"

I answered all his questions as if he were vetting a future son-in-law instead of the guy who wanted to stay as far away from me as possible.

He finally seemed satisfied, because he either ran out of questions or time. He turned to mom. "Any chance I can get some lunch after my dessert? I need to go back to the office."

"Of course." She collected our empty plates and went to the kitchen.

He sat back and looked me over. "How long are you staying?"

"A couple days. I have to be back at work Wednesday."

He stood up, pulled his wallet out, and handed me several bills. "Here."

"Dad, I don't need it. I have a job."

"Uh-huh. Take it."

I stood there, trying to decide how much it mattered that I felt like a child being handed my allowance when it came to letting my father help me the only way he knew how. I took the money and put it in my pocket.

"Thanks, Dad."

He didn't say anything as he turned toward the kitchen.

After he went back to work, I went up to my room and poked around in old drawers and felt the rush of past experiences flood over me. Everything I touched reminded me of a life I could have had. I could have already graduated from SFU with my degree. My father would be grilling me about some other guy he was suspicious of. I'd know all about the small things in my mother's life because I would have visited home on a regular basis. I sat on the floor with my yearbook and wiped a tear from my cheek. My whole life, everything that I thought I was going to have, never happened.

"Victoria." My mother's voice floated up the stairs.

I went to the top of the landing and looked down. "What?"

"Would you mind going to the store for me? I forgot to get onions for the pot roast."

"Sure."

I hopped down the stairs, and she handed me a twenty dollar bill.

"How many onions do you need!" I said, staring at the bill.

"Just keep the change," she said smugly.

"Mom, I don't need your money."

"Two onions will be enough."

"All right. I'll be back."

I went out the front door and down the steps. I walked three blocks to Main Street and hesitated. There was a small market on the corner I knew my Mom meant me to go to, but instead I turned left. Save-U-Mart was six blocks away, but the walk didn't bother me. At least it was flat. San Francisco had hills.

I walked into the grocery store terrified I might see someone I knew but hoping that I would. I saw the store manager on his knees, stocking cans of tomatoes. I remembered him, but forgot his name. Other shoppers ignored me, but I didn't know any of them. I went to the produce section and grabbed two onions that looked like ones Trish would use and dropped them into a plastic bag. I looked up and saw Cassie standing on the other side of the onion bin.

She looked older, but still the same. Seeing her wearing a blue store apron was weird.

We stared at each other for a few seconds.

"Hi, Cassie." I finally managed.

"Hey, Victoria," she said quietly. "My Mom said she saw you get off the bus. You look different."

"You look the same." Almost. Instead of her dark hair blow-dried and pinned into a fancy hairstyle, it was pulled back into a ponytail. She wore small blue stud earrings instead of the huge chandelier earrings she used to love, and her makeup was far less dramatic than in high school.

She leaned in over the onions. "You're not wearing *any* makeup."

I smirked. "It's been years since I wore makeup. Probably since the last time you saw me.'"

"Wow. So . . . how are you?"

Suddenly I was sucker punched. *How are you* is a question you answer a million times in your life, but when I tried to say anything, my throat refused to obey. After seeing Cassie, plus all the stuff in my bedroom and walking through town, that simple question unleashed more emotion than I was prepared for. I'd lost so much—my whole life, every ounce of respectability.

I choked and leaned against the bin. I wiped my eyes on the cuffs of my sleeves and looked away.

"Victoria," Cassie whispered. "I'm so sorry. I'm so sorry." She sobbed and grabbed a tissue from her apron pocket and buried her face. "It was my fault." I could barely hear her voice.

"What?" I looked up in shock. "Cassie, it wasn't your fault. It was mine. All mine. If I wasn't texting you, it would have been someone else."

She sniffed and wiped her eyes. "But I didn't care if you were driving or not. You said you were and I didn't care. I just wanted to hear from you, what it was like in San Francisco, and your dorm, and who you were meeting. I was so jealous."

"Jealous!"

She played with an onion skin and tore it apart. "Your parents could afford to send you to SFU. I had to go to junior college. You were going to live in San Francisco. I had to live at home and commute."

"Turns out you got the better end of the stick, don't you think?" I said.

A woman with a baby in her shopping cart watched us as she pushed passed, and kept glancing over while she picked through apples.

"I'm sorry I didn't keep in touch," Cassie said in a low voice.

"I know. What could you say? Really, I understand."

She looked up through wet lashes with mascara blurred under her eyes. "Was it bad? I mean, was it really bad?"

Flashbacks of prison life flew through my head. I grimaced involuntarily, but shook my head. "No, it wasn't that bad."

She visibly relaxed. "That's good. So, what are you doing now? Are you moving home?" I thought I detected a hint of worry. I wasn't sure she was prepared to see me on a regular basis.

"No, I'm not moving home. I have a job in San Francisco at a copy store."

"Oh." She nodded, understanding. "Do . . . you want to get together later?"

I felt ice melting. "Maybe tomorrow. My parents want me to be with them tonight."

"Oh, right. Well, call me." She reached into her pocket, pulled out a small note pad, and tore off a sheet. She fished out a pencil and wrote her number on it and handed it to me.

"Cool." I looked up at her and managed a smile. "It's good to see you, Cassie."

"It's good to see you, too. Call me."

"I will. We have a lot to catch up on."

She smiled with the uncertain way she always used for people she wouldn't let into her real world, that place where we could share our secrets. Maybe we would never get back there again, but it was good to try. I missed her.

Forty-two

I actually had a pretty good visit with my parents. I think my mom felt better because she could feed me, and my dad kept slipping me money. It was Cassie who never really relaxed. She never went too deep, like explaining why she dropped out of college. I suspect it was because she was so shaken by what happened to me, but maybe it was something else. She wouldn't really let me in.

I sat on the edge of her bed and watched her close her bedroom door. Her mother eyed me like I was a pariah. It was clear she believed it was my fault her daughter dropped out of school and ruined her life.

"What are you going to do, Cassie?"

She shoved clothes off the small bench in front of her vanity and sat down. "What do you mean?"

"I mean, are you going to work at a grocery store the rest of your life?"

"Why not? It's not a bad job. What about you? You work in a copy store."

"Fair enough." I glanced around at her room. It looked much like the last time I saw it. The only difference was all the jeans and T-shirts she used for work. I wasn't used to seeing her dressed like that. The Cassie I remembered was a girly-girl. She used to be more into stilettos than tennis shoes.

244

"Hey," I said. "Want to come down and spend some time with me in the city? I can show you around."

She looked down and shook her head. "I don't think so." She didn't look up right away, so I got that she didn't want to talk about it.

"Okay, well, it would be okay if you wanted to sometime."

"Yeah," she said, still avoiding my look.

"You ever hear from Sherrie?" I asked, leaning back into the bed.

"No. Her parents moved to Texas and she's going to school there somewhere. She never answers my texts, so I stopped sending them. You should get on FaceBook if you want to catch up with everyone."

I shook my head. "If anyone was really wanted to keep in touch with me, they would have. I'm not interested in opening up old history for people to start gossiping about again. Besides, I don't have anything to say that I need to post online."

"Not like the old days, huh?" She smiled at me slyly. Hints of the old Cassie.

I shook my head. "Not even."

"Do you think you'll ever get over it?"

Her question surprised me. "I *am* getting over it. I became a Christian. I carried so much guilt around that it was killing me, and Jesus took it all away."

She looked at me amazed, almost appalled. "What? Are you serious? You turned into a Jesus freak?"

"I know! Weird huh? But, Cassie, seriously, it saved my life." I looked away and took a deep breath. "I know I said it wasn't that bad in prison, but it was. And when I got out, it wasn't any better. I'd see . . . " I couldn't finish the sentence. I couldn't bring up all the grief and guilt one more time. "If I hadn't become a Christian, I would have killed myself."

"What?" She dropped to her knees and settled on the floor.

I nodded. "It was so bad, and I didn't know how to deal with it. I met this guy who kept telling me that God could fix anything, and he finally got me to pray to Jesus and read the Bible. It changed my life. I was happy, for a while."

"Then what happened?"

"Turned out, get this, he was the father of the kid I hit."

"Shut the front door!"

"I know. It was totally random."

"So, what happened?"

"When he found out who I was, he kind of lost it. He hasn't talked to me since."

"Wow. And he was a Christian, too?"

"Yeah. A really good one."

She got quiet while my story sank in.

"Cassie, this is not for FaceBook, or for sharing with anyone, okay?"

"Yeah, okay. Thanks for telling me though."

"Hey, you're my old friend, remember?"

She gave me a weak smile. "I remember."

***

I processed all the history and emotion that was stirred up as I rode the bus back. The visit wasn't as bad as I dreaded. I was just sorry about Cassie. She told me about our other friends. They were all away at college or moving on with their lives. She kept up with them when they came home on visits. She said they always asked about me, but I knew that wasn't the truth. I had been removed from local history. Victoria Johnson was the one whispered about and remembered as the child-killer who went to prison, not acceptable in polite society. I could almost hear them telling each other they always knew I'd turn out bad. Or maybe I still needed to let go of a lot of guilt and unforgiveness.

Pulling into San Francisco was as bewildering as finding myself in Connerville. The noise, the cars, and the buildings all ganged up to wrench me back to my real world. The world where

Crazy Igor and Crazy Ahab kept me grounded in the knowledge that I was only one stupid move from sleeping on a park bench myself.

Trish was out when I finally got home that evening. I tossed my bag into my room and stood there, readjusting to my real life. The past few days had been bittersweet. I was happy to have a relationship with my parents and Cassie again, but all the reminders of who I could have been were hard to reconcile.

I needed a long, soothing bath in the big bathtub. Laying back in the hot water was the best feeling in the world. I left the water running at a slight dribble so the water level would keep spilling into the spill drain under the faucet and the tub would stay hot. I rested my head on a folded hand towel on the edge of the tub and closed my eyes. The previous days had been so emotionally exhausting that, even though I was telling people Jesus changed my life, I wasn't actually talking to him very much. I'd forgotten about my peace and the tension in my body was proof.

As the heat soaked into my muscles, I talked to God. I said I was sorry for not reading my Bible while I was gone, even though I took it with me. I told him about how hard it was to see my parents and Cassie. I told him how much I hated not having his peace and that it was what I wanted. I remembered the scripture where Jesus said he would carry our burden because it was easy for him. I asked him to take all the tension I'd been carrying.

I turned off the hot water because it was getting too hot and settled back again. It was quiet. I was home. The bath was perfect and peaceful.

Forty-three

Going back to work was almost a joy. Well, not really joy, but I looked forward to it. Wrangling the monster was familiar, and Lenny and Laurel were real with me. I didn't have to tiptoe around or wonder if they were judging me. But every day I thought about Jess. It had been weeks with no word from him. I had expected I wouldn't hear from him, but it still hurt that I didn't. Where was he? What was he thinking?

When I finally got the call from Bill on my way home from work, I was startled. Just seeing his name on my phone sent me into panic. I stopped walking and stepped next to a building to answer.

"Hello?"

"Hey, how's it going, Jenna?"

No, I couldn't tell him. "Fine."

"I think he's ready to meet with you. Want to get together tomorrow?"

Tomorrow! That soon? As much as I wanted to get past the actual meeting with Jess, I really didn't want to face it. My brain scrambled to think of a reason why tomorrow wasn't good, but it couldn't. "Oh, um, sure."

"Cool. A friend of mine has a coffee shop on Geary, just over from Divisidero, called Bean Me. Want to meet there? He's got a little room at the back we can use."

"Bean Me. Okay."

"Cool. I've got stuff going on in the afternoon, so can you come about 10:00?"

"In the morning?"

"Yeah, in the morning."

"Okay," I said, pretending like I was all cool with it.

"Great. Hey, I'll see you tomorrow, Jenna. Hang in there. God's going to do some real work."

I hung up and felt anxiety surge through my veins like an old friend.

Trish asked if I wanted her to go with me the next morning, but I told her no. I knew she'd have to take time off of work, and Saturday was a busy day for her. I wasn't what you'd call a very brave person, but prison did toughen a person up a bit. Still, I wanted to throw up thinking about facing Jess.

I stepped outside the next day and looked down the block. I thought about taking the bus, but decided to walk and burn off some nervousness. James 5:16. I repeated it over and over. If we admitted our sins to each other and prayed, we would be healed. God knew we both needed it.

I wondered what Jess had been thinking this whole time. He was okay with meeting me. He might even forgive me. But what would happen after that? What we had, it was gone. I wasn't that stupid.

I turned the corner on Geary and walked a block before I realized I was going the wrong direction. Perfect. I turned around and backtracked then found Bean Me across the street. It was a jazzy little place—small, red tables, sax music. And it was full. Saturday morning in SF. What coffee shop wasn't?

Then I saw him and my heart stopped. How could you miss Jess Brown in a crowd? He turned heads, mostly women's, everywhere he went. He actually nodded to me from across the room. Bill stood next to him and waved me over. I made my way through chairs and laptops and followed them into an empty back room.

Bill closed the door and it got quieter as we sat down in overstuffed chairs and faced each other.

Jess gave me a little smile. "I'm glad you came, Jenna."

"Really?" I was shocked and relieved. I had to look at his eyes to make sure he was telling the truth.

"Listen." He leaned forward with his arms on his knees. "I'm sorry for running off like I did at Tyrone's office. It must have made you feel terrible. I just didn't expect to see you there. I didn't expect you to be . . . " He held his hands out as he tried to think of what to say. "It took me a while to get my head around it. I'm sorry."

Suddenly I couldn't talk or see. My eyes filled with tears and I got a massive lump in my throat. I put my face in my hands and burst out crying. I couldn't bear what I had done to him, to his family. It felt like all the pain and guilt I'd carried since that terrible moment in the car all piled up and grew bigger now that I sat in front of him. It seemed like the only way to feel any better was to die first. I didn't even try to stop crying, it just came out in big waves of emotion. I felt something on my hand and looked at a handkerchief Bill held out. I wiped my eyes and started to blow my nose, but I stopped and looked at up at him and sniffed. He grinned and waved me to go on.

Jess just sat and waited for me to pull myself together.

I took a deep breath and worked hard to exhale smoothly.

"One more time," said Bill.

I took another deep breath and let it out, this time easier. I looked up at Jess's patient face and actually felt a little better. I ran my finger over the frayed edge of the upholstery on the chair. "Jess, I'm so sorry. I'm so sorry for David. I'm so sorry. Can you ever forgive me?" I tried to maintain eye contact, but lost my nerve.

He reached out and lifted my chin. "I forgive you, Jenna, Victoria."

I smiled, embarrassed. "Jennifer is my middle name. I started using Jenna after I got out of prison. I thought it would be a new start and all."

He nodded and let go of my chin. "I understand. You said you'd been through some bad stuff. I understand not wanting to talk about it. I'm sorry for not handling the truth very well. I thought I had forgiven you from the very beginning, but when I saw you—" he shook his head. "I'm sorry. I tried hard not to fall into the misery that Darla, my ex-wife, fell into. I don't know why these things are allowed to happen, but I trust God. I have to. That's why I never wanted to go to the trial. To sit and accuse you wouldn't bring David back. I knew you were going through your own hell. I checked on you in prison and found your parole officer. I prayed for you every time I thought of David. I guess God wanted to be sure I really did forgive you when he showed me the picture of you sitting in the park that first time."

I wiped my eyes again and sniffed. "Jess, it's so remarkable of you to be like that."

"I had to trust God, Jenna. I had to." He blinked quickly to push back tears but managed to not break down like I did.

"I read something in the Bible," I said. "'So admit your sins to each other, and pray for each other so that you will be healed.' It's in James. That's what we're doing, isn't it?"

Jess looked down and started to laugh, then looked back at me with a big grin.

"That's exactly the same verse God gave me."

"You're kidding!" I thought I'd stumbled onto it. Turned out God wanted me to find it.

"Now that's just awesome," said Bill. He sat back in his chair looking like a happy sultan.

"So, how do we get healed? 'Cause I know I need it," I asked, looking from Jess to Bill.

Bill sobered up and leaned forward. "You *have* confessed your sins to each other, so now we pray for the healing."

He got up and stood between Jess and me and put his big hands on our heads. Still freaked me out a little when people did that, but I got it. There was something about that connection when you prayed for people.

"Father God," prayed Bill. "It's by your mercy that you brought these two saints together. They have been obedient in confessing their sins to each other and to you. I ask you now to heal them both of deep wounds. Holy Spirit, go deep inside and heal anything that has been wounded and scarred. Pour in the balm of Gilead to bring peace and healing. Take away what the enemy tried to use for hurt, and fill them with the peace of your presence. We ask this in your name and give you all the glory. Amen."

Bill pulled his hands back. "How do you feel?"

I looked up through a dream. "I feel it."

Bill smiled. "What do you feel?"

"Peace," I said. "It came down over me like warm chocolate sauce. Sweet and peaceful, all the way inside." I took a deep breath and felt like I'd lost ten pounds. I looked at Jess. "How about you?"

He smiled and nodded. "Good. I feel good. Do you feel forgiven?"

I tilted my head and thought about it. I thought about David and seeing the look on Jess's face at Tyrone's office. I felt a twinge of pain, but only like the memory of pain. I thought about Darla, Jess's wife, at the trial. She used to give me the most grief. It was different now. I looked up at Jess. "Yes, I do feel forgiven." I was smiling. I was amazed. "I never thought I would, even when I read it in the Bible, even when I thought I had killed the giant."

Bill nodded his big, bald head. "Sometimes these things come off in layers. There may be more to deal with later on, but looks like you got hold of God there."

Jess reached out and laid his hand on mine. He didn't say anything, he just squeezed it.

Bill slapped Jess on the back. "Okay, my work here is done." He grinned. "I'll leave the two of you to talk it out more." He looked at me. "You okay?"

I smiled and nodded. "Yep. Thank you, Bill."

"You're welcome. I'll keep praying for you," he said as he walked out.

Jess and I looked at each other like we'd just escaped Mount Doom. It felt like we were both surprised to see each other alive.

I pulled out my wallet, took out the beat-up letter I had carried for years, and unfolded it.

Jess stared at it. "You carry it with you?"

"Yeah. I've looked at it a lot, you can tell," I said, fingering the worn folds. "You said you forgave me a long time ago. When I felt the worst, I would pull it out and look at it and try to feel forgiven. It never worked." I looked down at the letter and pointed to signature. "You didn't sign it with your name. *David's Dad*. That's why I didn't know who you were."

Jess kept looking at the letter. "It's so strange to see you holding that. I had no idea who I was giving it to, but I did want to forgive. And I did, to some extent. I thought I had."

"What should I do with it?" I asked. "Burn it or keep it?"

He ran his fingers over the bent edges then dropped his hand. "Keep it. Forgiveness is the key to both our lives. I'm glad you still have it."

"So, you really forgive me," I said quietly and put the letter back.

He got kind of a sly smile and reached out and took my hands and pulled me forward onto his lap. We hugged each other like it was the first time. In a way, it was like starting over again. It didn't seem possible. For weeks, I'd just wanted to die because of what I had done to him, and here I was in his lap, feeling my hug returned even tighter. It just wasn't possible.

I pushed against his chest to look in his face. "How do we keep this from coming up again? 'Cause this would be a huge problem."

He shrugged. "We both refuse to let that happen. It's always going to be there, but as long as we are honest about how we feel, it doesn't have to be an issue."

"Okay." I was so relieved. I was pretty sure I could do that. I just had to believe that he would too. "I guess it really is a trust thing isn't it?"

He nodded then pulled my face to his. "I missed you." He kissed me so tenderly I knew then that it was going to be fine.

Suddenly the door flew open and a group of teenagers in skinny jeans poured in with paper coffee cups.

"Oh, dude!" said one as he turned back to his friends, grinning.

I jumped off of Jess's lap, totally embarrassed, and he stood up.

"We're leaving anyway," he said.

The kids grinned at us as we walked past them. We made our way through the shop, then Jess took my hand as we got outside.

"I know you walked, so we can take my car," he said, leading me down the block.

"Where are we going?"

"You've never been to my place." He unlocked the passenger door of his car and held it open for me.

"Oh!" I was excited. I always wondered what his place was like.

Forty-four

We drove through the city to the Noe Valley district and turned onto Liberty Street. Beautiful homes boxed up next to each other, with covered porches and long, steep stairs from the street up to the front doors. A garage door opened slowly as we pulled into a driveway, and I knew Trish would kill for a house like that—one with a garage. Well, not kill really, but maybe maim.

I got out of the car and looked back at the street. "You live on Liberty Street."

"Yeah! I love that," said Jess. "It's one of the reasons why I bought this place. I'm glad you caught that."

He unlocked the door and led me inside. It looked like I thought it would—clean, neat, nothing fussy. I peeked into a room that looked like a den and my heart jumped at the sight of a wall of fully stocked bookshelves. I couldn't wait to go through all the titles and see what he had.

He waved me into the living room and pointed to the couch. "Have a seat. Want a soda or something?"

"Yeah, sure."

I was pleased his furniture wasn't all leather. Seemed like that was what guys tended to buy. He had a comfortable cloth-covered couch in dark brown with matching pillows. I was about to comment that his house looked very Jess-like, when I saw the shelf of pictures—pictures of David.

Suddenly I didn't feel like talking. I went over and looked at all of them. David as a baby. David as a toddler. David on his first day of school. There he was, frozen in time, forever a child. His little smile and blue eyes beamed the kind of joy only a small child can express. I could practically hear his little tiny laugh.

I picked up a picture of David sitting on Jess's lap. They were outside. David looked about two. He was wearing a small baseball hat and Jess was holding a little baseball. It was a moment of joy frozen forever. So much promise. So many games to be played. They both wanted there to be more games.

I felt Jess's hand on my shoulder as I put the picture back.

"I wanted you to see." He set my soda down, but his eyes were on David.

I was surprised that I wasn't more emotional. What I saw was beautiful and heartbreaking. I couldn't say anything. I didn't know what to say. I turned and looked into his face to see what he was feeling.

He was looking at the photo I'd picked up. "He was a perfect child." He ran his finger over the picture to touch the little cheek under cold glass. Then he turned and stroked my face. "I miss him. I really do. But I'm so glad you are here. I don't want you to look at these pictures and think you have to beat yourself up every time you see them. They are just a part of my life, part of my past." He pulled me close and held me. "We'll move on together. We can do this, Jenna."

I closed my eyes and breathed a prayer of thankfulness. I didn't know why it hadn't occurred to me that I'd see pictures of David in Jess's house, but now that I saw them, I was glad. I was glad that Jess wasn't putting his love of his son in a box in the attic. David was a part of him and should be remembered. I was also thankful that God healed me so I could see the face of that boy and not fall apart. I knew I would always feel sadness when I looked at the pictures, but they would also remind me of God's great mercy.

I hugged Jess back and pressed my cheek against his shoulder. "Thank you for letting me be part of your life."

He kissed the top of my head. "Let you! Like I have a choice. You made your own place with me the first time you brushed me off."

"I didn't brush you off!" I pushed back against him and looked up at his grin. "Well, maybe."

He took my hand and walked me to shelves of vinyl records.

"What do you like, the Beatles, Sinatra, or Death Eating Mothmen?" he asked as he opened the top of a turntable and turned it on.

"Death Eating Mothmen? Never heard of them."

"Okay, so the Beatles or Sinatra. I made up the other one." He reached into a shelf and pulled out a Beatles album I didn't recognize.

"Yeah, okay," I said. "I don't know all the Beatles' music, so that one's good."

He set the needle down gently and sat next to me on the couch, so close I practically rolled into him. He put his arm across my shoulder and we laid our heads back and listened to John Lennon sing about love.

Then I started to cry. Not big wailing sobs, but the leaky kind. The kind that happens when you suddenly feel overwhelmed with joy and security. I'd ruined my life and God fixed it, just like Jess said he would. I sat back on the couch with Jess, listening to the Beatles sing yet another song I didn't know, and looked across the room at pictures of David. I felt real peace, just like it says in the Bible. Why had I fought against this for so long? What was I thinking?

I tried not to make my crying obvious, but I couldn't hide it from Jess.

"Jenna, what's the matter?" he asked, searching my face.

I wiped my eyes and shook my head. "It's okay. I'm just so thankful that everything worked out. I'm so thankful you forgave me, Jess. Sitting here with you, it's just so perfect. I never, ever believed I could feel like this." I took a breath. "Like it's okay to believe that the balloon won't break, 'cause it's not a balloon at all. It's more solid than that."

He reached back somewhere and handed me a tissue. Of course he would have a tissue handy when I needed it.

He leaned down and kissed my head. "I'm thankful too. I didn't even realize how much healing I needed myself. It's amazing how we go on thinking we know ourselves better than anyone, and it turns out we don't even know that."

"Jess." I looked at him face on. "I feel like we need to be really honest with each other if this is going to work."

"I agree. Isn't that what we're doing?"

I bit my lip and debated in my head. How much honesty was too much honesty? It had been disastrous telling Manish up front.

"What's going on?" he asked.

I exhaled and decided. "You know that day at Tyrone's office?"

He nodded slowly and frowned, like it was a bad memory.

I couldn't look at him while I told him. "I was so broken up, because I knew I'd hurt you like no one should ever hurt someone. Ever since the accident, I'd carried this guilt. I . . . always thought about killing myself, because it was useless to think about living life like that. I didn't have any hope for anything, you know what I mean?" I stopped. I wasn't sure I should go on.

"I understand." He shifted around to look at me better, but I wouldn't look up. "You know, I was so caught up in my own misery of not forgiving you, that I forgot how broken you were when we first met." He reached out and stroked my hair. "Now I understand. You really were torturing yourself, even before you met me."

I rolled my eyes. "Yeah, I was pretty good at that. Well, that day I saw you at Tyrone's office, I got some pills, some depressants. I was going to take all of them. I was so ready to just end it." I played with the hem on my shirt, rolling it up and pulling it back. I glanced up at him. "It was freaky, Jess. I sat on the beach and thought about my life just ending. I couldn't think about God or what was right or wrong, I just wanted it to be over, forever. It was kind of scary."

"I'm sure. What happened?"

I let out an exasperated breath. "You wouldn't believe it." I looked up at him. "A seagull grabbed the bag of pills out of my hand."

"What?"

I gave my head an exaggerated shake. "Stupid birds. I couldn't even kill myself right."

"Oh, ho, ho." He put both arms around me and pulled me to his chest. "Jenna, my Jenna. God wouldn't let you do that." He leaned his head against mine and held me tighter. "I'm so sorry you were so broken. I'm so sorry I hurt you so much you wanted to do that."

"No, Jess. It was all my own guilt. Seeing you at Tyrone's office was just the icing on the cake. I'd been carrying it long before I met you. You have no idea how many times I played it out in my head. I just finally got the courage to try to do it that day."

He didn't say anything but rocked me a little. "It's over. Now it's over." He sat back and straightened up. "But I think we need to pray that suicide off of you."

I shook my head. "But there's no reason to feel that now."

"I know, but those urges don't come from God and they don't just go away by themselves. I don't want you to ever be confronted with that again."

"Okay. So, what do we do?"

"We tell it to go." He put his hand on my head and told suicide to leave me and never come back, in Jesus' name. Then he blessed me with the peace of God, so I would never again feel driven to take my life.

"Okay." I wiped some stray tears from my face. "Good. Thanks."

"That's what I'm here for," he said. "That's how we support each other. I want you to pray over me as much as I pray over you."

"Oh, no problem," I said, smiling at him. "I could pray for you all day."

I reached for my soda, feeling happy that I decided to be open with him. It worked out after all.

He watched me take a drink. "You like chicken piccata?"

I set the glass down and wondered how not to look stupid while I wondered what chicken piccata was. "I don't know."

"Well, then. You are in for a treat tonight, young lady. Chicken piccata happens to be *my* specialty." He looked smug and crossed his legs.

I laughed. "Okay, then."

I was pretty sure who would be doing most of the cooking in this relationship.

Forty-five

An argument in a language I didn't recognize woke me the next morning. Someone from the next building was yelling near an open window, and the sound filled my room like it was right outside. I rolled over and peeked at the clock. 7:12. I rolled back and closed my eyes. Surely I could get ten more minutes of quick sleep before I got up, but no. My phone rang.

I picked it up off the floor and smiled. "Good morning, handsome."

"Good morning, beautiful. Are you up?"

"No, are you?"

"Yep. Been up for a while. I just didn't want to wake you too early. How did you sleep?"

I sighed. "I slept great. I really did."

"Is Trish coming with us to church?"

"Yeah, she'll come with us. Is that okay?"

"Of course. What about Laurel?"

"She told me no before, but I'll call her in case she'll change her mind." I started to close the phone and heard him call out.

"Hey!"

"What?" I asked, pulling the phone quickly to my ear.

"I miss you now."

I giggled. "Jess. I'll call you back in a bit. Bye."

I heard him sigh. "Bye."

"Hey, Laurel," I said when she answered.

"Jenna?" She sounded groggy. "You want to talk *now*? What time is it?"

"It's a little after seven. I'm sorry to call you so early, but did you want to come to church this morning? Jess is driving and I want to let him know."

Laurel was quiet on the other end.

"Laurel?"

"Wait—Jess?"

I forgot I hadn't told her what happened, so I filled her in quickly. I felt bad about rushing through it but we would need to time to pick her up.

"So?" I asked.

"No thanks, Jenna. I know you want me to, and I know you mean well, but I can't."

"What do you mean? I thought you were getting that cross tattoo and everything."

"I thought about it, but decided not to. I just, I don't believe it all the same way you do. I see you all excited about this church stuff, and I'm just not."

I kind of expected her to say that, but was still disappointed. "Okay. You'll still be friends with me even though I'm all into it?"

"I hope so," she said. "You're the only other freak at work I can talk to."

I laughed. "Great. At least I have that going for me. Okay. I've got to get ready. See you at work."

***

We found Lenny at the back of the church comparing tats with another guy. I'm not entirely sure which one had more. They were like long-lost brothers, each so happy to find a kindred spirit. Wendy was standing around smiling her waitress smile and talking to anyone who stopped. She lit up when she saw Jess and I.

"Hi! There you are. You're . . . together! Lenny, they're here."
She lifted her eyebrows at me in surprise and jabbed Lenny in the
side.

"Oh, hey!" He came over and hugged Trish and me. He
started to hug Jess, but stopped and shoved his hands in his
pockets, looking self-conscious.

"Dude, it's okay," laughed Jess as he grabbed him and hugged
him.

Lenny turned to his new friend. "You guys know Coop?"

"Hey, Coop," Jess and Coop gave each other the back slap
hug. I guessed that was the manly thing to do. Then Jess
introduced Trish and me. It was nice to see Lenny connecting at
church. Trish, Wendy, and I were still trying to find our element.

Lenny pointed to the artwork on Coop's arm. "I know that
guy. He does great work."

Trish and I smiled and nodded, then looked around the
church as people wandered in and found each other. The band was
getting ready to play, so it looked like we should sit down.

"I want to sit closer to the front," I told Jess.

He grinned. "Okay, but why?"

"It kind of seems like that's where all the action is, you know
what I mean? Like if God is going to do something, then I want to
be close enough to get it." I glanced at him to see if he thought I
was going off the deep end.

"You don't think God can find you at the back of the
church?"

I wasn't sure if he was kidding me or testing me. "I'm pretty
sure God can find me anywhere I am," I said, giving him the eye.
"But I want to put myself where I know I'll hear him."

"You can't hear back there?"

Still wasn't sure about the kidding or testing. "Are you giving
me a bad time about this?"

He chuckled. "No I'm not. I'm just curious about what you're
thinking."

"Well, look." I leaned into him so I could whisper. "The people at the back don't get very excited about worship and the people at the front do, so I want to sit next to the people who are having the best time!"

He chuckled again and nodded. "I get it, I get it. Let's do it."

We all filed into a row close to the front and sat down. I was excited. Going though the forgiveness thing with Jess took so much weight off my shoulders. I hadn't realized how much I'd been carrying. I wanted to get in closer to God, to whatever was going to happen during the service. If he was going to do anything, anything at all, I wanted in. It felt like I had so much to catch up on. Those days I was so depressed robbed me of my time with him.

When the music started, I stood up, raised my hands, closed my eyes and waited to feel God in the room. And I did. Even the pastor said the Spirit of God was thick. It was an interesting way to put it. It did feel thick. I felt my heart get full and I was so grateful for what he had done in my life. I started crying, just because I felt so grateful and happy. I was sorry when the music finally stopped. I wanted to stay in the middle of that atmosphere for ever.

But then the pastor started talking about how God can do anything in us if we let him. If we let him? I lost track of what he said after that because I was thinking about that. I always thought God could do whatever he wanted. Why did he need me to let him?

So, then I started talking to God. *God, you can do anything you want with me. I've already been through hell, so there's nothing you can do to scare me. I don't know what it really means to let you do stuff in me or through me, but have at it. I'm in all the way.*

I was so happy sitting in church, looking around at where I was. I couldn't believe how my life had changed. I'd gone from being a broken shell, struggling to hold my life together, to being safe and healed and blessed. I had Jess and I had friends and I was sitting there listening to how great God was and it felt right and good. I shook my head as I thought about what everyone always said about Christians. They said Christians were boring and mean. I guessed some probably were, but not where I was sitting.

After the service, Jess got to talking to people so I read through the bulletin again.

"Trish, what do you think of going to this women's group thing?" I said, pointing to the announcement.

She pulled out her copy, read it, and nodded. "Sounds good. We should go. We're women." She grinned and poked Wendy. "Wendy, want to come to this women's group with us?"

Wendy leaned down and looked at it and wrinkled her nose. "I have to work."

"Oh, how's your job going?" asked Trish.

Wendy smiled. "It's so much better than working in the bar. And it's a lot classier."

"What would you really like to do, if you could do anything in the world?" asked Trish.

"I don't know," said Wendy. "I always liked little kids. I'd do something with little kids I guess." She looked at Trish smiling at her. "What, you think I should stop waitressing and find a job working with little kids?"

Trish raised her eyebrows. "I'm just thinking that you might like it better."

"But, how do I do that?" asked Wendy. "I didn't do that good in school."

"Maybe you could volunteer a few hours a week at a daycare and see if you really like it," said Trish.

Wendy got a far off look in her eyes. "Yeah, I could do that." She turned back to Trish and smiled. "Thanks, Trish! You're pretty smart!"

Trish rolled her eyes and shook her head.

We didn't all go to lunch together because Lenny wanted to go out with Coop, and Trish wanted to do some shopping. So we dropped Trish back at the apartment, and Jess and I went out for Thai.

I sipped green tea from a small, white cup while we waited for our food, and I thought about all the stuff I'd learned about God. It wasn't a lot, but I wanted to be sure I was getting things right.

"Jess."

He looked up like he was going to be ready for whatever I said next. I guess I sounded serious.

"I'm trying to understand what God means to me," I said.

"Oh." He looked relieved. "What are you having trouble with?"

"Not trouble really." I turned the cup in my hands and tapped the sides. "It's just that God could do anything if we let him. And it says in Psalms to commit your way to the Lord. It's like you have to really be real about this, like your whole life."

Jess nodded. "That's exactly what it means."

"So what does that *really* mean? Do I have to join a convent or something?"

He laughed, a lot. "No. It means you do whatever God has called you to do."

"Well, what is that? How do I know what he wants me to do?"

"What do *you* want to do?" he asked back.

I was confused. "I thought you just said to do what God wanted."

He nodded, like that made sense. "The hopes and dreams you have all came from him. He put them there. Don't stop trusting your own decisions, because he gives you the ideas in the first place."

"But, I don't feel like being, I don't know, what's a woman pastor called?"

"A pastor. But that's okay. Not everyone is called to do that. Not every Christian should go into ministry. You still want to do geology?"

I nodded. "Yeah."

"Then do it," he said, like he was throwing down a challenge.

"But, how is that committing myself to God?"

"Jenna, this is going to be easy for you," he said, leaning forward and putting his hand on mine. "You already believe what you read in the Bible and you already hear from God. Go back to geology and keep doing what you're doing. He wants you to enjoy your work. He'll probably show you things in geology that other people miss because they're not listening to him and you are. You might find things that go against the whole evolution argument. Who knows? Committing yourself to him means that everything you are belongs to him. If he changes things up and tells you to go do something else, you should do it. You do your best to listen to God and he'll bless you in whatever you do."

"Okay. I get it. Just seemed like it was going to be more complicated than that." I squeezed his hand. "Thank you."

He squeezed back and gave me his dreamy face, but got interrupted by the waitress setting down Rama Beef and rice.

I spooned rice onto my plate and felt something fluttering in my stomach. I had to set the spoon down and process.

"What's the matter?" asked Jess. "Did we forget something?" He looked around for the waitress.

"No," I said. "I have butterflies in my stomach. I feel kind of excited." It felt stupid saying that out loud, but it was true.

He tilted his head and looked at me puzzled. "Why?"

It was hard to put into words, and I had to take a deep breath and let it out. "It just feels like my life is happening, for the first time. You know what I mean?"

He smiled and picked up the beef. "God fixes things, remember? When we let him, he can fix them better than we can imagine."

"It's just so amazing. Who would have thought that I'd be sitting here with . . . you, and talking about committing my life to God?"

"And the best is yet to come."

"What do you mean?"

"You're just getting your toes wet. Wait until you learn to trust God even more. He'll do things that would make your head spin if he told you now."

"You mean like scary stuff?"

"It would be scary if he told you now, but it won't be when the time is right." He stabbed a strip of beef. "Wouldn't it be cool to be so caught up in worship that you saw angels and heaven? Anything can happen with God."

"Wow, have you ever seen stuff like that?" I almost forgot about the food.

He shook his head. "No, but I want to."

"Me too." I realized the only way that kind of thing would happen was if I trusted God with everything inside me. But that's what I wanted—the real thing, and all of it. The butterflies got bigger.

We took our time at lunch, making dreamy faces at each other, then walked down the street looking into shops and holding hands. There wasn't any rush to the day. We had forever to do what we wanted.

And then the world blew up.

I was reading the titles of books in a bookstore window, when I happened to look up and see the face of Darla Brown, Jess' ex-wife. She saw me the same time I saw her from the other side of the glass. Her face went from blank to terrorist in a split second. Then she saw Jess with me, holding my hand.

Jess didn't see her and I couldn't warn him. Nothing would come out. I tried to say something, but my whole body froze—my brain, my voice, my heart, my lungs. I was probably turning blue.

She flew outside like a banshee, screaming. "Murderer! Murderer! You killed my son and now you're walking around with my husband! Why aren't you in prison, you murderer! YOU SHOULD BE DEAD! NOT MY DAVID! YOU!"

It felt like time closed around me as her words hurled themselves at my body. I felt every blow. Each one would leave a mark. Jess turned in slow motion and held his hand out against her as she threw herself at me. She struggled against him to get at me. She wanted to kill me, to use herself as a weapon to scratch, kick, punch, and bite. Her fury sent tears streaming down her face as she continued to scream and swear at me.

Jess held on to her with both arms, holding her tight. People came out of the store and stopped on the street. Someone asked if they should call 911.

I was frozen. All I could do was watch in horror as a woman deteriorated before my eyes. Her grief and hatred turned her into a thing. She wasn't a person any more. She was terrifying.

I couldn't defend myself. She was right. I had taken her son, her only son. It wasn't right that I should be free and with Jess, but I was forgiven. I knew I was forgiven, but I still couldn't defend myself. Nothing I could say would take away her pain. There was nothing I could give her or do for her. She would still live in pain if I was dead. She just didn't know it.

Finally, she stopped screaming and started sobbing into Jess's shoulder.

"I miss him, Jess. I miss him." She held onto him with a familiarity that twisted my stomach.

"I know," said Jess. "I miss him too." He held her more gently and stroked her hair.

She pulled herself back and looked up at him darkly. "Why are you with her? Why were you holding her hand?" She glared at me, and her grip on his arms tightened.

"Darla, you and I aren't together any more. You left me. You divorced me. I forgave her a long time ago."

"Why isn't she in prison?" She nearly spat the words out.

None of the lingering crowd moved on. They all stood around to listen and look at me.

"She did her time. She's out," said Jess. "It's over."

Darla dropped her hands like she suddenly realized she was holding onto the enemy. "It will never be over," she said in a sinister whisper. She glared at me again. "Never."

"Darla," Jess started to say.

"Don't you speak to me!" She turned her glare on him and walked away in a cloud of fury.

Jess came to me and put his arms around me. "I'm so sorry," he said quietly in my ear. "I'm so sorry." He held me out at arm's length. "Are you okay?"

I was still in shock. It felt like I'd been beaten with rubber hoses.

"Come on. Let me take you home."

I let him walk me back to the car. I was grateful he didn't expect me to say anything. He just drove.

When we got to my block he asked, "Do you want me to come in, or do you want to be alone?"

I had to say something, so I stiffened up to speak. "I need to be alone." I said it like a normal person even.

He just nodded and double-parked in front of the building. "I'll call you later, okay?"

I barely nodded back and got out. He didn't drive off, despite the honking from other cars—not until I got inside. Trish was still out. I was glad. I couldn't talk to Jess, and I certainly couldn't talk to Trish.

I lay on my bed with my arm over my head. How could the universe turn in on itself so fast? I was so excited and happy in the restaurant and then in a heartbeat I was facing the devil himself. I knew it wasn't fair to even think that about Darla, but she'd done a good job of imitating evil.

I closed my eyes and saw her face, distorted and screaming. She looked like a fright mask, twisted in hate. I heard her words again, and the pounding started in my head. Every word sent a shock of pain through my skull. The pain was coming back.

Murderer! Murderer! You killed my son! You should be dead! You should be dead!

I rolled into a protective curl and pressed my palm into my temple. *Make it stop! Make it stop!*

Then a thought rolled through my head, light as a feather—*You make it stop.* I blinked through my tears and wondered if that was God. In my panic, I wondered if I could really hear him.

And then I remembered David, the Bible David. He was always fighting. He never really found much peace in his life. For all the trust he had in God, he was always fighting against someone. Life didn't turn peachy for him after he killed Goliath. He still fought wars, but he won them. God was always with him.

I pushed myself up and hugged my knees. I recognized this. This was an old giant trying to beat me down again, but this time I was armed. I had a sword—my trust in God, the name of the Lord of Hosts, the God of the armies of Israel.

"In the name of Jesus, I defeat you—guilt and depression!" I shouted into the atmosphere and threw my hand out like I actually was stabbing with a sword. I didn't know exactly how to address invisible giants, but I didn't care. "In Jesus name, I am free and I am forgiven. Leave me alone and never come back!"

The pain in my head stopped, just like that. I was free. I was free. I picked up my Bible and flipped it to Psalms. I just turned pages then stopped and read. *Lord, see how badly my enemies treat me! Show me your favor. Don't let me go down to the gates of death. Then I can give praise to you at the gates of the city of Zion. There I will be full of joy because you have saved me.*

I set the book down and leaned against the wall. Just like God to point me to a verse so fitting for the moment. *You protect me from the gates of death.* Yes, oh yes, I will be full of joy because you saved me.

It suddenly dawned on me that little David actually saved my life. If he hadn't died, I never would have been driven to ask God for forgiveness, which I needed anyway, I just didn't know it. By

271

the life of little David, I found the sword that delivered me, the sword that kills giants. I mourned the loss of such a young life. It wasn't fair. It wasn't fair for him and it wasn't fair for Jess and Darla. But it happened. I was forgiven and I knew I was forgiven. I suspected that the old giants would come back from time to time if I let them, but why should I?

I asked God to help Darla. She was in so much misery. I asked him to take her pain away and help her find forgiveness, like Jess did. She didn't need to tell me she forgave me, but she needed to find it. She needed to find life and let go of death. I asked God to bless her and give her peace.

Then I thanked God for what he did for me. I was a new person. I had a future. I sighed just thinking about it. I had peace—the kind that stays even in the middle of the world blowing up. Then the tears started. I was so grateful that God was so good. I was so grateful that Jess could forgive me. I asked God to be in the middle of our relationship so we'd never, ever let our past divide us again.

I curled up on my bed and closed my eyes. Bad things could happen to me, but now I knew God would always be there. I must have drifted off to sleep, because the ring of my cell phone startled me. I pulled it out and smiled.

"Hi," I said and sniffed.

"How are you?" asked Jess.

"I'm okay. I'm okay."

"Good." He sounded relieved. "Do you want me to come over?"

I smiled again. It was so good to hear his voice. "Yeah. I'd like you to come over."

The End

The Story of the Crucible

I heard a story once of a visit to a gold mine in South Africa. The demonstration area had a working furnace where gold was being refined. The visitors, seated several yards away, could see the glow of fire from the cracks around the furnace doors. When the doors were opened, the heat, even from across the room, was almost unbearable. Two men wearing asbestos suits took a crucible out of the fire with long tongs. The vessel was filled with molten gold. The audience was told that the fire was heated to a certain degree to melt off the impurities in the gold. After the impurities are removed, the furnace is heated even hotter and the gold was put back in again. The impurities were again removed and returned to an even higher heat. Each level of purification corresponds to a grade of the gold standard, i.e. 14k, 18k, 24k. The gold technician knows when the gold has reached its peak of purification when he can see his face reflected in it. Pure, molten gold is nearly clear.

When our hearts are purified by God's grace, he can see himself in us.

Thanks to Scott Abke for sharing this.

19929210R00151

Made in the USA
Charleston, SC
18 June 2013